Praise for Chris Manby

'Devour it in one go' *Company* on *Ready or Not?*

'Nothing short of brilliant' *Marie Clare* on *Seven Sunny Days*

'Very funny, hugely feel-good and the perfect antidote for anyone who worries that the only career ladder they've achieved is a run in their tights'
Fiona Walker on *Lizzie Jordan's Secret Life*

'It's a great idea for a plot, and Manby's writing more than does it justice' *Marie Clare* on *Getting Personal*

'A deliciously comical novel that's peppered with characters who are so endearing you'll want to take them home and introduce them to your mum . . . *Girl Meets Ape* is charming, funny and as compelling as your favourite soap . . . a rip-roaring good read.'
Heat

'Manby's hilarious novels still shine out' *OK*

Also by Chris Manby

Flatmates

Second Prize

Deep Heat

Lizzie Jordan's Secret Life

Running Away from Richard

Getting Personal

Seven Sunny Days

Girl Meets Ape

About the author

In 1995 Chris Manby met a New York psychic who told her she would write seven novels. This is her ninth. Which means she probably won't marry that millionaire, either. She is also editor/contributor to the *Girls' Night In* anthologies, which have so far raised more than £900,000 for humanitarian organisation War Child, and topped book charts all over the world. Raised in Gloucester, Chris now lives between London and Los Angeles. Her hobbies include reading in-flight magazines and she hopes that continually crossing time zones is an effective anti-ageing strategy.

CHRIS MANBY

Ready or Not?

HODDER

First published in Great Britain in 2005 by Hodder and Stoughton
A division of Hodder Headline

A Hodder paperback

7

A CIP catalogue record for this title
is available from the British Library

ISBN 978 0 340 83866 2

Typeset in Plantin Light by Hewer Text Ltd, Edinburgh
Printed and bound by
Mackays of Chatham Ltd, Chatham, Kent

Hodder Headline's policy is to use papers that are natural,
renewable and recyclable products and made from wood grown in
sustainable forests. The logging and manufacturing processes are expected
to conform to the environmental regulations of the country of origin.

Hodder and Stoughton Ltd
A division of Hodder Headline
338 Euston Road
London NW1 3BH

To Guy Hazel

With thanks to:

My fabulous family, everyone at Hodder, all my lovely friends at The Board, Barfy, Peter Dailey, Debbie Deuble, Tony Gardner, Antony Harwood, Guy Hazel, Marcus Hoffman, Danuta Kean, Peyvand Khorshandi, Shappi Khorshandi, Hector Macdonald, James Macdonald Lockhart, Jennifer Niederhauser, Sheryl Petersen, Alex Potter, James Pusey, Dan Rhodes, Sally Riley, Jane Royce, Shelley Silas, Frank Strausser, Martin Weaver and Jane Wright. Who variously gave me advice about radio, rugby, six-month-old babies, made me money, made me laugh and generally stopped me going bonkers during the process of writing this book.

I

What was there left to do but call the wedding off?

As my fiancé Ed stood on the doorstep in the early hours of the morning one Sunday early last February, I fancied I could see a dream flying away behind him. Almost twelve months of planning, 150 RSVPs, thousands of pounds already laid out on booking the venue, the caterers, the ceilidh band . . . But as I looked at him right then there was no way I was going to be able to walk down that aisle to stand beside him.

'Heidi, I lost my key,' he said.

It wasn't the only thing he'd lost that weekend.

'Ed,' I sighed. 'Where are your clothes?'

When I was younger, struggling hopefully with a series of brief and hopeless relationships, I heard all the clichés. After each uniquely painful break-up my family and friends would rally round and utter such gems of advice as 'Love will only come when you're not looking for it' and 'You'll find love where you least expect it'. I hated to hear those things. But the fact is that love did come when I wasn't looking for it and it certainly wasn't where I expected to find it.

'So, you'll need to book another appointment as soon as possible to have that temporary filling replaced,' said the dentist. 'And, er, I wonder whether you'd like to come to the theatre next Thursday night.'

Yes. That was how I met him. I lost half a tooth at a friend's dinner party, accidentally crunching on a stray olive stone in the puttanesca sauce, and Ed Gordon was the emergency dentist who patched me up. He was a locum at the time, standing in for my usual dentist, Mr Orpington. Mr Orpington was a fifty-something whose yellowing pegs and bad breath were far from the best advertisement for his profession. Ed Gordon had the straight, white grin of a Hollywood film star, though I'd find out later on that his front two teeth were a bridge to replace the two he lost to rugby.

'It's just that I noticed you reading the theatre brochure in the waiting room and I've got a spare ticket to see *An Inspector Calls*,' Ed explained.

It would be a few months before I admitted that I only picked up the theatre brochure because the single tattered copy of *Hello* was an issue I already owned. 'Er,' I replied. 'Isn't it against the rules to go on a date with a patient?'

'But you're not my patient,' said Ed. 'Not really. And I promise never to go near your mouth again. At least, not with a drill bit . . .' He grinned at me like a naughty schoolboy who thinks he might have got away with something wicked.

'I'd love to come,' I told him. 'I think.'

After all, any man who asked me out having seen my crumbling molars had to be a pretty genuine sort of bloke. Not overly concerned with looks, at least. Or perhaps he was just as desperate as I was.

Needless to say, our first date went wonderfully. Ed greeted me in the lobby of the theatre with a single, perfect rose. I spent the entire performance sneaking glimpses at his impressively masculine profile in the semi-darkness and being very pleased he was much more handsome than I remembered. We followed up on that theatre date with a Saturday afternoon at London Zoo, then a day at the races and, three weeks later, we spent our first whole night together – a weekend in a posh hotel in Brighton that was as romantic as it was dirty. And almost two years after that fateful filling Ed Gordon finally proposed. Valentine's Day. Paris. Top of the Eiffel Tower. The most perfect cliché in the world. We saw four more proposals while we waited for the lift to take us down again and one of the girls actually fainted. I felt pretty giddy myself.

We spent the rest of that weekend in Paris on a high, floating around like a pair of teenagers, holding hands and periodically congratulating ourselves on our good fortune in having found each other in a world full of so many strangers. On our last night in France we climbed up to the gardens in front of the Sacré-Cœur and looked back across the city towards the sparkling Tower, where the defining moment of our lives so far had taken place.

'How did you know it was me?' I asked Ed then. 'How did you know I was "The One" for you?'

It wasn't the way I looked, or the way I talked. It wasn't the way my nose wrinkled up when I giggled (which it doesn't). It wasn't my way with a baking tin or my incredible skill in the sack. It was the way I packed my suitcase.

'Your ability to travel light,' was at the top of Ed's well-considered list of reasons why he loved me. 'The fact that you can get out of the house in less than five minutes whether we're going to the supermarket or a black-tie ball, and the way that you cook scrambled eggs.'

Strange as it may sound, I wasn't disappointed with that answer.

'And I love you,' I told him, 'because you always warn me when you're going to fart in bed.'

We set the date for sixteen months after the proposal. Ed had some relatives in Australia and was keen for them to be able to attend, while I wanted plenty of time to make sure our big day was a suitably fantastic expression of our love. Before Ed asked me to marry him, I would have sworn I wasn't interested in the extravagant white wedding thing: registry office on the King's Road or a cheesy Elvis chapel in Las Vegas would have been good enough for me. The only guests I needed were my parents, my best friend Kara and my younger brother James . . .

After the proposal, I turned into Bride-zilla. I told myself I was only doing it for my family, but I discovered that I secretly wanted a church. I wanted a white dress. I wanted brides-maids. I wanted small boys dressed as Little Lord Fauntleroy (my younger brother was very lucky he had just turned twenty-five). And as the date grew nearer, every spare moment seemed to be taken up with finalising details: dresses, flowers, table decorations. Food suitable for just about every allergy known to the medical profession – peanuts, dairy, *tomato pips* for goodness' sake. It was stressful beyond belief, but I thought I had every eventuality covered.

Then, with just four months left to go, Ed went and lost his trousers. And his jacket. And his T-shirt. And his pants.

'What the hell happened to you?' I asked him.

'I fell asleep,' he said. 'So they punished me.'

'They' being the other members of Ed's amateur rugby club.

That weekend the club had hired a minibus and driven from London to Gloucester to play a few friendly matches there. They celebrated a weekend of wins with the traditional com-bination of a curry, drinking games and dirty songs. Unfortu-nately for Ed – and for me, as it turned out – that year's captain, Richard (orthopaedic surgeon on working days and lunatic on Saturdays), decided to introduce a new weekend-away tradition, imported from his posh Oxford college. The first man to pass out through fatigue or too much alcohol forfeited his clothes. And in their place, the unlucky sucker got a fine layer of sticky black treacle and feathers.

Ed was the first man to pass out.

'You're not coming in till I've put down some newspaper,' I shrieked as he tried to step inside.

'But Heidi, I'm cold,' Ed said pathetically.

'Serves you right.' It was two degrees below outside and I was in no mood to be kind, still smarting from a spat about place settings we'd had before Ed left on the Friday night.

I laid a trail of old Sunday supplements from the front door to the bathroom. 'Why on earth do you have to hang out with such perverts?' I asked as I surveyed the damage. Ed's team-mates had sensibly driven off at high speed after depositing him and a plastic carrier bag of suspiciously wet clothes in my care. 'This is never going to come off.' He was covered from ankles to ears. Ed grimaced manfully as I pulled away the first handful of feathers and half his leg hair. Half an hour later, we had to resort to shaving the damn treacle away with *my* Gillette Venus ladies' razor.

'I'm cancelling the wedding,' I said.

'You won't, will you, Heidi? You know how much I love you,' Ed slurred.

'Well, I don't love you any more. You're supposed to be a bloody grown-up. How could you let them do this to you? I'm calling the caterers tomorrow.'

'Heidi, please don't do that. You've got to marry me; I've told all my friends.'

'The same friends that covered you in this mess?' I ran my hands through my hair in exasperation and immediately regretted it. The treacle was getting everywhere. The news-paper hadn't protected the carpet at all and there were three sticky handprints on the bathroom wall where Ed had reached out to steady himself. 'If any one of those jokers actually turns up to the wedding, I will cut off his balls with the cake knife.'

'I love you most because you always have such a calm reaction to disasters,' Ed told me with a burp. 'I can't wait till you're my wife.'

'But I am never going to marry you, Ed Gordon,' I said flatly.

It felt like I was only half-joking.

2

Treacle notwithstanding, to anyone looking in from the outside, my life was pretty much perfect at that moment in time. Not only was I about to get married to a wonderful man, I was one of the rare people I knew who didn't dread Monday mornings; work was going very well.

I joined the BBC as soon as I left college, using my university radio experience to wangle a place on their graduate trainee course. At the end of my training, I was given a placement at Radio Four. After that, I followed the usual path, from lowly 'meeter and greeter' – making tea and coffee for guests on the show – to broadcast assistant to assistant producer to full-blown producer with a desk of my own and a PC I didn't have to share. Well, not often.

Just before Ed's Eiffel Tower proposal, I was headhunted to co-produce a new general interest show on an independent station. The show was to be called *Let's Talk London*. I knew that the station, London Talk Live, didn't have a fraction of Radio Four's listening figures, but something convinced me it might be the right moment to take a leap into the independent-radio unknown. You see, though I had been steadily creeping up through the ranks in the BBC, there were still some people at the corporation who refused to see me as anything other than the work-experience girl I had been when they first met me. I had a feeling my glass ceiling was looming. In fact, I had a feeling I was already smearing that glass ceiling with my Aveda styling serum. I took the new position.

Let's Talk London was great fun from the very beginning. The new gang all started on the same day, which really helped foster team spirit. We were all enthusiastic and hardworking and were soon putting together a show that was gradually, by word of mouth, becoming *the* morning talk show to listen to in the capital city: I knew we had made it when I got into a cab one day after work and noticed that the cabbie's radio was already tuned into my station. When he struck up a conversation about an item that I had produced a couple of days before, proving that he hadn't just tuned in to London Talk Live accidentally, I could have kissed him.

It was a very fast-moving job. The hour-long show went out live three mornings a week and there was rarely any time to congratulate ourselves on a particularly good one before we had to start all over again on another. As soon as each show ended, we would have a meeting to discuss what should feature on the next edition and launch straight into finding the guests who could offer an expert opinion. Sometimes the issues we confronted were serious, sometimes far from it. During my time on the show, *Let's Talk London* had covered everything from the war in Iraq to the threatened demise of Heinz salad cream. Everyone from pop stars to freedom fighters to a man who had been arrested twenty-seven times while attempting to break the world record for visiting every Tube station on the London Underground naked had walked through those studio doors. And yes, Mr Underground came naked to the studio, too – an even less appealing sight than my fiancé in treacle and feathers.

A few days after Ed's rugby-club debacle, a new government study into single parenting was released. The statistics were astonishing: it seemed there were hardly any children with two parents any more. Britain, however, was still largely geared towards catering for a nuclear family that hadn't existed since the end of the Cold War. Single parents were expected to go out to work and yet there was little childcare provision to help them juggle jobs and homelife. Those few childcare places that did exist were so expensive the gap between money earned and money spent, in order to be *able* to earn, had shrunk to such an extent it hardly seemed worth leaving the house in the morning anyway. Every newspaper, from the tabloids to the broadsheets, had covered the study and the dilemmas it revealed. It was front-page news pending the next Premier League footballer's indiscretion or former royal butler's revelation. We really couldn't afford not to cover it ourselves.

'What we need,' said Eleanor, the show's editor and my boss, 'is something that examines single parenting from a new angle.'

I have no doubt that exactly the same conversation was being had in fifty independent-radio production offices throughout the country that afternoon.

'Single mothers: what kind of shoes do they wear?' asked Robin, the office funny boy. It was a running joke that Robin would include shoes in every proposal he made at the programme meetings. Apparently it was all we girls ever talked about. Manolos, Jimmy Choos, or, more realistically on our wages, Dolcis and Ravel.

'A *sensible* new angle,' said Flo, the show's beautiful presenter. She always tried to be stern with Robin but a smile was never far from her lips when she spoke to him. In some ways Robin used his boyish good looks around our oestrogen-filled office like a male version of a buxom girl flashing her cleavage on a City trading floor. He could make Flo flirt like a teen, though she was old enough to be his mother. At least, I assumed Flo was old enough to be his mother. She had a very mature CV but her soft black skin was still as smooth and shiny as a wet pebble and she laughed like someone who had never been let down.

'Everyone assumes that a single parent is a mother left by a feckless man,' piped up Nelly, our other trainee. If Robin was class clown, then Nelly was definitely class swot. 'But what about a *father* bringing up the kids on his own?' She pushed her glasses further up her nose and squinted through them expectantly as she waited for us to respond.

'That sounds good,' I said. If not entirely original, I thought. Still, there were only two flavours of single parent, weren't there?

Eleanor nodded.

'Single fathers and their shoes?' Robin muttered.

We all ignored him.

'Single father works for me,' said Flo.

It would work for me too. That close to lunchtime I just wanted to get out of the office and into Pret A Manger.

'Right. A lone father it is,' said Eleanor, 'pending any better ideas.'

'Single shoes?' said Robin.

We continued to ignore him.

'Nelly, perhaps you should start by ringing some of the single-parent charities,' I suggested.

Nelly, as usual, was way ahead of the game. 'Oh, I already did that,' she said. I caught Robin rolling his eyes. 'I'm waiting to hear from a couple of men who should be available at short notice.'

'Great. Let me know as soon as they get back to you,' said Eleanor.

'Will do.' Nelly made herself a note before going off to fix us some coffee and shine her halo.

Once again, Robin found himself in the humiliating position of researching the shorter, more lightweight part of the show. He was set to finding someone to talk to us about yet another calendar made up of nude pictures of unlikely models. We'd had the naked WI girls, naked footballers, naked firemen, naked vicars . . . (okay, so that last one I made up). This time the nude models were all professional cyclists raising money for an arthritis charity. Strategically placed bicycle pumps kept us from finding out whether the rumour that cyclists put bananas down their Lycra shorts was true. It was surprisingly disappointing when Robin announced, after some very light research, that it *was* true: cyclists do put bananas in their Lycras. But only the skins. Between their buttocks. To stop chafing.

'Can we use the word "chafing" on our show?' I wondered aloud.

'I'll look it up in the network guidelines,' said Nelly.

3

Later that same day, I met up with my very own link to the world of the single parent.

My best friend Kara had recently become a single mum. Her son Forester was almost six months old, but Kara hadn't seen Forester's musician father since she told him she was going to keep the baby. Nine months after the whirlwind romance in Goa, that resulted in one very-much unplanned pregnancy, relations had quickly deteriorated to such an extent that when Forester was born, Kara merely included the man who gave him half his genes on the list of recipients for a birth announcement via round-robin email.

I wouldn't say Kara was exactly thrilled to see the little blue line in the results window of the pregnancy test, but after it appeared there was never any question that she would be a mother. It was the ultimate expression of sod's law. The weekend before Kara flew off for some winter sun in Goa and got herself pregnant, she and I had visited our old college pal Mary and her newborn baby boy in hospital. Mary had us both crossing our legs with her tales of in-depth investigations at the fertility clinic and the subsequent horrors of pregnancy and labour without drugs; not so much as a whiff of the laughing gas (or so she claimed). Ed didn't get anywhere near me for a week.

'I don't think I have a maternal cell in my body,' Kara announced that evening as we drank red wine and told each other what we really thought of Mary's pig-ugly bundle of joy.

Kara certainly had a maternal cell in her body when she got back from India.

'Great,' she said, tossing the white plastic stick into the wastepaper bin and clapping her hands together as though she had just made a decision about what to have for lunch. 'I'm going to be a single mother. Better than getting myself a cat and being a common-or-garden single woman, I suppose. At least people will know I had one good shag before my life ended.'

'But . . . how . . .?' I began.

'How what?' Kara asked. 'How did I get pregnant? Well, Heidi, it goes like this—'

'How will you do it on your own?' I interrupted seriously.

I didn't know why, but I suddenly felt quite breathless. My heart beat like a trapped bird in my chest, as though I had been the one peeing on the spatula. I was much more worried than Kara was.

Kara Knight always gave the impression that she glided through life. Certainly in the twelve or so years I had known her (we met on our first day at university in Leeds) she had managed to avoid most of the crises that afflict the average twenty-something girl. She breezed through her degree – even final exams couldn't stop her from going to see her favourite band in London the night before her last paper. She managed to get a first without ever spending all night in the library. In fact, I don't think she even knew where it was. While the rest of us trudged from interview to interview on the corporate 'milk round', desperate to find graduate placements so we could start repaying those student loans, Kara never bothered to impress the corporations. Kara met the man who gave her her first proper job (for a glamorous film company) at a London nightclub, when she spilled her pink drink on his white suede jacket.

Not that Kara needed a job; her parents were loaded. Her father was something big in stainless steel. She had her credit card bills sent straight to his office and Daddy Knight was more than happy to indulge his only child. That alone should have made me hate her, but I recognised at once that Kara was slightly embarrassed by her fortunate situation and that writing her off as a spoilt rich girl would have been as unfair as the way some of her former private schoolmates wrote people like me off as proles. She was fun and kind, and she gave me my first ever spliff. Hanging out with Kara was an education. Of sorts.

In short, Kara had every modern girl's dream life. Rich, intelligent, adored by men and women alike. She even had beautiful toes. It was as if a fairy godmother had waved a wand over her head as she emerged into the world with her silver spoon already firmly clenched between her perfect teeth. And that fairy had remained by Kara's side throughout her days, deflecting all the boredom and ugliness and low-level unhappiness that touched the average existence, making sure Kara never cried over boys, books or the size of her bum. Until the fateful night on Baga Beach when the fairy went AWOL, Kara met 'what's-his-name' and conceived her son.

'How will you do it?' I asked again. 'How can you afford to have this baby on your own?'

At the age of thirty, Kara had only recently decided she would take no more handouts from her parents but try to make her own way in life. She had cashed (so she said) the last cheque and was wavering between careers in massage therapy, past-life regression and feng shui consultancy.

'What will you do without a partner to support you through this?' I persisted.

Kara was thinking about cheese.

'I'll save loads of money over the next nine months,' she told me optimistically. 'Even if Mum and Dad refuse to help out, which they won't. There are plenty of things I can cut back on. Alcohol, cocaine, unpasteurised cheese. Bloody hell. No red wine *or* Brie for a whole nine months. I don't know which is worse. But at least I know I'm not going to be tempted to go mad in the summer sales this year. Not if I'm going to look like a blimp.'

Of course, Kara never really looked like a blimp. Over the next three seasons she was the perfect exemplar of that mythical pregnant woman who glows. No varicose veins. No spots. No piles. Hardly any weight gain at all apart from the neat little bump that was as round and tight as a basketball. Her glossy, thick hair just got glossier and thicker. And nothing seemed to bother her, not any of the physical symptoms of pregnancy that tortured mortal women or the terrifying thought of what she was about to take on for the next eighteen years. Kara was the very model of a modern Madonna. She gave *me* morning sickness.

'I don't know how you're going to do it,' I told her the day she found out.

She just did.

That evening in February we met, as had become our custom, at a little Greek restaurant equidistant between our two houses. We'd completely overlooked the place until Kara got a craving for taramasalata in her second trimester. Now we favoured Little Athens as our restaurant of choice because it was one of the few places we knew that had a door wide enough to admit a fully laden pushchair.

'And my post-natal arse,' Kara sighed.

As Kara wheeled his pushchair in from the cold, Forester already looked faintly disgruntled at having to be out with the girls again. His trendy fur-trimmed cap with ear-flaps made him look like a mini Elmer Fudd. He strained his little body against the straps that held him safe like Hercules trying to break his bonds. But even when he was pouting Forester Knight was a cutie. He had his mother's lips, her Valrhona chocolate eyes and a perfect fuzz of dark brown curls – 'Must be from his father,' said Kara, whose own dark hair was long and straight as a Japanese girl's. But she wasn't sure – Forester's dad had a shaved head during the brief time Kara knew him. But whatever his father looked like, Forester was not one of those babies you compared to a pickled walnut. He was Botticelli beautiful. A Christmas card cupid. An angel.

I pushed the brim of his cap back to coo at him. 'Haven't you grown!' I said. 'I swear he grows an inch a day.'

'Stop with the growing stuff,' said Kara. 'You'll be pinching his cheeks next.' But I could tell she was pleased when I noticed the way he was changing from day to day. She undid the harness that held Forester in his pram. 'Hold him for a second?' she asked me.

She lifted Forester out and handed him over. I took him from her, concentrating hard on getting that ideal soft yet secure grip on his wriggling torso, then I attempted to give him a cuddle. He protested at once, arching his body away from mine as though I was King Herod. I handed him back to his mum as soon as her arms were empty again.

'Hang on, will you?' Kara still had a packet of wet wipes between her teeth.

'He can smell I'm an amateur,' I explained, deftly swapping baby for baby product.

Kara tutted and rolled her eyes at me. 'Well, practice makes perfect,' she said.

But I knew that both Forester and I were very much happier when he was on Kara's knee at the table, grabbing everything within reach and trying to get it into his mouth before his mother spotted and intervened.

'Not the knife!' said Kara. 'He's started grabbing.'

'I noticed,' I said when I leaned too close to admire his tiny wee nose and he gave the silver pendant around my neck a hefty tug.

'Give your Auntie Heidi a smile,' she suggested, when she had freed me from his determined grasp. 'He's got the smiling thing totally down now. He's been doing this really cute grin.'

Forester immediately turned his face away from me, arched his back again and started preparing himself for a scream. No cute grin for Auntie Heidi then. Like I said, he could smell my fear.

'He's tired,' Kara sighed, and indeed his eyelids were drooping. My shoulders relaxed slightly at the thought that he might soon be asleep for the whole meal. He yawned and seemed to close his eyes tightly. After a moment, to be sure, Kara carefully laid him back down in his buggy. The second his bottom touched the canvas seat, however, his eyes flipped wide open like the eyes of an evil baby doll. He protested until Kara picked him up again and cuddled him close to her shoulder, then he yelled as though she was pinching him. My shoulders were back up by my ears and I found myself looking around the restaurant apologetically even though Kara and I were the only customers there. Kara just kept on chatting above the fray.

'Did you read that piece about that footballer's boyfriend in the *Sun* today?' she asked.

I couldn't concentrate on a word she was saying.

'Have to say I always thought he wasn't entirely straight.'

Forester yelled so hard I had to sit on my hands to stop myself covering my ears, but Kara didn't even flinch as she got the full force of his yell in her face. I was shaking by the time our bottle of wine arrived.

'Do you think I'd get arrested for putting some of this in his bottle?' Kara joked with the waitress. 'He's so bloody active now,' she added to me. 'Oh, for the days when I could carry him around like a rather cumbersome handbag.'

'I look forward to you guys coming in; he's so adorable,' the waitress clucked.

Forester threw back his head and gave her a view of his tonsils, complete with Sioux warrior battlecry sound effects.

'Don't you think much of our restaurant, eh?' the waitress asked him as she stroked his reddening cheek. 'Don't you like to eat Greek food? Not good enough for you in here?'

Forester squealed.

The waitress cooed, 'Awww!'

Awww? Sometimes I felt like I was the only person who could actually hear it when Forester bawled. Like the boy who noticed that the emperor's new clothes were in fact a birthday suit, I seemed to lack the filter that turned a baby's cry into song.

Forester was to struggle on for quite a while that afternoon. It took an emergency bottle of milk and a good deal of cuddling from his well-practised mother before he closed his eyes again. But, as usual, once his face was all angelic and serene once more, it was almost impossible to remember what he had looked like while screaming. Kara and the waitress gazed in awe for a moment. I gazed along with them.

'Quick,' Kara said then. 'We've got approximately forty-five minutes to gossip before he wakes up.'

The waitress poured us both another glass of wine.

'Here's to not breastfeeding.' Kara downed hers in one and slammed the glass on the table.

Being a mum had hardly changed my best friend at all.

Personally, I didn't have much gossip. I was getting married. Apart from Ed's brush with the treacle, my life had become a thrilling round of weekdays at the radio station and weekends spent buying shelving units at Ikea. We seemed to have an infinite appetite for new shelving units though I wasn't quite sure where Ed was putting them any more. Lately, even the wedding planning was starting to lose its appeal as a subject of discussion for me. Just after the engagement, I never travelled anywhere without a bridal magazine in my handbag and I couldn't wait for the year to tick away. Now the feeling I had as I flicked through the pages of my diary was more akin to the way I felt in the run-up to my GCSEs. It had started with six months to go but I didn't feel I could talk about it. Who would understand?

Kara, by contrast, always seemed to have some juicy tale up her sleeve, even though now she was a stay-at-home mum.

Just the previous week she had announced that she was ready to jump back into the dating scene. It didn't seem that long since she had been complaining about her intimate stitches and claiming she would never have sex again. Never ever. Not even if George Clooney and his heretofore undiscovered twin brother dropped by with flowers. But then, all of a sudden, it was as if the sun came out in her life again and she decided she was *dying* for a flirt.

'I feel as though I've been invisible for the past fifteen months,' she had complained to me. 'First because I was pregnant. Now because I have so obviously just *been* pregnant, with the big jumpers and the wild "got no sleep last night" hair thing going on.'

She didn't look that bad and I told her so. In fact, I had been admiring the dark-blue sweater she now described as a Cornish fisherman's cast-off.

'Well, it's time to get back into the game,' she said, batting away my compliments. 'I want someone to flirt with, even if it's just in cyberspace. I've been thinking about Internet dating.'

We had done a couple of segments on cyber-dating in the show. 'It's the perfect place to start,' I agreed. 'You don't even have to change out of your pyjamas.'

'And I can post a photo taken before I got pregnant,' said

Kara. 'You've got to help me think of something funny to put in my profile. I need a good name.'

'Kara at Gagging For It dot com?' was my first suggestion.

'Already taken,' Kara quipped back. 'But I'm serious, Heidi. If I don't get some adult male company, some *flirtatious* adult male company, soon, I am going to have to buy a cat. Except I can't even buy a cat any more.'

'Why not?' I asked.

'In case the baby catches something horrible and dies.'

She whipped out a sanitising wipe and carefully cleaned her hands before she even thought about reaching for the pitta bread. When I kissed Kara 'hello' these days I always caught a faint whiff of something antibacterial.

'Try Internet dating. It could be the best thing you ever did,' I said encouragingly. 'And what possible harm can come of it, so long as you're careful and don't go meeting up with a virtual stranger in the middle of the night on a deserted beach?'

Kara grinned. I was talking to a girl who had conceived her son under almost exactly those circumstances.

Just seven days later, back in Little Athens, Kara was proud to announce that her mission to fill that flirtatious gap in her life was going well. Very well, in fact. She had joined three online dating sites as soon as she got home from discussing the idea with me and claimed to have had more than a hundred 'hits' in the first twenty-four hours after her profile went live.

'Any good ones?' I asked.

'Oh yes.' Kara reached into the tray beneath Forester's pushchair and pulled out a handful of printouts. These were her favourite emails and some grainy-looking photos.

'You're very popular,' I said, as I started to leaf through them.

'Well, KarmaKara is.'

'KarmaKara? What is that?'

'That's my log-in name.'

'Yuck. You'll be besieged by hippies.'

'That's not such a bad thing.'

'As long as you've got no sense of smell.'

'Just help me suss out the losers, will you?'

So while Forester snoozed on in his pushchair, his mother and I sifted through the candidates for stepfatherhood. I quickly whittled the contenders down to the three who'd dared to post photos, then read some of their emails and immediately had to discount the best-looking one on the grounds that he asked what kind of underwear Kara liked to wear in his very first attempt at correspondence. In line one, in fact. Top of a list of ten questions. 'Bikini-style or thong?'

'What's wrong with him?' Kara asked, as I flipped him onto the reject pile.

'Where do you want me to start?'

Question two was 'Au naturel or Brazilian?'

'So he's a little bit forward.'

'Forward?' I snorted. 'He's a pervert. You can forget any man who asks whether you're wearing tights or stockings before you've even had a coffee.'

The other two were better correspondents, sticking to niceties such as their favourite music, towns and food. At least until email five, by which time Kara's own smutty sense of humour was creeping in.

'Oh no,' I said, handing back a couple of particularly steamy pages. 'Too much information.'

'I'm going to keep that one,' said Kara, lips twitching upwards at a joke she might have kept more private.

'All very funny. But how do you propose to take it from email to real life?'

'I sent one of them my phone number,' Kara admitted. She pushed the guy in question's profile back towards me.

His name was Duncan Stevenson. He was single, six feet tall

and thirty-two. His profile said he enjoyed eating out and dancing, city breaks and classic cars. There was no photo – which is why I had previously consigned him to the reject pile; you've got to be suspicious of someone who won't post a pic. 'Perhaps he's intimidatingly gorgeous,' I joked. But now I was examining the evidence more closely, I found that his emails were not only impressively long but witty, charming and thoughtful. I liked him.

'I emailed him my number first thing this morning,' Kara continued, 'but he hasn't called yet. I guess that part of dating hasn't changed at all since I was last out there. The girl always ends up waiting for a call.'

Said the girl I had never known to wait for a call in her life. Kara could have written *The Anti-Rules*. Call him ten times a day if you want to. Be funny if you feel like it. Have sex on the very first night. She always got away with it and wouldn't have wanted any man who didn't like the way she played anyway.

'Perhaps I was too pushy. What do you think? Perhaps I should have waited for him to give me his number instead.' She fished her mobile phone out of her bag. 'Heidi, will you just call my phone for me? Perhaps it's on the blink.'

'It's not on the blink,' I said firmly.

'Then why won't he ring me?'

'Maybe he's a little bit shy. Maybe he hasn't checked his email yet today. Maybe his computer exploded and he was run over by a bus on his way to the Internet café.'

Kara grinned at that thought.

'Give him a chance,' I said. 'He will call.'

'And when he does call, he'll turn out to be some twelve-year-old kid who's been pretending to be a grown-up for a dare.' Her shoulders slumped. Meanwhile, Forester had woken from his all-too-short nap. Kara quickly started unbuckling him to pre-empt any screaming.

'Or he could turn out to be as gorgeous as him over there,' I said, nodding towards a bloke who had just walked into our empty restaurant looking like he should be followed by paparazzi. 'In fact, that could be him! We've got no photo. We just can't tell.'

'Quick,' said Kara. 'Hold Forester and pretend he's yours.'

She handed me the baby and started to preen. Her best pouty-lipped face sent us both into hysterics, which certainly drew the attention of the gorgeous guy now being shown to a table right next to us. And his boyfriend . . .

'I *so* knew he was gay,' whispered Kara, as the guys huddled together over a menu and shot us the occasional worried glance.

'Yeah, right. You can have Forester back now,' I said. 'I think there's something going on with his nappy.'

'There's always something going on with that child's nappy!' Kara lifted her baby until his well-padded bottom was level with her nose and took a sniff. Forester gave us his gummy smile. 'Can't smell anything now, though. Are you sure you haven't just farted, Heidi? Fancy trying to blame it on a baby!'

4

Kara and I decided to have coffee at my house. We settled Forester to snooze in the sitting room and retired to the kitchen so that Kara's shrieking laughter wouldn't wake her son as we got down to some serious character assassination. Kara had some great gossip about a girl we knew from university who claimed to have gone from 32B to 34E overnight using nothing but the power of meditation.

'*Ommmm, must improve my bussssssttttt . . .*' Kara sat cross-legged on the kitchen floor and chanted until I couldn't breathe for laughing.

We both turned a little guiltily at the sound of Ed's key in the front door.

'I could hear you two cackling all the way down the street,' he claimed, as he walked into the kitchen.

'We don't cackle,' said Kara.

'Like a pair of witches. Got some good gossip?'

'Swapping knitting patterns. Hello, handsome.'

'Kara.' Ed kissed her hello.

'Phew!' Kara pretended to reel from alcohol fumes. 'Been out with the lads again?'

'Been next door with Mrs H,' said Ed.

'Your fancy woman,' Kara laughed. 'You want to watch him, Heidi.'

'Oh, I do,' I played along with the joke.

Mrs H was eighty-two years old. On a Thursday night, Ed played cards with our elderly neighbour. He was always round there: opening pickle jars, taking out the rubbish on a Tuesday night, making sure the front steps were clear of ice and well-gritted in the event of a freeze.

'Where's my little man?' Ed asked now. Kara had appointed Ed her son's godfather, without the ceremony. Unless you count the bottle of vintage port we toasted away on Forester's behalf. Kara's mother was still furious that her daughter had refused a nice service at their local church, or even a proper secular party. Secretly, I thought Kara might have indulged her parents a little more.

'Forester's asleep in the sitting room,' I told Ed.

At least, he had been asleep. Kara suddenly frowned. Her ears were attuned like those of a mother bat's to the little squeaks and rumblings that came from her son's tiny body. She reacted to Forester's cry before I even really heard it. Possibly even before Forester himself knew what was going on. 'Ed,' she said, 'Will you do me a huge favour and bring Forester into the kitchen for me while I warm up some milk?'

I had expected Ed to appear at the kitchen door with the pushchair, which is how I would have done it, but instead he appeared cradling Forester in his big arms, tucking his little finger into Forester's mouth to keep him occupied and cooing one of the few rugby songs with cleanish lyrics that he knew. I was astonished. As he stood in the doorway, Ed looked like something out of an early nineties Athena poster. Only not quite so attractive, obviously, on account of his having more than a slight beer belly and very little hair.

'Wow,' said Kara. 'You actually picked him up.'

She was clearly as shocked as I was. Even Forester seemed to be blinking in surprise.

'Of course I picked him up,' Ed said defensively. 'What else was I going to do?' Then he added, 'Am I doing it right?'

Kara nodded. 'If he isn't screaming, then you're doing it right. You do look awfully comfortable like that, you know.'

Ed smiled straight at me. I gave him the thumbs up. 'Looking good, Mr Gordon,' I agreed.

'Ow!' That was when Ed discovered Forester's first tooth.

'Oh yeah,' said Kara. 'I meant to tell you I've stopped putting my body parts anywhere near his mouth.'

She handed Ed a clean dummy to replace his finger and set a bottle of milk to warm in the microwave. After twenty seconds, she tested the temperature on the back of her hand.

'Is it cool enough?' Ed asked, all concerned.

'Well, I'm not coming up in a blister.'

'Kara!' Ed exclaimed.

'Of course it's cool enough.' She passed the bottle to Ed. 'Here. You're doing so well at holding him perhaps you want to have a go at giving him his bottle, too?'

'All right,' Ed said gamely. 'I reckon I should be able to do this.'

'It's so easy, even a woman can do it.' Kara winked at me.

Still cradling the baby in his arms, Ed lowered himself very slowly onto one of the rickety kitchen chairs and tried to find a comfortable position. He shifted so that Forester was almost completely prone across his knees. Sensing that all was not quite as usual, Forester swivelled his wobbly head and looked to his mother in alarm.

'You'll need to lift him up a bit more than that,' said Kara. 'He still can't sit up too well but he likes to try to hold the bottle himself.' Ed moved accordingly but I could see he was finding it hard to manoeuvre.

'Give me that for a second.' I took the bottle back off him.

Ed finally got Forester into the right position, resting in the crook of his arm against his soft green sweater.

'This okay with you?' he asked the baby.

Forester made serious eye contact and attempted a half-smile as if to say that it would do for now. Ed held the teat of the bottle to Forester's lips, but Forester turned his head as though the bottle was filled with poison.

'He doesn't want it,' said Ed in dismay.

'He does. He always moves his head away like that at first. He gets so excited he forgets what he was crying about. You've sort of got to shove the teat in his mouth,' Kara instructed.

'Shove it?'

'Yeah. Don't be quite so delicate. Press it against his lips again.'

Ed did as he was told. 'Here you go, little man.' He put just a little more pressure behind the bottle. And it worked. This time Forester sucked the teat in greedily, grabbing at the bottle with both his hands. But he took just one big gulp before he squawked and spat what little milk he had taken over the kitchen table. The speed with which Ed handed him back to his mother was comical. He offloaded Forester almost as quickly as my own record time.

'Forgot to set the video,' Ed muttered as he headed back to the TV. Kara just shook her head and laughed.

'At least he wanted to have a go,' Kara whispered when Ed was gone. 'I know plenty of blokes who have never even really looked at a baby until they get their own, let alone tried to feed one. He'll make a good father, I reckon, your fiancé.'

'Hmm,' I agreed.

'You've got to have a girl first so that she and Forester can fall in love, get married and make us in-laws,' she continued. 'Make our friendship more official.'

'But will any girl your son falls in love with ever be good enough?' I asked. 'I don't want to have to fall out with you over my daughter's sloppy housekeeping practices.'

'Then you'll have to teach her by example,' said Kara,

running a finger along my kitchen table and tutting at imaginary dirt. 'I can't wait till you have a baby and I have someone decent to talk to about the whole nappy thing. The girls from my antenatal class have turned into a bunch of zombies. No sense of humour about it at all.'

Kara chuntered on for a while about the few girls from her antenatal group who were still doing their best to keep a support network going now all their babies were born. Kara particularly hated one called Julia, who was actually on her third baby and had made a point of telling all the 'beginners', as she called the rest of them, how it should be done. Natural birth. Breastfeeding. Recyclable nappies. Doing it like the twentieth century never happened. I had met Julia once, while Kara and I were walking Forester through the park. Julia had her youngest in a big old-fashioned Silver Cross pram – a genuine reconditioned antique. Her middle child ate dirt in the sandpit while the eldest hit smaller children who tried to climb up the slide he was monopolising.

'STILL BREASTFEEDING?' Julia had shouted to Kara from the other side of the playground.

At the sound of the word 'breast', a dozen Saturday fathers' heads swivelled towards us like dogs hearing 'WALK!'

I went beetroot on Kara's behalf.

'YES, THANKS,' Kara gamely shouted back. 'AND HOW ARE YOUR STITCHES?'

'ABSOLUTE AGONY. TELL ME, DID YOU GET ANY PILES?'

I was very relieved when, after quite a stand-off during which they competitively yelled out their birth-related ailments across twenty feet of tarmac, Kara deigned to push Forester's pram over to Julia. The alpha mother.

'Jonathan is still rubbing cocoa butter into my perineum every night,' Julia confided in a whisper. Thank God.

I crossed my legs and looked anywhere but at the new

mothers while Julia chattered on. *Cocoa butter in the perineum?* It didn't sound much like foreplay to me.

'And don't even get me started on my cracked nipples,' Julia continued.

I won't, I promised inwardly. I won't.

'Oh dear,' Julia giggled then. 'Talk of the devils. I'm leaking again.' She looked down at the front of her blouse, where a wet patch bloomed in the blue cotton like a dandelion, and promptly started to unbutton it. 'Must be lunchtime.' She flopped her left breast out of an enormous flesh-coloured bra. 'Are your nipples looking like this?' she asked Kara, pointing one in her direction.

'Mine are more like raspberry fruit gums,' said Kara.

Julia insisted that we stay and chat while she fed baby Fergus and the dozen Saturday fathers tried very hard not to look on.

Nipples, belly, perineum.

Cracks, stretch-marks, stitches.

'Your body becomes public property. Derelict public property at that,' was the minus-point of motherhood I added to my increasingly long list that night.

Kara had in fact given up breastfeeding long before that hideous afternoon in the park. Forester was just too big, and she couldn't produce enough breast milk to stop him from going hungry. After the first bottle of formula, the guilt was gone and the relief of being able to leave her son with his grandparents for a few hours every so often took its place.

That night, Forester sucked hungrily on his bottle and it was empty within a couple of minutes.

'Well, I don't have to worry about this one not feeding.' She tipped Forester forward to burp him. An enormous belch racked his little body before he pulled another familiar face: eyebrow-knitting effort and then eyes-wide-open relief.

'Oh no,' said Kara, as Forester filled his nappy. 'Not already. Talk about in one end and out the other. I don't know how he's managing to get so big when he spends so much time pooing everything I put into him straight out again. The nappies we go through! He's responsible for the contents of an entire landfill site on his own.'

'I'll get us both another drink,' I said, eager to make sure my hands were busy before Kara found me something altogether messier to do with them.

'I did pretty well with Forester, didn't I?' Ed said, when he climbed into bed beside me that night.

'You held him for a whole five minutes,' I agreed.

'You know, I think I'm getting pretty good with kids. I can usually stop them crying when they come into the surgery.'

'That's the sugar-free lollipops,' I said meanly.

Ed ignored me. 'We're going to have a boy first, you know.' He wrapped his arms around me and blew a warm raspberry against the back of my neck. 'Within a year of our wedding. Mrs H says so.'

Mrs H could get quite psychic on the Harvey's Bristol Cream but I preferred it when she used her special powers to pronounce on the marital prospects of the ex-Spice Girls.

'And we're going to call him Johnny, after the greatest man who ever lived,' Ed continued.

'Who?' I played dumb.

'Sir Johnny Wilkinson, you clot!'

'We are not going to call him Johnny,' I replied. The name Jonathan would now, to me, always mean cocoa butter in the perineum. But at least the England rugby team's 2003 World Cup victory meant that Johnny Wilkinson had replaced Winston Churchill as Ed's all-time favourite Briton. Winston Gordon. Now that definitely wasn't a name I wanted to conjure with. And neither was Winstona Gordon, for a girl.

'Johnny Winston Churchill Gordon,' Ed murmured into my neck. 'Future captain of the England rugby team. Future head of the Association of Dental Surgeons. Future prime minister of the United Kingdom of . . .'

'Sounds great,' I interrupted, gently removing Ed's hand from my breast. 'But we're not going to start making him tonight. I'm tired.'

It was true. I was *very* tired. But I was still awake long after Ed started snoring. I must have changed position a dozen times, and turned my pillow over and over to let my cheek rest against the cooler side. I stuck one leg out from beneath the duvet. I counted sheep. I tried to remember what sheep really look like. I cursed the fact that Ed liked to wake up to sunlight filtering through cream-coloured curtains while I really needed blackout blinds. (We had compromised on navy blue.)

In the end I gave up, went to the fridge and poured myself a big glass of milk. I drank the milk sitting at the kitchen table, thinking back to earlier that evening when Kara had been sitting in the chair opposite with Forester on her knee pulling his best infant Buddha face while she told a story about a comically bad blow-job that had me laughing until my nose ran.

'For goodness' sake,' I said. 'Not in front of your son.' I had taken to saying 'blimey' instead of 'fuck' since Kara started bringing her little one round. I was even spelling more adult vocabulary out letter by letter.

'He won't remember this,' Kara assured me. 'But I can see his biography now. He'll describe evenings when, dressed as if for a ball, I came into his room to wish him goodnight, the scent of *Arpege* still hanging in the air like a fragrant cloud as I

31

drifted out through the door in my rustling silk gown . . .' She waved her elegant arm dramatically. 'That's how I remember my mum. Though she didn't wear *Arpege* and the dresses were always horrible and never really silk. It being the Seventies . . .'

'I don't think my mum and dad ever went out,' I said.

5

What is your earliest memory? It's probably not as early as you think. I read somewhere that those people who think they can remember lying in the cot wearing a baby-gro are probably just remembering their parents' memories of them. When you think back to what you believe to be your very early memories, it's just as likely that you are remembering a photograph someone once showed you. Or perhaps your mother told the story of the time she lost control of your pushchair on the steep hill that led towards the busy road so often that you think you can remember it too. You can't. You slept all the way through it. Believe me.

One of my earliest true memories is of my mother's back.

I must have been four years old. I had a baby doll called Kelly. She was an ugly-looking thing, with a head shaped like a plastic onion, but I loved her with a passion. Almost more than I loved the puppy who decided the doll would be fun to play tug-of-war with. As I wrestled my doll free from the puppy's jaws one of her legs came away in the fight. I picked up the loose limb, dented with sharp puppy tooth-marks, and went running through the house, crying for Mum to mend the doll and make me happy. Mum could always make me happy.

But this particular day she didn't answer my call. By the time I found her I was in a total panic and thought someone had kidnapped her. I'd been listening to too many Grimm fairy-tales. Mum hadn't been kidnapped, of course. She was just sitting on the back doorstep of our Sixties semi, slightly hunched over something I couldn't yet see. It was cold outside but she wasn't wearing a cardigan over her thin blouse. When I put my hand on her shoulder, she flinched and turned to look at me with a face I didn't recognise. She was lighting up a cigarette.

'Heidi, don't creep up on me like that,' she said.

'I've been looking for you everywhere,' I told her accusingly. 'Beano broke my doll.'

Beano the puppy stood beside me, still wagging his tail. He was waiting for me to take my eye off the doll for just one second so he could run down the garden and bury her next to his bones, I was convinced of it.

'Mummy.' I held the sorry-looking baby doll and its broken leg towards my mother again, but she didn't take it from me and immediately work Mummy magic.

'Show it to Daddy when he gets home from work,' she said instead.

'Is that a cigarette?' I asked.

Mum looked at the glowing tip as though surprised to find the fag in her hand. Then she said, 'Yes. I think it is,' and took a long drag. She exhaled luxuriously. And, while I'm sure she didn't mean for it to happen, some of the smoke got into my eyes. I screwed them tightly shut against the pain but didn't complain. I think I already knew that complaining wouldn't be appreciated that morning.

As I waited for my eyes to stop stinging, my little brother James started crying upstairs. He was only six months old.

'James is crying,' I said.

'I know.'

But Mum didn't race into the house to see what was upsetting him. Instead, she got up slowly and walked straight past, without looking at me, to the end of the garden. She stayed there and watched the washing blowing on the line until she had finished her cigarette.

*　　*　　*

Mum certainly doesn't smoke any more, which makes me wonder if I ever really did see that woman on the doorstep. Perhaps all these years I've really been remembering a photograph of someone else, or a scene from a movie. Not a Hollywood blockbuster but one of those films about urban isolation made by some gritty director from the North of England who grew up without any shoes. It doesn't seem possible that the soft, cuddly woman who greets me with a hug at the door of my parents' house these days ever walked straight past me so coldly when I wanted her to console me about a broken doll.

But sometimes when I think back over my early childhood, it does seem unusually quiet. I remember going to friends' houses, playing music loud and jumping on the beds, screaming round the garden, hollering through the hall, but those memories never take place in the house where my brother and I grew up. We played quiet games at our house – lots of hiding-under-the-stairs games. Games that involved lots of whispering. And we never had our schoolfriends round.

I stood at the kitchen sink and rinsed out my milk glass, shivering as I had done on that distant morning. I had been thinking about Mum and the strange cigarette moment quite often lately. Her face would pop into my mind at the oddest times: while I was watching the TV news, getting miserable about people starving in countries I hadn't heard of, or while I was sitting on the Tube opposite a Saturday father trying to entertain an unhappy pre-teen, or while I waited for Ed to hold open a shop door for some overburdened woman struggling alone with a pushchair and a toddler. When I say I saw Mum's face, I mean that odd, expressionless mask she had on that day twenty-five years ago, so different from the smiling, open face in the framed family photograph taken around the same time that now sat on the bookshelf in my sitting room. Which was the real one?

'Hey, what are you doing out here in the cold?' Ed appeared in the kitchen doorway.

'Just thirsty,' I told him. 'Sorry. I didn't mean to wake you up.'

'You didn't. My bladder did. Knew I shouldn't have had that last sherry. Do you want me to get your dressing gown for you?'

'No,' I said. 'I'm coming back to bed now.'

'Good. I can't sleep without you beside me.'

Ed kissed me on the top of the head. I smiled and reached up for his hand.

'Only because the electric blanket broke,' he added.

6

The following day, I was bleary-eyed as I glanced at the lists of guests who would be interviewed about the dangers of chafing and single parenting on *Let's Talk London* that morning. So bleary-eyed that I didn't even notice his name, let alone make any kind of connection.

I hadn't slept much at all. It had turned into one of those nights where you watch the shadows creep right across the ceiling until they disappear into the dawn before you finally start to lose consciousness. My face was scrubbed clean of make-up. The only colour to my pasty complexion came from the black shadows beneath my eyes and a 'time of the month' zit on my chin so large it actually had its own pulse. I was wearing my oldest jeans and my Ugg boots. 'Is that because they make men go "ugh" when they see them?' Ed asked every time I put them on. I hadn't washed my hair that morning because, having dropped off so late, I managed to sleep right through my alarm.

Nelly was organising all the show's guests, fetching them from reception, endowing them with the neatly printed name badges that would get them past the power-crazed security guard (ex-Territorial Army) and offering them their choice of disgusting coffee or horrible tea (we made Nelly and Robin fetch the team's coffee from Starbucks). It was quite usual that I didn't get to see the guests until the very last moment, just as Nelly walked them through from the shabby waiting area we rather grandly called the 'green room' while we connected to traffic news or weather. Often I didn't actually talk to the guests at all, except to ask them to introduce themselves into the microphone so that Jack, the studio manager, could check their voice levels. Jack was too shy to ask them himself unless he really had to. I think he would have preferred not to have to deal with other people ever. He reminded me of a Hobbit.

I had my head down, counting out the seconds of a traffic report, casting my eye over the schedule, as Nelly led that morning's guests into the studio. So the first I saw of him was when I looked up to see him sitting next to Flo.

Isn't it strange? For five years, you see someone almost every single day. You go to bed next to them. You wake up with your nose on their shoulder. They know everything about you: your childhood, your family and friends, your fantasies and your phobias. They know who said what to whom in the restaurant where you work at the weekends. What your English Lit tutor thought of your latest essay. Your hopes and fears for the future. What drives you mad. What turns you on . . . And you know everything about them, too. About the town they grew up in, the football team they support so zealously, the origins of all their scars . . .

Then, all of a sudden, they're not part of your life any more. You wake up together for the last time. You argue for the last time. You move out of the flat you once shared. You move to another part of town. You stop seeing the friends you had in common. Twelve months later you think of them around their birthday but you're no longer really sure whether it's on the sixteenth or the twelfth. And then, seven years on from the moment when you thought you would never, ever be able to stop that one particular person from being the first thought to enter your mind upon waking, they pop up in your workplace. You don't immediately recognise them. And they have a child you didn't even know was born.

'This morning we're going to be talking about the latest government report into the state of the family,' Flo began on the other side of the soundproof screen, totally oblivious to my sudden discomfort. 'Steven Gabriel, you're a single parent . . .'

Steven Gabriel was also my ex-boyfriend.

'Heidi,' Eleanor nudged me as Flo launched into her spiel. 'Are you okay?'

I was not okay. I felt as though I had been whacked in the stomach with a length of two by four. I ducked under the desk and started choking on a mouthful of coffee.

'Heidi?'

For months after Steven and I broke up, the mere mention of his name had a visceral effect on me. There were a couple of occasions when, walking down the street in some town he had probably never visited, I caught a glimpse of someone who looked a tiny bit like him and had to lean against a wall until my heart stopped thudding and my breath came back. It passed, of course. I had to get over it just to get into work. But that morning, I felt winded all over again, almost as badly as the first time.

Perhaps it was seeing him on *my* territory that did it; reawakening the small, broken part of me that had drawn a new map of London in my heart in the aftermath of our break-up and avoided whole swathes of the city for years to prevent any such unexpected meetings.

What on earth was Steven Gabriel doing in my studio?

'Steven is a representative of the Lone Parents Network, an organisation that supports parents of both sexes who find themselves bringing up children alone. You have one daughter,' Flo continued. 'Isabelle. Aged three and a half. Is that right?'

'Actually, she's just turned four,' said Steven with a grin in his voice at the thought of her. 'She'd be very upset if we didn't get that right.'

Flo laughed. 'We girls all know how important those few extra months can be. Particularly on the wrong side of thirty. Isn't that right, ladies?' Flo looked through the glass towards us. But I was busy mopping up the coffee I had spluttered all over the console, and Eleanor and Jack were still too busy staring at me, wondering whether I had just had a fit.

Over the next three minutes, all the questions I had secretly hoped I might one day find answered on Friends Reunited were answered right in front of me, live on air.

'Tell us about Isabelle,' asked Flo.

Four-year-old Isabelle was the only child from Steven's short-lived – very short-lived apparently – marriage to a French woman called Sarah.

Marriage. *Marriage*? You have no idea how strange that word sounded from his mouth.

'And where is Sarah now?'

Sarah had felt trapped by marriage and motherhood and decided she wanted to go back to university. In the South of France. On her own.

She left him? I was still reeling from the fact that she'd captured him at all.

'How did that make you feel?'

Understandably, Steven felt gutted.

'And how did it affect your work?'

Now Steven, who was a high-flying copywriter in an ad agency, had made arrangements to work from home two days a week in order to be able to look after Isabelle, with the help of a part-time nanny, until she started school full-time.

'And how has that arrangement been working out?'

Steven felt honoured to be able to spend so much time with his child, but at first he had been worried that his career would never fully recover from the time he now spent away from the office. He used to be a workaholic, which was another reason he thought Sarah might have chosen to leave.

'Some companies find it difficult to believe that you can be committed to a family and your career simultaneously,' said Steven. 'It's an issue women face all the time. I'll certainly be more sympathetic when I'm back in the office full-time.'

'Do you think lone fathers get more sympathy than lone mothers?' Flo asked.

'I come up against a lack of comprehension more often than sympathy,' he told her. 'It isn't often that a woman walks away from her child. There's a myth that motherhood comes naturally and women who choose not to stick with it are somehow wicked . . .'

'That's an interesting observation,' said Flo.

I didn't know where to look. I felt like an eight-year-old again, watching the Daleks on *Doctor Who* from behind the sofa. As it was, I had both my hands to my forehead, shading my face as I sneaked another little peek through the glass. He hadn't actually glanced my way for a second so far and was keeping his attention firmly on Flo.

Perhaps it wasn't him, I told myself. I mean, how likely was it that my ex-boyfriend would turn up on *Let's Talk London*?

Very likely.

The blond hair Steven had worn long and sun-bleached when I knew him was short and serious now and clearly hadn't seen much sunshine for a while. It started a little further back on his forehead, too. But his long, straight nose was unmistakable. As was his strong, square jawline and his summer-sky blue eyes, as Kara had once described them. His perfectly shaped pink lips. The sound of his voice. And of course there was the fact that the name 'Steven Gabriel' was neatly printed on my schedule in black letters twelve points high.

'Choosing a nanny was another headache,' he continued. 'I

could never understand why the girls in my office made such a fuss about it. I assumed that all women were somehow born with the right temperament and skills to look after any child. Just about anyone without a criminal record would do, I thought . . . Nothing could be further from the truth: allowing someone else to look after your child requires a huge amount of trust.'

'And money,' Flo chipped in.

'You're telling me,' Steven inhaled. 'It was while I was looking for a reliable, responsible and *affordable* childminder that I came across the Lone Parents Network.'

'How did you find them?'

'Via Google. They've got a great website.'

'And what do they offer the parent who finds him or herself alone?'

'They hold weekly meetings in cities all over the country. Social events. With crèches, of course, so you don't have to worry about childcare. And they offer a kind of local buddy system whereby newly single parents can call people who've been parenting alone for a while and find out how they cope.'

'And you liked them so much that you joined the committee.'

'I felt I had to. They helped me so much in those early days, and with my particular experience – having been able to persuade my bosses to allow me to work from home in a pretty serious role – I knew I had something to offer that might help someone else in my position later on.'

Steven was incredibly fluent. Flo had been chosen to front the show for her ability to do exactly that – *flow* – when the interviews she conducted got sticky. But Steven was good, too; no wonder he had been chosen as a spokesperson. Then he glanced away from Flo and finally caught my eye. And the cup of coffee he had been nursing toppled over onto the green baize of the table.

'Shit,' he said.

Flo's eyes widened.

'What do I keep saying about drinks in the studio?' groaned Jack.

'This is live, isn't it?' Steven cringed.

'I'm afraid so! But there is a tiny time lag so all anyone out there will hear is a beep! Sorry about that, ladies and gentlemen. Bit of an accident here in the studio. Not the first time, Steven, I can assure you,' Flo lied. 'These thin plastic cups really are no use to anyone. Still, I imagine you're well used to mopping up little spills with a three-year-old. I mean, just turned four-year-old . . .'

Steven looked towards me again and his eyes narrowed. I'm afraid I ducked under the table once more, on the pretence of looking for something in my handbag.

Nelly dashed into the studio with a handful of napkins she had thoughtfully pinched from Starbucks while fetching altogether better coffee for me and Eleanor.

'All under control now,' Flo was saying. Her voice was calm but when I popped back up her eyes were still asking frantic questions of mine. As were Steven's.

'What is going on?' hissed Eleanor. 'Do you know that man in there or something? You do, don't you?'

I shrugged at her in reply.

'Tell me the truth.' She gave me a pinch on the arm.

'Let's get back to the Lone Parents Network and your experiences,' Flo the pro continued. 'What would you say has been the hardest thing about being a single parent? I know it's not really the done thing for a man to admit he ever sheds a tear about anything except England losing the football or winning the rugby, but has there been a moment that really brought tears to your eyes?'

'Well,' Steven pulled himself back into the conversation. 'There have been so many. But the hardest thing . . . well, the hardest thing is witnessing the milestones in Isabelle's life on my own. My wife left us before Isabelle even took her first step. She hasn't seen our daughter walk, except in the little videos I send to France every month or so. She hasn't heard our daughter talk, except on the telephone. She certainly hasn't heard Isabelle's version of "Wuthering Heights". Isabelle's nanny is a big Kate Bush fan,' Steven explained. 'Every time Isabelle does something new and exciting, I have to hold back the tears – tears of happiness that she's turning into such a fabulous young lady, and tears of sadness that Sarah is missing it all. Sarah's definitely missing out by not being in Isabelle's life.'

Flo picked up one of the Starbucks' napkins and dabbed at her eyes theatrically. 'Oh, Steven,' she said. 'You're making my mascara run.'

On the other side of the studio, the telephone lines were already lighting up. Nelly and Robin started logging the calls so that Eleanor and I could filter the nutters and decide who might be safe enough to put through. They moved without pause from one call to the next. I clearly wasn't the only metropolitan woman being reduced to a pile of goo by Steven Gabriel that morning.

'Well, it looks like we're getting some calls,' said Flo. 'Steven, there are some people on the phone lines who would like to ask you a few questions about life as a single parent. Do you mind?'

Flo normally ended the show with a Jerry Springer-style round-up of the 'issues' raised by the topics discussed in the previous couple of hours, but that morning she didn't get round to it. We had been worrying that Flo would have to talk for longer than usual because the cyclist booked to talk about the calendar and his unorthodox ways with a banana skin hadn't made it to the studio, stuck on a broken-down train somewhere between Brighton and Victoria. ('Why didn't he bloody well cycle?' Eleanor asked.) But the callers kept their questions coming.

'Alice from Walthamstow wants to know what you think about the MMR vaccine debate . . .'

Isabelle had been vaccinated.

'Anna from Barnet is interested in your view on the new childcare voucher system . . .'

Extremely unwieldy, thought Steven.

'Fiona from Clapham would like to ask whether you've tried to find another female role-model for your daughter since Sarah left . . .'

'Elizabeth from Hammersmith says she would like to fill that vacancy,' Flo laughed. 'As would Jane from Hampstead, Sarah from Kennington, Maria from Stockwell and Adela from Golders Green.'

Heidi from Chiswick just wants to know what the hell you're doing walking back into her life on a Friday morning four months before she marries someone else.

'It's just like *Sleepless in Seattle*,' said Eleanor, as Steven handled the questions and accepted the sympathetic murmurings of several more women who sounded as though they would be only too happy to step into the position his wife had vacated. 'And they can't even see what he looks like. Isn't he lovely?' Eleanor added. 'So bloody handsome.'

'Hmm,' I replied. There was a touch of rakishness to his face when he was smiling, as he was right then in response to Clare from High Barnet's offer of babysitting help.

'That's very kind of you,' said Steven.

The woman gave him half her phone number on air before Flo could stop her.

At last the show came to an end.

'Well, thank you so much for coming to speak to us, Steven,' said Flo eventually. 'It's been wonderful to hear the single-parenting story from a man's perspective. Isabelle is a very lucky girl to have a dad like you.'

'No, Flo,' said Steven. 'I'm the lucky one. Every man should have the chance to get to know his child so well. Isabelle has made my life complete.'

Eleanor clutched at her heart and Flo gave a mock swoon for the benefit of the people behind the glass. She just about managed to introduce the news and bid her listeners 'good afternoon' without blubbing for real. The red light went off. The next show's team were already in place at the control desk on the other side of the station's single studio, ready to segue seamlessly into their show while we went for a quick break before beginning the business of planning the following programme's feelgood fest.

'That was unbelievable,' said Eleanor when Steven emerged. 'I've never seen call volume like it. At least it proves it isn't just my mum who listens to this show.' She clasped Steven's hand between both of hers when she shook it, but his eyes had already moved on to me.

'Hello, Heidi.'

'Hello, Steven.'

'You two know each other?' asked Flo, wide-eyed.

7

'We were at university together,' I said.

'That's right,' said Steven. 'Up in Leeds.'

'You're kidding! You didn't mention it,' Flo said to me.

'When would I have mentioned it?' I said defensively. 'I didn't make the connection between the person and the name on the list this morning. It's been a very long time.'

Steven nodded as he looked me straight in the eye. 'It certainly has. Seven years.'

'Well,' said Flo. 'It won't be so long next time. Heidi, we have got to have this man back on the show.' She grabbed his arm. 'Perhaps we can have a dating call-in with Steven as the prime catch! What do you think of that?' She gave him an exuberant kiss on both cheeks, leaving behind a big splodge of the signature bright-pink lipstick she had just reapplied. 'Fix it, Nelly.'

Nelly darted forward with a Starbucks' napkin and dabbed at Steven's cheek.

'Not his face! I mean fix a dating show,' said Flo. 'Honestly, she's so keen, that girl.'

Nelly blushed and went back to her notes.

'Got time for a decent coffee with us, Steven?' Eleanor asked coquettishly. 'I'll send Robin out for some cappuccinos. Or are you more an espresso kind of man?'

'I would love to join you but Isabelle's playgroup finishes at twelve,' Steven said, before Robin could protest at being cast as dogsbody again. 'I've got to pick her up today. Nanny's got the afternoon off.'

'Aww,' the assembled girls sighed.

'I'll make sure your taxi's ready,' said Nelly. 'And walk you to the door.'

'No. *I'll* walk you to the door,' I told him.

'Of course. You two must have loads to catch up on,' said Eleanor.

She didn't know the half of it.

'Gosh, well this is . . .'

'Strange?' Steven suggested.

We crossed the lobby and found a quiet place to stand on the pavement outside the London Talk Live building while we waited for his car.

'You look . . .' I said.

'So do you,' said Steven, nodding in what I hoped was an approving sort of manner, though I knew I looked as though I'd done a dive into the laundry basket.

'You've got a . . .'

'Little girl. Yes. Isabelle.'

'I had no idea.'

'I didn't know where to contact you when she was born.'

I nodded as if I thought I might in a million years have been on the list of people to whom he would send a birth announcement.

'It's a lovely name,' I said.

'Thank you. She's named after her grandmother. On Sarah's side,' he added unnecessarily. I knew very well that his own mother was called Jean.

'Well, I . . .'

I didn't know what to say next. Neither, it seemed, did he. I nudged at a piece of gravel on the pavement with my toe.

'What have you been doing with yourself?' Steven eventually pushed the conversation forward. 'You work in radio. Obviously.'

'Obviously . . .' I snatched at his question with relief. 'I'm a producer. Second in command in there after Eleanor.'

'That's great. It's what you always wanted to do.'

'Yes, it is. And you . . . you obviously got into advertising, just like you said you would.'

'Yeah,' he nodded. 'Though copywriting at Green and Grievson hasn't quite been the path towards a glittering career as a film-maker I thought it would be. At least, not yet. You may have seen my work for Amazin' Raisins,' he added, gently mocking himself with a parody of a Los Angeles accent. He had always been good at accents. 'We shot it in California; nearest I'll come to Hollywood for a while.'

'Amazin' Raisins?'

'You know the ad.'

'I don't think so.'

'It went like this.' He sang the Amazin' Raisins song for me.

'You should be locked up,' I said, when he finished singing about dried grapes in a scary elf voice. 'I remember that ad – couldn't get the jingle out of my head for weeks.'

'That was the idea.'

'I could sue for Persistent Song Syndrome.'

'But I bet you bought more raisins.'

'Uh-uh. No raisins in my house.'

'Whyever not?' Steven feigned shock. 'They're delicious, they're nutritious . . .' He threatened to reprise the song.

I found myself laughing. For more than two years after our split I had planned for this moment at least once a day and in my plans I was going to be frosty. I was going to be looking my best and feeling invincible and I was going to sweep straight past him to my limo. Yet there I was standing on the pavement outside work, wearing no make-up and Ugg boots, laughing with Steven Gabriel. I was just marvelling at how easy it was for him to make me smile again, when the following words popped out of my mouth.

'Ed doesn't like them.'

'Ed?' Steven's eyebrows shot up questioningly. 'Got yourself a cat at last?'

'No,' I told the ex-love-of-my-life. 'Ed's my boyfriend.'

My boyfriend. Ed's my *boyfriend*?

Why did I say that? Why didn't I say 'fiancé'? Since Ed had popped the question at the top of Eiffel's Parisian folly, I sometimes felt like I couldn't stop saying the bloody word. Fiancé. Fiancé. *Fee-yawn-say*. But to Steven I said 'boyfriend'. I might as well have said Ed was my flatmate, someone with whom I shared nothing more than a kitchen and a phone bill. Steven's momentarily surprised expression was soon replaced by an easy grin that told me he didn't feel threatened by the idea of my having a *boyfriend* at all.

'Your boyfriend, eh?' he said, nodding.

'Uh-huh,' I replied.

'Mm-hmm.'

Feeling the heat rise in my cheeks as it always did when I was caught in a lie, I looked away from Steven and searched the street for the account car that was suddenly taking way too long. I kept my hands in my pockets. It was cold for the time of year. And when Steven handed me his card, I reached out to take it with my right hand. Why wouldn't I? I am right-handed. The diamond as big as a peanut remained safely out of view.

'You should give me a call,' Steven said, as I admired the smart black font announcing his name and numbers. 'It would be nice to catch up when we've got a bit more time.' He paused then added, 'Get reacquainted *properly*.' His mouth curled up at one side.

Had he meant that to sound flirtatious?

'Yeah. Some time soon,' I said. 'I'd better get back to the office now. I daren't even go to the loo for fear that Nelly will use the opportunity to steal my job.'

'She seems pretty ambitious.'

'Gordon Gecko in a skirt . . . Look, there's your car.' I recognised with relief the black Audi A8 that the cab company often sent on account jobs.

'I guess I'm off, then.'

I nodded. 'I guess you are.'

Steven hovered.

'Thanks for coming in,' I said eventually.

'My pleasure.'

'Bye.'

He seemed to sway towards me as though thinking about giving me a kiss farewell and I stuck out my hand like a barrier coming down in a car park. Right hand, of course. We shook on it instead.

'It was nice to see you,' I told him.

'Yeah,' he said. 'A really nice surprise.'

The account car pulled up to the kerb and I waited as Steven climbed inside. It was a courtesy I would have afforded any of the show's visitors. He closed the car door but immediately wound down the passenger window and stuck his head out to continue our conversation.

'Heidi, do give me a call,' he said. 'I mean it. You've got my number now.'

'Of course,' I said brightly. Too brightly.

'He's a lucky guy, your boyfriend, Heidi Savage.'

And then, at last, the car pulled away.

I turned for the revolving door at once and made my way back to the lobby on shaky legs. I was a romantic Judas. I instantly began the process of beating up on myself, running back through the conversation and cringing at my moment of betrayal. Disgusted with myself for being so dishonest by omission, I paused by the big silver ashtray-bins at the entrance to my strictly non-smoking workplace and tossed

Steven Gabriel's card inside. It felt like throwing salt over my shoulder to blind the devil. I exhaled with relief immediately the card left my hand.

I took two more deep breaths.

Then, having made sure no one was watching, I gritted my teeth against the thought of God knows what else might be in that bin and fished the card back out again. I shook it clean of fag ash, took my wallet out of the back pocket of my jeans and tucked the card in there.

Why did I do it? Why didn't I just leave that card in the bin? At the time I told myself this: Kara and Steven had single-parenting in common now. And they had been good friends at university before the split forced Kara to choose sides. That was water under the bridge now. I should give her the opportunity of reconnecting with him again if she wanted to. She might be interested in calling him.

I was sure I *never* would.

8

When I got back into the office, I discovered that the rest of the team had been running a book on exactly how well I knew the lovely Steven Gabriel.

'I cannot believe that man is single,' said Flo. 'There must be a girlfriend he wasn't telling us about. Nelly, find out.'

Nelly automatically scribbled a note in her pad as the joke flew right over her head. If she ever quit radio, she would have a great future in international espionage. Robin had once suggested that the only thing Nelly couldn't track down was her own sense of humour.

'At least we know he's not gay,' said Eleanor.

'Lots of gay men have brief relationships with women in order to have children,' Nelly piped up. She was a veritable fount of conversation-stopping information. 'Don't you remember that item we did last year about same-sex parenting units?'

'*Units*? Oh Nelly! Shut up, for God's sake. Is he gay?' Eleanor asked me. 'He is in pretty good shape for a straight guy. That's always a bad sign. Tell us, Heidi. You must know if he went out with anyone at college. Were they male or were they female? Does he like big girls? Blondes? Brunettes?' she added hopefully, patting her own dark brown curls.

'I think he's into black girls,' said Flo. 'There was something about the way he smiled . . .'

'I went out with him at college,' I admitted then.

Eleanor's mouth dropped open in shock and, I think, slight admiration.

'See! I told you!' Flo whooped and slapped her palm down on her desk. 'What did I say? I knew it. Tell her what I said. I could tell from the look on her face when she saw him. Horror of the kind that only the unexpected appearance of an ex-lover can cause. Woo-hoo! I win. That will be a pound from you please, Robin.'

Robin tutted with annoyance and handed over the cash.

'And you, Eleanor.'

'What was it like?' Eleanor wanted to know. 'You lucky, lucky cow.'

'I'm not telling you.'

'Tell me or you're fired. I lost a whole quid on this.'

'I can't remember. It was a very long time ago,' I said.

'How long?' Flo probed.

'I haven't seen him for at least seven years and it's almost twelve years since I first met him.'

I saw Nelly's eyes narrow as she immediately tried to work out exactly how old that made me. I knew that Nelly was constantly measuring her career up against mine and was keen to know how long she had to go before she could be sitting in my seat.

'I went to university when I was fifteen,' I said to annoy her. 'But enough about me.' I sat down in my usual place at the round table covered in newspaper and magazine cuttings where we held our afternoon meetings. 'Shall we start? What have the papers thrown up as tomorrow's hot topic? Anybody?'

'Meeting your long-lost love in the workplace,' Robin suggested wickedly.

'Can bygones be bygones?' asked Eleanor.

'You're assuming there must be some bygones,' I replied.

'Has your long-lost lover turned out like you expected?' Nelly threw into the mix. 'Or even *better*?'

'Is there still a spark?' asked Flo.

'Oh, for God's sake,' I interrupted them. 'Will you lot behave yourselves? Yes, it was a shock to see him. And yes, it was a shock to see how much he's changed. He used to have long hair, you know. Down to here.' I indicated my shoulders. Eleanor and Flo shared an approving nod. 'But no, it didn't make me question my entire existence since we broke up and see that I'm marrying the wrong man, my life has become a meaningless shell and I won't be complete until my ex and I are together again. Steven Gabriel is just an ordinary man I happen to have gone out with in my dim and distant past. My very distant past. He is history.' My voice started to rise. 'I have put that man behind me. Ladies and gentlemen, I thank you very much.'

The whole team looked at me in faintly stunned silence for a second or two.

'Where did *that* come from?' asked Eleanor eventually.

'Oh, PM-bloody-T,' I snapped.

Robin, the only boy in the room that morning, nodded wisely.

'Nelly,' I continued. 'Perhaps you would like to start the meeting by telling the rest of the team about that article you found in the *Daily Mirror* on pet owners who grow to look like their dogs.'

That afternoon's meeting progressed without any further reference to my shared past with Steven Gabriel, but as soon as I got out of the office and turned my mobile phone on again, it was buzzing with messages from someone I knew would be far more persistent in uncovering the truth about my feelings on the matter.

Kara always listened to the show. She had switched allegiance from Radio Four's *Woman's Hour* while pregnant and she was still listening to *Let's Talk London* now that she was at home full-time with Forester (her parents had insisted on funding some proper 'maternity leave'). In fact, she had once even been a call-in guest on the show, for a segment about the year's most popular baby names. She had been chosen to illustrate the small group of people who bucked the Sophie, Jack and Thomas trend and went for something ridiculous instead. I didn't tell Kara that 'ridiculous' was the exact word Eleanor had used when briefing the piece at a meeting.

That morning, Kara had sent me six text messages.

'Was that him?'

'Was that *really* him?'

'Why didn't you tell me he was going to be on the show?'

'Are you with him now?'

'Are you having sex with him in a seedy hotel in West Kensington?'

Not having had sex with anybody since Forester was conceived, Kara had become obsessed with the idea that everyone else was having lots of it, shagging simply *all* the time. I definitely wasn't, being engaged.

'For God's sake pick up your phone!!!!' was the last text.

I grudgingly sent a reply. 'Yes. Yes. Didn't know. No. No! NO!!!!!.' She must have called me the second she got it.

'Heidi Savage! Have I got you out of bed?' she began.

'I am walking to the Tube station,' I said flatly.

'That was quick.'

'Kara, I have not been having sex with Steven Gabriel. I did not even kiss him goodbye. Why does everyone assume I want to jump on him?'

'Does everyone assume?'

'You obviously do. And everyone at the studio did – they wouldn't let it go.'

'Because that's exactly what would happen in a soap opera. A face from the past reappears. Neither of you can control yourself. The chemistry is still there . . .'

I snorted.

'It's the Friends Reunited syndrome. Hundreds of relationships starting up again after years apart. Unfinished business,' she added wisely.

'Steven Gabriel and I have no unfinished business.'

'Whatever. How did he look? Fat? Old? Balding?'

'No. No. No.'

'Shaggable?' Kara persisted.

'Nooo!'

'Wow. All that stuff he said to Flo. Incredible. Can you believe that a woman actually left Steven Gabriel? Can you believe he actually got married in the first place? What on earth can she have been like? I'd like to say she must be amazing but since you're the most amazing woman I know the whole thing must have been a shotgun affair. And she walked away from him? I almost choked on my coffee,' she told me.

'I did choke on mine.'

'I bet you want to call her up and offer your congratulations. We should buy her a medal for services to womankind.'

'I don't want to do anything of the sort,' I said firmly. 'It's horrible being dumped, especially if you've got a child. I wouldn't even wish it on someone who dumped me.'

'Dumped you *horribly*,' Kara reminded me.

'Not even someone who dumped me horribly.'

'That's very big of you. Bigger than I would be in the same circumstances. Good girl.'

'Thank you.'

'So . . .'

'So what?'

'So, you must have had some kind of conversation with him off air as well?'

'Yes.'

'What about?'

'I don't know . . . He sang me the Amazin' Raisins jingle.'

Confused silence from Kara's end.

57

'Amazin' Raisins?'

'He worked on the adverts,' I explained.

'You talked about *adverts*?'

'What else were we going to talk about?'

'Er, I dunno . . .!' Kara put on her village-idiot voice. 'What do you think, you daft cow? So many things left unsaid since the last time you saw that man.'

'Right. That would have been a *very* easy conversation to start on the street right outside my office,' I said sarcastically. 'Kara, we had about two minutes before the account car came to take him home and I had to get back to work. That's all.'

'He dumped you seven years ago without giving you a proper reason and this morning all you managed to talk about was some bloody raisin advert. I don't believe it. You might have missed your opportunity to ever know the truth.'

'Who says I want to know it? What difference could it possibly make to me now?'

'It could heal all those years of pain,' Kara joked.

'Perhaps they *have* healed and going back over them would be just like picking a scab.'

'Charming image,' said Kara. 'But I still don't believe you really don't want to know. Unless you've secretly arranged to see him again and you're just not telling me . . .'

'Of course I haven't.'

'You gave him your number?'

'I didn't.'

'Then you took his number, didn't you?'

'No.'

'But they must have it in your office.'

'I expect they do.'

'Did you tell him about Ed?'

'Yes.'

'And you said you were getting married?'

'Yes.'

'And you showed him the ring?'

I hesitated.

'Of course.'

Kara made a little snorting noise. A disbelieving noise, perhaps. Though there was no reason on earth why she shouldn't have believed me, given that I was nuts about Ed Gordon. Absolutely crazy about the man I was going to marry. Ed Gordon was the centre of my universe. He was the love of my life. Why wouldn't I have wanted to tell Steven? Kara didn't really know that I hadn't. I was just transposing my guilt into her questioning.

'Did you show him the ring?' she asked one more time.

'Kara,' I insisted, 'I showed him the bloody ring.'

9

When I finally managed to get Kara off the phone, having promised that I would see her first thing the following morning to sift through another set of replies to her online personal, I called Ed at his surgery. I felt a need to hear his voice, as though it might block out all the sudden noise in my head. But he couldn't talk to me – he was up to his elbows, or his knuckles at least, fixing some poor sod's broken crown. His receptionist promised me that she would let him know I called as soon as he was free.

'Thanks, Roberta.'

'He's mortified about the treacle thing, you know. He told me you were really pissed off about the mess.'

'I guess we'll just have to get everything cleaned professionally.'

'Don't be too hard on him, will you? Those rugby mates of his, they're only daft. And I'm sure I'm not letting the cat out of the bag when I tell you that Ed can't believe how badly he's cocked up. He keeps asking me how he can make it up to you. He loves you more than anything. You know that.'

For all his macho posturing with the rugby lads, Ed was a great big softy who, when he couldn't get away from the chair, often got his receptionist to call me to tell me that he loved me. I was much more embarrassed than he should have been.

'Thanks,' I said. 'I do know that.'

'You arranged your hen night yet?' Roberta asked then.

'Not yet. The wedding's still four months away.'

'Those four months will be over in no time. Before you know what's happened, you'll have been married for fifty years with ten grandchildren.'

'Yeah,' I said.

Fifty years? *Ten* grandchildren? An image of a worn-out old sow popped into my mind's eye, unbidden. Seriously. An actual pig.

'Don't forget to invite me, will you?' Roberta said, while I was still trying to shake the porker.

'You're number one on my list. Look, Roberta, I should let you get back to work. Have a nice weekend.'

'Bye-bye, darling.'

As I slipped my phone back into my pocket, I found myself nervously twisting my engagement ring. It didn't really matter that I hadn't shown it to Steven, did it? It would have been a bit forced: not having seen him for seven years – seven years since I told him I didn't care if he fell under a Tube train – then suddenly thrusting my diamond in his face. There just wasn't a moment when it wouldn't have seemed like showing off in the worst possible way.

Besides, I would be showing the ring to plenty of people that night. Once a year, Ed's rugby team hosted a proper formal dinner to which wives and girlfriends were invited. It was a black-tie affair, a 'thank you' for the patience the girls had shown throughout the season. And their laundry services. Though to his credit, Ed had always managed to put his own jock-strap in the washing machine.

That night, Ed came home from work slightly earlier than usual and by six o'clock he was as excited to be shoe-horning himself into his slightly-too-small dinner jacket as any teenage girl slipping into her high-school prom dress. He had me tie his bow tie – though he inevitably complained that I didn't do it properly and retied the thing himself when he thought I wasn't looking – then he pulled James Bond poses in the bedroom mirror while I put on my make-up.

'Do I look like Sean Connery?' he asked me. 'Or Pierce Brosnan?'

'More hair than Connery and much better than Pierce Brosnan,' I said.

Ed was satisfied I had given the right answer.

That night, I would be wearing a dress I had bought for the radio station's Christmas party the previous year. It was black velvet – a bit boring perhaps, but very well cut. And expensive. I was damned well going to get some more wear out of it, particularly since I had already had to have it dry-cleaned twice to restore the nap after Ed spilled a pint all over the skirt. When eventually I was ready, Ed grabbed me by the waist and threw me backwards over his knee in a ballroom-dancing style swoon so that my carefully arranged hairdo was instantly ruined.

'Don't we make a gorgeous couple?' he said, when I had finished shrieking.

'We don't look too bad together,' I sighed.

Before we left, Ed popped next door to show Mrs H how handsome he looked in his black tie and to drop off a pre-scription he had picked up for her on his way back from work. After that, we got a taxi to the venue where the party was being held. It was unthinkable that Ed wouldn't get too drunk to drive that night and I knew I would need a drink or seven to put up with him and find the naked rugby songs even remotely amusing.

When we arrived, most of the team were already there, propping up the bar and making excruciatingly polite small-talk with the wives and girlfriends of their mates. The girls were all in boring little black dresses like me, but the variety in the men's outfits was pretty impressive. They all wore the exclusive rugby-club tie (gold skull and crossbones against a burgundy background) but accessorised with a wacky waist-coat here, a Simpsons' cummerbund there. And when I say Simpsons, I mean *The* Simpsons, America's favourite dysfunctional TV family, not some smart Jermyn Street tailor.

Ed greeted his best friend Zach with a gentle punch to the solar plexus, then James 'Scotty' Macdonald kicked off an impromptu scrum by grabbing hold of Ed's head and trying to force it down between Zach's thighs.

'Bender!' was the accompanying call. 'Eddy Gordon is a bend-errrrrr!!!!'

'But I'm getting married! Tell him, Heidi!' Ed appealed to me.

'He is a bender,' I agreed with Scotty and left Ed to fend for himself. He was a big boy, after all.

'Hi, Heidi,' Zach's wife Sophie kissed me on both cheeks, as did Scotty's girlfriend Clare.

'Heidi, hi!' hollered another of the boys in passing before throwing himself on top of Ed, Scotty and Zach.

As far as greeting rituals went, any alien zoologist watching the men and women at that party would have been forgiven for thinking we were from very different branches of the evolutionary tree.

'Are you ready for this?' Sophie asked me, as the men continued to fondle each others' crotches in an orgy of the kind of homo-eroticism they otherwise spent so much energy denying.

'Can one ever be ready? I'm going for the "can't beat 'em, join 'em" approach this year,' I confided. 'I'm getting absolutely wasted *before* the trousers start coming off and Ed auditions for puppetry of the penis again.' Sophie and I both winced at the memory of the previous year's impromptu entertainment. 'Who wants a drink?' I asked. 'Double V and T's all round?'

'Yes, please,' said Clare.

'I can't,' said Sophie.

Clare was immediately wide-eyed. It took me a moment or two longer to work out the huge significance of Sophie's throwaway line.

'Oh my God!' Clare put her hand to her mouth. 'You're not?'

'Yes,' Sophie confirmed. 'Yes. I am. We're pregnant! I had my twelve-week scan yesterday afternoon.'

'Congratulations!' Clare shrieked and actually jumped up and down at the news. There was much more kissing. 'I thought you were glowing! I knew it. I didn't like to ask.'

Sophie smoothed the fabric of her dress over an as yet non-existent bump and adopted the coy look of a Renaissance Madonna. 'I would have told you earlier but, well, we wanted to be really sure. Can you believe it? I'm going to be a mum.'

'You'll have rugby kit *and* baby-gros to wash this time next year!' said Clare. 'You lucky, lucky thing.'

'Very lucky,' I concurred. 'If you really like doing the laundry that much.'

I thought of Kara's friend Julia and the stinking dustbin of soiled reusable nappies in the corner of her kitchen that Kara had described to me. I said, 'Congratulations, Sophie. Zach must be very pleased.'

'He's over the moon. He's been broody for years, just like Ed has.'

I blinked at that comment.

'Zach's already been out and bought a train set,' Sophie continued. 'I told him he better not be disappointed if it's a girl and he said he wasn't intending to let the baby anywhere near it anyway, boy or girl. It was his treat for proving he's such a fertile man.'

Clare guffawed.

I caught the barman's eye at last. 'What can I get you?' he asked.

'Double vodka and tonic,' I said. 'Actually, make it a triple. Save me coming back to the bar,' I explained to Clare and Sophie, who had stopped laughing rather suddenly, I thought, when they heard my order.

By the time my drink was ready, a small group of women had already lined up to place their hands on Sophie's stomach in veneration. She lifted her floaty black chiffon top proudly to expose her ever-so-slightly convex belly-button. For the rest of the evening, you could almost chart Sophie's progress around the party by the girlish 'ooohs' and 'aaahs' that followed her happy announcement.

Zach and Sophie were seated on a different table from Ed and I. I have to admit I wasn't entirely disappointed. It wasn't long before the ultrasound picture came out of Sophie's beaded handbag and there's only so much you can say about the fuzzy black and white picture of TV interference that is a prenatal scan. Sophie flashed hers as proudly as if it were a Mario Testino cover shot for Vogue.

'There are the fingers,' she said. 'Or perhaps they're the toes . . .'

Perhaps they're the horns, I always wanted to suggest. I liked Sophie. I really did. But baby scans, to me, were only slightly more interesting than a scan of a ruptured appendix. I could only widen my eyes in disbelief when Clare claimed she could actually see a resemblance between the black and white dots and Sophie's husband.

Our table of eight was completed by three other couples. Jack and Lucy (him in the City, her *extremely* busy mother of three. Triplets. IVF. 'I don't think you have any idea how stressed out I am,' was her catchphrase), Gids and Virginia (I think that was her name. They'd met at a speed-dating event just two weeks earlier. She was a primary-school teacher from Barcelona and hardly spoke any English at all, which was probably how Gids had managed to hang on to her so long), and then there was Scotty and Clare.

Scotty was an estate agent. He'd started out at a big branch of the Foxtons chain as soon as he left school but now, twelve years on, he had a small agency of his own and, like Ed with his surgery, was working all hours to get it off the ground. His girlfriend of two years, Clare, worked in the accounts department of a little Mayfair art gallery that specialised in Victorian paintings. She was eager to work her way out of the accounts office and into art dealing proper, having studied fine art at university. She looked a little like a watercolour herself, with a bob of blonde hair as fine as a baby's and a strangely melancholy look in her pale-blue eyes.

Clare and I had met at several of these occasions. I remember how nervous Scotty had been to introduce Clare to his friends the very first time. He had even called Ed at home before the big event (the rugby-club annual dinner, of course) and begged him to tone it down a bit. Not to take the piss too much. Not to scare her off. Scotty called all the boys and asked the same, because he really liked Clare. Clare was special, he said.

I got along with Clare well enough, though it was very difficult to get her off the typical London dinner-party subjects: the daily commute, congestion charging, house prices. Especially house prices since Scotty had set up on his own estate agency. For a while, I wondered whether she found me too boring to bother taking the conversation further. Later, I would realise that even as she seemed to be talking directly to me, she was always keeping one ear on whatever conversation Scotty was having on the other side of the table. If he was talking to another woman, she became as nervous as a rabbit, straining her hearing to make sure that he wasn't flirting.

Unfortunately, Scotty usually *was* flirting. Less than two years after Scotty had announced that this one was 'special', it was clear that the lustre had worn off, for him at least. Clare was still besotted. Her eyes had started to look perpetually tearful, like a devoted spaniel's.

'You must be so excited about the wedding,' was her opening gambit that night, as the silver-service staff began to circle the room with their baskets of rock-hard bread rolls that would later be used as the first missiles in a food fight.

I started to tell her about local politics at the beautiful sixteenth-century church near my parents' home where Ed and I were to be married. We were having trouble persuading the old-fashioned vicar to allow us to record the service on video.

'And he's vetoed outright our plans to process from the church to the strains of "A Thing Called Love" by The Darkness,' I joked.

Clare didn't laugh. In fact, her eyes glistened as I spoke, I thought. Became perceptibly wetter. And then she zoned out completely. One ear on Scotty's conversation again.

'*Dos birra por favor*,' said Scotty. 'See Gids, I can speak Spanish too. I could chat up your girlfriend. Piece of piss.'

'I think you mean *cerveza*,' said Virginia seriously. 'Cerveza is Spanish for beer.'

'Whatever,' said Scotty. 'It's all French to me.'

The meal was predictably terrible. You can't expect much for fifty pounds when forty of those pounds are budgeted on booze. Everything was the wrong colour. The chicken was still pink on the inside. Sophie was practically in convulsions as she passed by our table on the way to the ladies' room. 'That was raw chicken!' she exclaimed. 'Salmonella could have killed the baby! I've told Zach to complain.'

Conversely, the colour of the vegetables had been obliterated by three days on the boil. Broccoli, cauliflower, beetroot? Who knew? Pudding wasn't much better: a black-forest gateau of true Seventies vintage with 'cream' that hadn't ever seen a cow. I couldn't touch it. Ed, on the other hand, didn't seem to care what anything looked like. He might as well have been eating dog food. To him, it was all about lining his stomach for the next pint of Bordeaux. That's right. The boys were drinking red wine *by the pint*. Ed was on his second but he was determined not to be the first man to pass out that night.

'How long till the big day now?' Lucy swapped places with her husband so that she could grill me about the wedding as well.

'Four months,' Ed shouted across the table. 'Heidi's still got the chance to lose a few more pounds.'

'And he's still got a chance to grow up or find himself alone at the altar.' I launched a pellet of bread roll in his direction.

'I didn't mean it, my little chick-a-dee. Your curves are in all the right places.' Ed got up from his seat and kissed me on the top of the head as he paused on his way to the bar.

'You've been engaged for a whole year, haven't you?' Lucy observed, as though there might be some sinister reason behind the delay.

'We didn't think we'd have enough time to arrange a proper wedding if we tried to do it last summer,' I explained.

'But we can't wait too much longer because Heidi isn't getting any younger and I feel the need to breed.' Ed beat his chest.

'Oh God. Ed,' I groaned, 'you're not a bloody silverback.' I hated it when Ed did his gorilla impression. I felt my pelvic floor muscles contract involuntarily – and not in a good way – whenever Ed talked about sex in animal husbandry terms.

Lucy rolled her eyes in sympathetic recognition. All around the room, barristers and surgeons and management consultants were connecting with their animal ancestry. 'We'll just have to hope that his sperm aren't already swimming in circles,' I added with a wan smile.

'What are you talking about?' Ed snorted. 'I've got super-sperm! I'm not some Jaffa who needs IVF.'

Lucy winced. Thankfully, Ed was dragged off to join the rest of his team in a scrum on the dance-floor before he could elaborate on his theme. 'Hold these,' he said, handing me his front teeth for safe-keeping as he went.

This bouncing scrum was the boys' version of dancing around their handbags. Funny how many men will only venture onto the dance-floor when the song being played is almost impossible to dance to. They don't make it easy for themselves, waiting for 'Come on Eileen' or 'God Save the Queen' (Sex Pistols version) before they step out. That said, Ed certainly looked far more comfortable pogo-ing up and down to The Pistols than he had done the one time I managed to drag him to a salsa class. God only knew what he would choose for our wedding song, given a chance. 'Tainted Love'? That was another boy-dance classic, offering the perfect opportunity for the rugby lads to camp it up and grab each other by the man-breasts.

'I'm so sorry about that,' I said to Lucy.

'About what?'

'About the . . . you know, the IVF thing. He didn't mean to sound so insensitive, I'm sure. Ed really doesn't know what he's talking about half the time.'

'Why should that bother me?'

I had momentarily forgotten that I wasn't actually supposed to know the triplets weren't conceived in the natural way. Sophie, who had always been much closer to Lucy than I ever really wanted to be, had spilled the confidential beans. Ed wasn't the only member of the rugby club who wanted it thought that he was a fully functioning breeding male. An alpha male. Who had Jack talked to when things got tough? I wondered.

In some ways, it was a shame we couldn't mention the

intervention. I would have loved to have asked Lucy what made them decide to go for it; what made them decide that having a child of their own was worth the pain of hormone injections and potentially fruitless egg-harvesting? Not to mention the money. Kara had once told me that going on IVF meant growing a moustache like a Lithuanian bandsman while your follicles matured. I felt pretty certain that given the same circumstances I would have just thrown up my hands and consoled myself with a lifetime of fabulously expensive child-free holidays instead. I found it very hard to imagine that anyone could really want a baby enough to suffer poverty *and* facial hair.

'Have you called the babysitter?' Lucy yelled at Jack as he pogo-ed close to our table. 'Jack? Jack? Have you called the babysitter yet? Has she given Petrina her Calpol?' Lucy looked exhausted at the thought. 'Honestly, sometimes I feel like I've got four children. You have no idea quite how tough life is with just one full-time nanny . . .'

'Show me the ring,' said Clare wistfully. Again. But I was grateful to get off the subject of babies.

I held out my hand towards her and couldn't help smiling. Every time I saw my engagement ring it was as though I was seeing it for the first time. Even a year on. The perfect diamond, which had exactly one hundred facets, Ed told me, seemed to be lit on the inside. It sent a little shard of reflected light onto Clare's cheek, where it hovered like a glittering tear.

'And he chose it himself, didn't he? Amazing he got you something so tasteful. In the two years we've been together, Scotty has never once managed to buy me anything I would be seen dead in. I'm always first in the refunds queue at Marks and Spencer's every Boxing Day.'

Lucy nodded sympathetically. 'What is the mother of triplets supposed to do with a red lace thong?'

'Can I try the ring on?' Clare asked.

'Sure.' I slipped it off and handed it over.

'Not on *your* engagement finger, Clare,' said Lucy. 'That's really bad luck.'

'Don't think my love luck can get very much worse. I'm so jealous of you, Heidi,' Clare told me, turning her hand from side to side to catch the light. 'Ed's an amazing guy. You're so lucky.'

'It will be your turn one day, Clare,' said Lucy.

Clare smiled bravely but I felt like thumping Lucy when she patted her on the 'engagement' hand in patronising consolation.

It was this kind of insistence that marriage was a state in which every girl eventually found herself that made it so hard to bear when you weren't anywhere near. All this talk of two by two as though there was no other way to get through life. I could remember being in Clare's position very clearly.

But then again, as soon as you did bag a man, you had to start outlining your family-planning arrangements to practical strangers every time you were out to dinner. I didn't know which was worse.

Clare handed back my ring and turned her wistful smile towards the dance-floor where the first brave lad had already lost his trousers.

'Oh dear,' said Lucy eventually. 'Looks like Ed's just passed out.'

IO

That was the end of Ed's big night out and the beginning of my nightmare. Richard, the captain, declared that there was to be no mercy when Ed was first man to pass out in front of his team-mates for the second time in less than a fortnight. Treacle and feathers didn't seem like much of a punishment compared to that night's torture. While Ed hopelessly struggled to regain a useful level of consciousness out there in the middle of the dance-floor, Richard draped a black handkerchief over his head and intoned in a deep judge's voice that this time Ed Gordon was to forfeit *all his body hair* – at least, what little had grown back since I scraped off the treacle. Richard waved aloft a ceremonial Gillette bought specially for the occasion and the team held Ed down while he was shaved.

Legs, arms, chest, head, eyebrows . . .

'Eyebrows! No! You're joking!' I shouted.

Richard wasn't.

I pleaded for clemency, to no avail.

'What will his patients think?' I asked, when it was clear that getting married in less than four months was not a good enough reason for the rugby boys to leave my fiancé looking vaguely human.

'He can tell them he's having chemo,' said one bright spark, drawing in a new set of comedy brows above Ed's startled eyes with what was probably an indelible marker.

'Richard,' I said seriously. 'You may well have ruined my life.'

★   ★   ★

Ed threw up in the cab on the way back to our flat. He threw up in the cab and all down the side of cab when I finally managed to direct his big, fat, bald head out through the window. The taxi driver made me part with an extra fifty quid on top of the already extortionate fare to pay for cleaning (though from the smell of his car even before Ed started spewing, I doubted the driver would bother to do much more than wipe the seat over with some kitchen roll before he picked up his next sickly customer). After that, there was no way I was going to let Ed get into bed beside me. I installed him in the spare room with a red plastic bucket within easy reach of the bed.

He had been barely conscious on the way home and was out cold as soon as his head hit the pillow. Mouth wide open. Teeth still out. Snoring like a swamp monster. I took off his tie and shoes but didn't bother to undress him further than that. I didn't know where to start. I definitely didn't want to touch his shirt, covered as it was with that vomit. Or his trousers, which were drenched in beer (please, only beer, I prayed). He could undress himself and strip the bed when he woke up the following day.

Instead, I stood with my hands on my hips and stared down at him, feeling a sense of nausea in my own stomach.

You have no idea how much eyebrows contribute to the beauty of a man's face until they're not there any more. Without his brows to add definition Ed looked like a great big ugly newborn and not a human one at that. It might have been funny had it happened to someone else's man. I put my hand to my own forehead and sighed.

How was it possible that this ridiculous man on the mattress before me was a respected professional? Ed had studied extremely hard for many years. People trusted him to take care of their mouths. He was allowed to administer *anaesthetic*. He was what might in the past have been called a 'pillar of the community'. And yet he was also a man who, on occasion, got so drunk he couldn't even stand up unaided. He was a bloke who hung out with a bunch of guys who thought that chemotherapy was something to make a joke about. And let's not even go near the hideous historical overtones of that black treacle and feathers stunt.

I thought of Lucy's tight-lipped smile as her husband Jack and Ed's best friend Zach helped me carry Ed out to the taxi. I thought of Sophie's concerned little moue. Clare's gentle squeeze of my shoulder. Even the other rugby widows pitied me. I didn't want their pity – these were women whom I had actually heard to tut 'boys will be boys' when their full-grown husbands were arrested for setting fire to the tablecloths in an Indian restaurant. But I certainly pitied myself right then, alone in charge of the biggest baby in London. I wondered briefly whether it was even safe to leave Ed alone in the spare room. What if he choked on his own vomit? What if he died? As I considered the scope for calamity he let out a wet-sounding fart in his sleep.

'I've had enough of this,' I murmured.

Who cared if he did die?

I slammed the door to the spare room behind me.

Why did I find it so difficult to hang on to my sense of humour that evening? In all probability, four months was plenty of time to grow back a pair of eyebrows for the wedding photos. Mine certainly never stayed neatly plucked for that long.

It wasn't as though Ed had suddenly started behaving out of character. Sure, he had got horribly drunk but he was only that horribly drunk a couple of times a year. The dinner was a special occasion and for all the time I'd known him, I'd been able to convince myself that Ed's rugby-club shenanigans were harmless. Just a form of release. Like many of his team-mates, he had a very difficult and stressful job. His dental surgery – which had been running for just over a year – employed three full-time staff who relied on Ed to be sensible day-in day-out so that he could pay their wages. Surely he deserved to be able to go a little crazy sometimes. And I shouldn't forget the fact that Richard had actually *auctioned* the opportunity to shave Ed's body hair off for charity. His friend George had paid three hundred pounds for the privilege and all that money would be going to support child victims of war.

One day I would look back on this and laugh. One day I would be proud that my future husband's humiliation had helped relieve another human being's pain. That's what Clare told me. But it was no use that night. The good in the situation simply wouldn't outweigh the bad.

I undressed in a fury. The pleasantly squiffy feeling I had developed during dinner was long gone; the taxi ride home made me sober up pretty quickly. I took off my dress and hung it on the outside of the wardrobe to air, though I knew that it would have to be dry-cleaned again. There was to be no getting away with a quick airing this time. Ed had slobbered all over me and wiped his sick-sticky chin all over my shoulder as he begged me to get him home safely during a brief moment of consciousness. I took off my jewellery. Earrings, necklace *and* engagement ring. I tossed the ring into my jewellery box not caring if it got scratched. A small, symbolic gesture. I was so straight by this point, I even remembered to decant my mobile phone and severely depleted wallet from my sequinned evening bag back into the black leather handbag I used every day. I tossed Ed's disgusting false front teeth into the water glass on his side of the bed.

And that's when I found myself sitting on the edge of the mattress, opening my wallet and looking at his card again.

His phone number. His mobile number. Steven Gabriel.

* * *

What was he doing that night? I wondered. Where was he? Was he at home? Perhaps he'd got himself a babysitter for the evening and was out on the town with his friends. I hadn't even had a chance to ask him where he was living these days. His card held no address.

Where would he live? I imagined him somewhere by the river Thames, in a cool, white-painted bachelor pad, walking from his designer sofa to his high-tech designer sound system. In my imagination, everything was show-home immaculate. Pale untreated wood. Perfect finishes on the walls and floors. But of course he had a four-year-old daughter these days. It was unlikely she favoured the minimalist approach.

What did she look like? Isabelle: the name immediately conjured up a fairy princess with jiggling ringlets of gold. Did she look like that? Did she look like *him*?

When Steven and I were together, I used to lay in bed beside him at night and trace his lips, so full for a man's, and tell him that I hoped our daughter inherited his mouth rather than mine. The memory of those conversations gave me a little prickle in the chest. Perhaps Isabelle looked more like her mother . . .

What was *she* like? I wondered. This Sarah. What kind of woman left her husband *and* her baby? More to the point, what kind of woman would Steven Gabriel have married in the first place? What kind of woman could he have decided was worth committing his life to in such a serious way?

As Ed snored on in the spare room (at least the noise told me he was alive), I sank back in the pillows and found myself imagining the ex Mrs Steven Gabriel.

I had an idea of the kind of woman Steven fancied, and I didn't fit the mould. When I first arrived at university, Steven was already going out with a girl called Anna. She couldn't have been more different from the girl I was back then.

Confident, gregarious, as dark as I was blonde. A sporty brunette who knew what to do with a lacrosse stick. I didn't even know what a lacrosse stick was, not having been to a private school.

I imagined Sarah to be the same as Anna. There was the French bit too. I pictured a woman like Beatrice Dalle. In my mind's eye, Sarah Gabriel was raven-haired with blow-job lips and moody *chocolat* eyes. Basically, my polar opposite. Just as Ed was the polar opposite of Steven. Steven was blond. When he had hair, Ed was dark. Steven was snake-hipped. Ed was built like the proverbial brick shit-house. Steven once played guitar and sang Cure songs in a pretentious student band. Ed couldn't play any instruments at all but occasionally sang rude rugby songs until he passed out . . .

Oh, God. Now Ed was snoring loudly enough to wake Mrs H next door, even if she had taken her hearing aid off. I tried to arrange my pillows so that they covered my ears. Steven never snored.

Since Steven and I had broken up seven years earlier, I hadn't dared to think well of him, or even really to think about him at all. I had tried very hard to never play the comparison game during my post-Steven dating life, but that night, I found myself unable to stop. I compared the dreadful evening I had just endured with the kind of evenings I used to spend with Steven. Intimate evenings in Ethiopian restaurants, Turkish restaurants, little Polish places well off the beaten track with a bunch of eclectic friends. I compared the stupid rugby-club widows and their meat-headed men with Steven's friends – his funny, clever crowd of musicians and artists and wannabe writers. What had become of them? Was he still in touch with them? And then, inevitably, I was leafing back through twelve years' worth of memories. All the way back to very first time Steven spoke to me.

★   ★   ★

77

I thought of me, aged just eighteen, standing in the lodge of the university hall of residence. I thought of Steven, bounding in from the football pitch with his friends and saying 'hello'. I'd seen him before of course, and I knew all about him. Everybody did. Steven was the most popular guy in the year above mine, if not in the university. Captain of the football team. Brightest student on his course. That afternoon, standing by the pigeonholes, was the first time he had acknowledged my existence. My heart immediately bloomed towards him like a crocus breaking through the frozen earth. And when his friends left the lobby and headed for the bar, Steven was still standing there.

'Heidi, isn't it?' he asked.

I could only nod in reply.

'You've got the room upstairs from mine,' he said. 'You must really like the Rolling Stones.'

It took me a moment to work out what he meant.

'I think you need some new tapes,' he continued. 'Because I'm fed up with hearing "Sympathy for the Devil" even if you aren't. If you like your music rocky though, I think I've got just the thing for you.'

He brought a Nirvana album round to my room later that afternoon. I made him a cup of tea with UHT milk in one of the embarrassing floral mugs that matched the floral kettle Mum and Dad had given me as a student-pad-warming present. Steven didn't leave my room until midnight.

Three weeks later, I lost my virginity to him. To a beautiful young man who had, over the course of a decade, become the bloke I didn't immediately recognise when he walked into the studio. Divorced. A single father. It wasn't how I had expected his life to pan out.

But I hoped he was happy, didn't I? After seven years of not wanting to hear anything but bad news of Steven Gabriel, I

78

could finally wish him well. Because all was finally well in my world, wasn't it?

Another snore like a hippopotamus farting through mud erupted from the spare bedroom.

11

Kara telephoned at half past eight the following morning.

'Did I wake you up?' she asked, not waiting for an answer before she continued. 'Can you believe I've been up for three bloody hours already? Forester wanted to play at half past five in the morning!'

'Which is about the same time I finally got to sleep,' I complained. Of course she had woken me up. 'You wouldn't believe what happened to me last night. Or rather to Ed.'

'Tell me over coffee,' she suggested. In the background I heard Forester yell out indignantly.

'Whoops. His master's voice,' said Kara. 'See you in an hour or so?'

'Make it two,' I pleaded.

At half past ten precisely, Kara and Forester were on the doorstep. I had fallen back to sleep as soon as Kara rang off and was still in my pyjamas when she rang the doorbell as though the house was on fire. She couldn't wake Ed, though. He would have burned to death in his tuxedo. But for the moment he was alive; I could tell that by the continued snoring. I didn't dare to look into the spare room. I didn't want to. I knew if I did he would somehow persuade me to deal with his mess by acting all helpless again and I was still in no mood to play mother.

'Coffee,' Kara demanded when I opened the front door.

'Come in,' I said.

'Come out,' she said. 'We're not going to stay here and drink your decaf rubbish.'

I was trying to stay off the caffeine and Ed only ever drank tea.

Kara stepped into the hallway. 'Ugh. This house smells of sick,' she said. 'Dress quickly.'

I assembled an outfit from the various garments I had cast off onto the bedroom floor after work during the course of the previous week, pulling on a pair of fleecy tracksuit bottoms and a T-shirt I had worn to the gym.

'For goodness' sake,' Kara said when she saw what I had put together without her supervision. 'I know you and Ed are about to get married but that really is no excuse to give up absolutely.'

'Tracksuits are very fashionable,' I retorted.

'If they're made by Juicy and worn by J-Lo. But that tracksuit is far from Juicy. You look like you're the one who gave birth six months ago.'

I dragged a sweater over my head and mumbled through the wool. 'If you really want me to leave this house before eleven o'clock on a Saturday morning after a night with Ed's rugby club – especially last night – I'm afraid you're going to have to bear the humiliation of being seen with me like this.'

'At least put some make-up on,' she pleaded.

'No. The walk to the coffee shop will bring colour to my cheeks.'

'We're too old to go natural,' said Kara.

'I'm too old to care.'

We headed for Starbucks, there really wasn't much choice, unless we muscled our way into the greasy spoon on the corner for some saturated fats and a cup of instant. We used to go there all the time – nothing like a chip butty with ketchup for a hangover – but these days Kara refused to enter that place on the grounds of protecting Forester's delicate lungs. It was going to be a long while before Sandro banned his clientele from having a fag with their breakfast, no matter what the EU ruled.

So instead we were bound for our nearest outpost of the Evil Empire and sugar-free muffins and fat-free lattes. Double decaf for me. In the twenty-first century even coffee and cake can be joyless.

'I'm buying,' said Kara.

'It's the least you can do after that wake-up call,' I snarled.

Kara just grinned at me. She had been grinning like a monkey ever since she rang my doorbell. Nothing could wipe that big smile off her face.

'Kara,' I said. 'What is *wrong* with you? You haven't taken an "e"?'

'I may have to ask you a favour,' she began.

It turned out that my faith in Kara's Internet beau had been well founded. The previous evening, after another flurry of flirtatious emails, he finally made the jump from virtual to vocal. The voice fitted. And I was the first to hear about it.

'I've got a date,' Kara almost shrieked. 'An actual date.'

I had a feeling I was about to find out why she was treating me that morning.

'He wants to see me tonight.'

Kara handed me my share of the chocolate muffin. 'The big half,' she pointed out.

'He wants to see you today?'

'Yes. And if I don't see him tonight then I probably won't be able to see him until the middle of next week, which is *aaaaaages* away. But I can't find a babysitter. Mum and Dad are insisting on going to their stupid golf-club dance. Heidi, I don't suppose there's any chance . . .'

I looked at her uncomprehendingly. Though part of my mind already knew what she was about to ask me, another, bigger part of it didn't think it was possible that she really would. Me? Heidi Savage? Be a babysitter? Had Kara gone quite mad?

'Just between eight and eleven,' Kara said. 'What do you reckon? Three hours.'

I didn't answer her. I couldn't. I felt slightly strange. I looked at Forester in his pushchair. He was busy gumming the cord around the hood of his sweatshirt into soggy strands. He was at his best when he was chewing his clothes. Just been fed. Content. Not screaming.

'He'll be asleep most of the time.' Kara reached out and stroked my arm. 'Please. Pretty please.'

I prayed for some sort of rip in the space-time continuum that would give me the opportunity to come up with a feasible excuse.

'Heidi?'

You see, even though Forester was already six months old, I had never actually spent any time alone with him, unless you count those extremely brief moments when Kara left me in charge of the pushchair while she dashed to the loo. Even then, I felt like a passenger without a driving licence left alone in charge of a four-wheel-drive on double yellow lines just as a traffic warden appears. Those minutes while Kara peed and I prayed that Forester wouldn't cry, choke or die always seemed to last for hours. And now she was actually asking me to look after him for three hours.

In my entire life, I had been left in sole charge of a minor for longer than three minutes only once. That was my brother, James. He was ten. I was fourteen. Mum and Dad couldn't find a babysitter to look after us while they went to parents' night at my school. They took a gamble and decided we were old enough to look after ourselves or at least call 999 if we couldn't. I spent the entire evening on the telephone while James played games on his computer. There wasn't really any risk involved. But a baby . . .?

'I can't tell you how happy just talking to this guy has made me. It's so special to feel like a woman again instead of just a mum. If I could just get to see him face to face . . .'

What was I supposed to be doing that night? There must be something. I tore through my mental diary in search of a reason why I couldn't look after Forester. I would have settled for a visit from my future mother-in-law. Then I flicked through my mental address book to find anyone, anyone on earth who might be a more suitable candidate for babysitting than me. Didn't Kara have any other friends for heaven's sake? Didn't she have any aunties? Perhaps she could drop Forester off at a children's home for the night.

'Of course, if you and Ed are already doing something . . .,' Kara sighed. 'I know what a busy social life you guys have.'

That last comment was heavy on the sarcasm. Even if Ed and I had been in the habit of partying all weekend, every weekend, Kara knew full well that the only thing scheduled in Ed's diary for the night after the rugby club dinner might be an appointment to have his stomach pumped.

'Ed could help you.'

The killer blow.

Kara fixed her big, brown eyes upon me. Forester fixed his big, brown eyes upon me too. Slowly, theatrically, as though he were a movie star making the most of a legendary smile, the corners of his lips began to twitch upwards. He let the soggy sweatshirt cord fall from his mouth.

'See. He loves his Auntie Heidi!' Kara exclaimed.

And I loved him. I did. I loved Kara, too. She was my best friend. She had been at my side through some of the greatest and the most difficult periods of my life. We'd never asked much of each other. Just someone to laugh with, shop with, occasionally cry upon. And she wasn't really asking much now. Three hours' worth of childcare. Three hours for the first time in six whole months since she became a mother. Three hours with the gorgeous baby who was beaming at me as though he could think of nothing he wanted to do more than spend time in my incompetent company.

A variety of the things a baby could choke on popped up in my mind like a slideshow: peanuts, fish bones, the earring I lost last weekend . . . So much responsibility. I couldn't do it. I couldn't do it. It simply wouldn't be right.

Just then Kara's phone rang. Saved by the bell, I hoped. But it was Ed.

'Is Heidi with you?' he asked. I'd left my own phone on the kitchen table.

'She's here,' said Kara, but she didn't hand the phone over. Instead she fixed me with mischievous eyes as she said, 'I'm just trying to persuade her to babysit for me this evening but she thinks you guys might be doing something else.'

'Not us,' Ed replied guilelessly. 'Not after last night. Where are you going?'

Kara explained about her date. I heard Ed laughing. And then, being the soft-hearted beast that he is, Ed volunteered us both.

'Good old Ed. Oh, Heidi,' Kara said with typical under-statement, 'you guys have saved my life.' She squeezed my face between her hands and kissed me on both cheeks. 'How can I ever repay you? Booze? Chocolate? A loan of my Jimmy Choo boots?'

'You just have to promise me a blow-by-blow,' I told her when I was able to speak through my shock. I would kill Ed the minute I got home.

'It seems a bit of a shame to have to have a real-life date at all,' Kara said then. 'It's been so lovely to check my mail each day and find a new message or two from him. The weird thing is, this first date feels as though it could be the end of it all. If we hate each other at first sight, my mailbox will be bereft from tomorrow morning Heidi,' Kara squealed. 'I've got a date. What on earth am I going to wear?'

Unlike babysitting, date shopping was a mission I was always glad to accept.

When Forester had been changed again, I offered to hold him while Kara had another coffee. It suddenly seemed important to get in as much practice as possible while Kara was still around to tell me what I was doing wrong. Maybe it would be okay. It was an odd thing, but there was something about holding the warm and sleepy bundle in my arms that made the sofa seem even more comfortable. I pushed a soft stray curl away from his face.

'He's so handsome,' I murmured. 'Which is more than can be said for Ed these days.'

At last I told Kara about the eyebrow shaving. The passing out. The vomiting. More vomiting. The chemotherapy joke.

'He looks like a maggot without his eyebrows,' I sighed.

'No wonder he doesn't want to go out tonight.'

'I'm not going to be able to go out in public with him for months. I can't even look at him without wanting to throw up.'

'Not good.' Kara pulled a face. 'But that's the rugby club for you. You know what they're like.'

'I wish he wouldn't spend so much time with them.'

'They're just a bunch of lads,' said Kara dismissively. She seemed determined to fight Ed's corner now that he had presented himself as her white knight. 'Ed's not like that all the time. And his eyebrows will grow back in time for the wedding. I think.'

'I know it probably seemed worse because I was tired and more than a little bit drunk myself. It's not as if this happens every weekend. Or even every other weekend. It's not the end of the world. But last night I just shoved him in the spare room, closed the door behind me and ten minutes later I found myself sitting on my bed and staring at this.'

I flipped open my wallet with my free hand and pulled out Steven Gabriel's card.

'Ah ha,' said Kara. 'The man you never think about.'

'I don't ever think about him. At least, I didn't until last week.'

'And now you can't stop thinking about him, right?'

'That isn't what I said.'

'No wonder you didn't have much patience for your lovely fiancé last night. Thinking about what might have been . . .'

'I wasn't.'

Kara didn't bother to contradict me, instead she peered closely at the number on the card, trying to work out where Steven might live from the digits of his landline. She approved of the central London prefix.

'Don't you think it's spooky that he's come back into your life just as you're about to get married?'

'Don't start with that psychic shit.'

'People come back into our lives for a reason,' she said.

'It's just a coincidence.'

'Some call it coincidence. I like to call it fate.'

'I'm engaged to be married. You're not supposed to be encouraging me to go off with my ex.'

Kara put down her coffee and looked at me like a teacher who knows her pupil is hiding something. 'Who was saying anything about you *going off with* your ex? You generated that little thought quite on your own.'

I blushed into Forester's hair.

'I was thinking more along the lines that your ex has come back into your life to show you how wonderful things are for you these days. To help you step into the future with Ed with no regrets. To show you what a great man he is, eyebrows or no eyebrows.'

'Right.'

'It's interesting, though – your assumption. And the way you went straight to it,' she added wickedly.

'It was just my assumption based on what I assumed you were assuming.'

Kara raised a single eyebrow this time.

'Oh, forget it.'

'So, have you called him?'

'Of course I haven't.'

'Why don't you call him? Meet up and have a proper chat.'

'No.'

'Where's the harm?'

'I don't know. It just doesn't feel right.'

'Why not?'

'Because he's my ex-boyfriend. Because he's part of my past. I only saved this card because I thought you might want to talk to him.'

Kara nodded but the amused curl of her mouth told me that she thought I was scrabbling for an excuse.

'You've got a lot in common now,' I ended weakly.

'Does he have stretch marks as well?'

'I just thought you might want to talk about having children. And, I dunno, about other things. You were his friend at university too.'

'And after you broke up, you made me swear that I would never speak to him again unless it was to warn him that I was about to cut his balls off with a rusty nail-file for hurting my best friend so badly. Remember?'

I shook my head in embarrassment at the memory. That was one of the milder pronouncements I had made at the time.

'I better go back home,' I said. 'Make sure Ed isn't trying to put his suit in the washing machine.'

'Okay.' Kara turned Steven's card over between her fingers with a magician's flourish, then tucked it back into the breast pocket of my denim jacket. 'But I'm not going to make this easy for you,' she said. 'If you want to see Steven Gabriel, you have to make the call.'

'Kara,' I insisted, 'I am never going to use that card.'

12

Ed hadn't tried to put his suit in the washing machine. Instead, it hung from the back of the bedroom door, gently scenting the whole house with vomit. All things considered, Ed had managed to get out of bed at a reasonable sort of time, but he was still like a bear prodded awake halfway through winter. I think he was slightly pissed off that I hadn't bothered to undress him when I put him to bed the previous night. I was still very pissed off that he looked like an alien from *Babylon Five* instead of the handsome man I had agreed to marry at the top of the Eiffel Tower. Really, he was hideous. It was worse than I remembered. Those marker-pen eyebrows simply would not shift no matter how many times Ed used my Clarins exfoliator. *All* my Clarins exfoliator – I found the empty tube in the bathroom bin.

'You've used at least twelve pounds' worth of my skincare,' I groaned. It was an insult to add to the injury of having been coerced into babysitting that night. I still couldn't believe Ed had volunteered us. To make things worse, he seemed excited at the prospect.

'Forester can watch *Starship Troopers* with me,' Ed said happily. 'Get his movie education going young.'

'Kara said he'd be asleep most of the time,' I snapped back, more to reassure myself than anyone else.

After lunch, I rejoined Kara in town to spend the afternoon date-shopping. Or, more accurately, she spent the afternoon shopping while I hung around outside department store changing rooms, pushing Forester's pram up and down aisles of dresses to stop him grizzling. He had developed very early a man's natural hatred of shopping with the girls.

But he wasn't the only one who got fed up by tea-time that day. Kara took half the stock of Harvey Nicks into the changing room over the period of three hours but we still went home empty-handed but for a tube of mascara (mine) and a cheesy Valentine's card for Ed. Though given the way he looked, I couldn't imagine I'd be feeling much more romantic towards him by the fourteenth.

'Nothing suits me any more,' Kara moaned as we rattled westwards on the Tube. 'I keep forgetting my body has completely changed shape since I last bought anything new. From hourglass to pint-glass in less than a year.'

I didn't dare contradict her but attempted to change the emphasis by suggesting instead that it was a good idea to wear a tried and tested outfit in a first-date situation in any case. 'You must have an old faithful in your wardrobe,' I continued. 'A lucky dress. Something you can just throw on and automatically feel confident and comfortable in.'

'Heidi,' said Kara. 'I had a whole wardrobe of clothes that made me look and feel like a million dollars. And then I had a baby. Nothing feels good to wear any more. I feel as comfortable as a walrus wearing a g-string in just about everything I own.'

She wasn't to be persuaded otherwise, so we parted again until the evening. When I got home, Ed was next door helping Mrs H tidy up her back garden for the spring. I found I was relieved to have the house for myself for just a little while, reading the papers with the radio tuned to music rather than rugby results for once. I was certainly relieved not to have to look at Ed's face.

*　　*　　*

At six o'clock, Kara reappeared on the doorstep with Forester, all ready for bed in his Moses basket, and a suitcase.

'Does he really need all that stuff?' I was horrified, imagining a whole branch of Mothercare's baby accessories I wouldn't be able to master.

'The suitcase is for me, stupid.'

As we set up Kara's date-preparation station in the spare room, I had a flashback to our university days. Back then, with nothing to do but study, we would spend whole afternoons getting ready for the big events in our social calendar: Christmas dinners, end of term balls, football club parties. Now Kara spread her bounty over the bed and I bounced Forester on my hip and tried to amuse him with a succession of bright-coloured bangles and strings of beads while she tried on each combination of clothes and shoes for my benefit. She must have brought across her whole wardrobe.

'I haven't worn anything without an elasticated waist for the past year and a half. I don't know if I can even fit into this any more,' she said, holding up a beautiful black dress that I had been particularly envious of when she brought it back from a secret assignation in New York while she and I still shared our bachelorette pad. I fingered the velvety hem with longing, just as I had done when she first tipped it out of a Macy's bag and onto my bed in that South London hovel.

'If this doesn't fit any more,' she said, 'you can have it.'

'I promise I'm not praying that I'll get it,' I told her with my fingers crossed beneath Forester's bottom.

She slipped the dress on over her head. There was an ominous tearing sound as she smoothed the skirt over her hips. 'I'm not even going to try to do the zip up,' she said, pulling the dress straight back off again. 'This is yours, I guess, if you can fix the rip.'

I tried not to look too pleased.

'You know what?' I said. 'I think you should probably go for something a little more low-key anyway. There's nothing worse than getting all dressed up to find out that your date was thinking more along the lines of two pints in a gastro-pub than three courses in a Michelin-starred restaurant. Do you know where he's taking you?'

She named an Italian restaurant in Chiswick.

'Oh, well,' I said. 'In that case you definitely shouldn't wear the dress. They'll think you've come to do the cabaret.'

Kara tried to laugh. She smoothed down Forester's fringe and his little mouth curled up at the edges, revealing his first and only tooth like the tip of a snowdrop poking through the winter earth.

'He's got such a lovely smile,' I sighed.

'It's probably wind,' said Kara. But I could tell she didn't mean that. Forester had been smiling properly for months. Kara gurned at him. He gurned back harder.

'You think this is very funny, don't you, Forester? Your old mum getting ready to go on a date. You think I should give up and stay at home in my tracksuit, don't you?' Forester bobbed excitedly on my knee, happy to be centre of attention again. Kara's own smile slipped away.

'He doesn't think you should stay in,' I interpreted quickly, much as I would have welcomed an excuse not to be left alone with her child. 'He wants you to go out there and get him a tall, dark and handsome stepfather. Preferably with a great car he can write off as soon as he gets his licence. Forester wants you to have the wonderful time you deserve tonight.'

'Tell me why I'm bothering again?' Kara sighed. 'I just feel so old.' She pulled back her cheeks so that her eyes slanted upwards and she looked like a Beverly Hills housewife who'd had just a little too much done.

'You're only thirty-one.'

'I'm so out of practice.'

'I'll give you that. But it really will be okay. You were always a mistress of the art of flirting. Everything I learned, I learned from you. And I managed to pull in the dentist's chair! At the very least, you've got a night on the town lined up – a night away from the baby and the television and another Marks and Spencer curry. That's got to make a change. Look,' I pushed a silky black sweater with a wide neck towards her, 'this is beautiful. You always looked fantastic in this. I've always wanted it!'

'It's five years old. Completely out of fashion.'

'Or timeless. It makes you look so elegant. Makes a feature of your long neck and your shoulders . . .'

'Instead of my bum and tum,' she said.

'Accentuate the positive!' I reminded her. When Kara and I lived next door in our university hall of residence and later, when we shared our flat, she had that very affirmation written on a Post-it note and stuck on her mirror. In those days, it was she who constantly acted the cheerleader, accentuating the positive in me.

Kara pulled on the sweater and gave herself a critical look in the mirror.

'Wear your hair up,' I suggested.

She held her hair on top of her head. 'It's not too bad, I suppose.'

'It's great,' I said.

'Then I'll wear it. Okay with you, Forester?' Kara picked him up for another cuddle. He immediately deposited a little dribble of sick over her shoulder and down her back.

'Perhaps it's lucky,' I suggested.

'Like bird shit?' Kara cried. 'Oh God. It's an omen, Heidi.' She sat back down on the bed. 'I shouldn't go out. This date is going to be a disaster. I shouldn't even be asking you to help me.'

'I don't mind babysitting,' I insisted.

'Perhaps I mind the idea of you babysitting,' she said.

13

It should have come as no real surprise that Kara was nervous about leaving me alone with Forester for the whole evening, even with Ed on standby. Sure, she brought Forester over to our place at least a couple of times a week, but though Ed and I always told her she should just relax and put her feet up while she was in our house, pretty much every time Forester squeaked, Kara was the one who raced to comfort him. I had given him his bottle plenty of times, but always under supervision. I had never changed a nappy. Kara had a knack of making it seem as though she was totally relaxed about Forester; she said she didn't want to be one of those 'helicopter mums' who swoops in every time the baby so much as wrinkles his brow. But I knew that she was actually hyper-vigilant.

So she was facing a night of double stress. Her first date in months and the first time ever that she had left Forester alone except in the capable hands of her own mother. Ed and I, for our part, were going to be babysitting together for the very first time – if Mrs H ever stopped drip-feeding Ed sherry in thanks for all his hard work and let him come back home, that was.

'Are you sure you're going to be okay?' Kara asked me.

'How hard can it possibly be?' I shrugged. 'I've just got to keep both ends clean, right? Besides, Forester isn't going to give his Auntie Heidi any trouble.'

He blew a bubble of saliva.

'You do understand how the nappies work? Perhaps I should show you one more time.'

'For God's sake. I know how to deal with a nappy. Or Ed does . . . Forester will be asleep most of the time.'

Forester was already rubbing at his ears, a sure sign that he was getting tired. Kara took him from me for a final time and gently settled him on the soft blankets in his Moses basket. He kicked his legs in half-hearted protest but his eyelids were already starting to droop. She leaned over him and cooed until they closed. A real baby hypnotist.

'I could still cancel,' she said as Forester tried and failed to hang on to wakefulness for just a little longer.

'You can *not*.' Good friend battled bad babysitter inside me. 'You have to go now. I know it's a good idea to keep them waiting for a little while on the first date, but there's late and there's so late he thinks you've stood him up and goes home to catch the end of the news.'

'I can't believe I'm doing this,' said Kara one more time.

'And I can't believe I'm going to be a babysitter.'

'Neither can I. Night night, Forester.' She kissed the tip of her finger and gently pressed it to his forehead. 'With any luck he should sleep until I'm back here, but make sure you keep looking in on him, won't you? And call me if anything happens,' she said to me. 'Anything at all. Even if he so much as sneezes.'

'Kara, we will be fine. If you stand there worrying any more, I'll start to think you're just looking for an excuse not to go.'

'Perhaps I am.' She chewed her lip.

'That isn't the Kara I know. Go.'

Outside in the street, the taxi driver honked his horn in agreement.

'I'm going,' said Kara.

'You'll have a great time.'

She passed Ed coming in through the gate on her way out.

He gave her a low, appreciative whistle that made her beam, then joined me on the step to wave her into the car.

'I'm glad I'll never have to do that first-date thing again,' Ed told me.

I looked pointedly at the grey smudge of marker pen where his eyebrows had once lived. 'Don't count on it, buster.'

I made him tiptoe into the house so as not to disturb our sleeping visitor.

Forester Knight was gorgeous from the very beginning. He wasn't born looking like Winston Churchill wondering who'd nicked his cigar, as most babies are. I didn't have to lie about how lovely he was while secretly thinking he resembled a frustrated prune. He didn't look angry to have been forced out of the comfort of the womb into the harsh fluorescent light of the delivery room. At least, I don't think he looked angry. I wasn't there at the time, though I was supposed to be.

Kara didn't always have a very easy relationship with her family. Though her parents were wonderful people – I had got to know them quite well over the years and loved them both – Kara often complained that she found them stifling. At the same time, Kara's life choices frustrated and bewildered Mr and Mrs Knight, especially since they had to bankroll so many of them. When she got pregnant, Kara's thoroughly respectable parents almost went insane trying to work out whether to be angry that Kara was having a baby outside marriage by a man whose surname she wasn't even sure of, or delighted that she was carrying their first grandchild.

After one particularly terrible row, Kara proclaimed that Ed and I were her chosen family and when the bump started to show it seemed to make sense that she would abandon the lease on the tiny flat she had been planning to take in Covent Garden and move further west to a bigger place just round the corner from us instead. And, when the moment came, I was the only person she wanted to be at the birth. Not her mother (though they had made up in plenty of time), not the father. Just me.

'That's wonderful,' I said when she told me. 'I'm really honoured. Truly I am.' But if you've ever wondered if there's anything worse than being asked to don a bridesmaid's dress at thirty . . . When Ed got home from work that night and saw how white my face was, he assumed I must have been diagnosed with something terminal.

Anyway, when I agreed to be Kara's birth partner, I also agreed to go to all the antenatal classes that were usually attended by a husband or boyfriend. I was able to skip quite a few, using work as an excuse – I've never had so many late nights at the office. Those I did attend I found excruciating: it felt weird as hell laying my head on Kara's bump to 'connect' with the little life inside it.

'Count ten breaths,' said the course leader.

I could only hear the rush of blood to my cheeks. I've never been what you could call a tactile person. I don't think Kara and I had ever really had any body contact at all before those classes, unless we were drunk and draping ourselves over each other in some faux lesbian display to titillate the boys while we lip-synched to 'I will survive'.

I got over it. Or rather I think I got away with it, with not looking like I hated the thought of touching something so 'naturally wonderful' as a pregnant woman's belly, though I would rather have put my head in a lion's mouth. I was fine at the synchronised panting too. The very worst class came when I was left alone with the men.

It happened about a month before the babies were due. While the mums-to-be bonded over biscuits, we 'partners' were taken into another room to watch a video of what we had let ourselves in for when we agreed to be present at the birth. The course leader explained that by having us watch the video without the soon-to-be-mums, she was giving us a chance to express what we really felt about the impending event. We could vent our deepest fears without risking offence to any of the mummies, she promised us. We could ask the questions we felt stupid asking. We could say whatever we wanted.

Horror. Horror. Horror. Those were the words that ran through my head as we settled ourselves on the grey plastic chairs in front of a tiny TV. I sat at the back. I hadn't made many friends amongst the daddies-in-waiting. I suspected they thought I was a spy for the girls. As the course instructor queued up the tape, the men joked about the 'video nasty' we were about to see, but their voices had taken on the timbre of teenage Vietnam conscripts about to be parachuted into the jungle. I knew exactly how they felt.

'The Miracle of Birth,' flickered the video title. A voiceover introduced the brave couple who had allowed their 'special moment' to be filmed. Melanie, the wife, looked fat and angry as she panted through her early contractions and Simon, her husband, looked petrified. Their smiles for the camera weren't fooling anyone. From their haircuts I guessed that the bump must be around twenty years old by now. One of the guys at the front of the room made a crack about this being the 'Joy of Sex' couple nine months after they'd been right through the book. I wondered if they were still together. Cut to the delivery room. The midwife. The doctor. All smiling. Nothing to worry about. This was something they did every day.

There was a brief overview of the kind of equipment you might see in a delivery room: monitors for the mother's heart-beat and the baby's heartbeat, oxygen, gas and air. I thought I saw the epidural needle. Longer than my palm.

Melanie shuffled into the room while Simon supported her elbow, then she climbed onto the table. I thought about that scene in *Hitchhikers' Guide* where the alien cow is wheeled into the restaurant live to describe its own best cuts.

'Your wife might choose to squat,' interjected the course leader, which made me think of mud huts and witch doctors.

There was some talk of enemas and shaving, which I tried hard to block out. Meanwhile Simon took his place at the head of the bed and Melanie clutched his hand.

'And there's the money shot,' announced the 'Joy of Sex' joker as we zoomed in between the mum-to-be's legs.

'Melanie has been having contractions for a little over three hours,' the voiceover continued gaily. 'Her cervix has already dilated to ten centimetres and it won't be long before we can see the top of the baby's head. This is what is known as "crowning".'

Crowning? More like drowning. When Melanie pushed and her vagina edged still wider, I held my hand to my breastbone as though I had just seen a dead cat in the road.

'Push,' someone funny shouted from my left.

'Breathe,' someone funnier replied.

'Push.'

'Breathe.'

'Push.'

'Breathe.'

The instructions were coming from the video now.

'You can breathe along with Melanie if you like,' said the course leader. 'Just like we've been teaching you to breathe along with your partners.'

No one took her up on her suggestion.

In fact, after the initial burst of cat-calling, which I had feared would set the tone for the whole film, the room very quickly grew silent. The wisecracks stopped. I could hear my pulse thumping in my ears as the on-screen action grew more urgent. The grown men shifted in their chairs like children who wanted to be able to duck behind the sofa for the scary bits and I sank down as far as the hard plastic seat would allow, putting my hand to my mouth.

It wasn't long before you could see the baby's head clearly. It had hair, slicked dark black with mucus. While Melanie pushed harder, her anus winked like an evil eye and even though Melanie was thoroughly dilated by this time, it still didn't seem quite possible that anything but a baby with a head shaped like a carrot was going to be able to get out.

I crossed my legs, realising that I was experiencing the female equivalent of these boys being forced to watch a video of a fellow man being repeatedly kneed in the nuts. My pelvic floor muscles tried to take refuge in my intestines. And then there was the screaming. How long did it go on for? Certainly not as long as it went on for in real life, I'm sure. But the pushing, the breathing, the wailing just wouldn't seem to stop. Was it always like this? It was probably worse. I mean, they wouldn't have chosen the footage of a really painful, horrific labour for an educational video, would they? The human race would die out in one TV-watching generation. Or perhaps, I struggled to think more optimistically, this actually was one of the most agonising labours the film crew captured during the video's making and they decided to run with this one because after this horror movie, a real live birth would seem like a children's cartoon. It was a good idea to show the worst. I was a big believer in being prepared for the worst because then you could only be pleasantly surprised.

'You utter *beep*!' shouted Melanie. 'You beeping beep beep.' They'd bleeped out all the cursing.

'It's nearly over,' said her husband. He'd said that fifteen times. 'It's nearly over.' Please let him be telling the truth this time.

I closed my eyes completely for the final push.

'Aaaaaaaaggggghhhhh! You beep.'

'It's a boy!'

Slap.

'Waaaaaah!'

Cut to Melanie and her husband in the aftermath. The baby, washed and wrapped in a white blanket but still the colour of a kidney, slept in his mother's arms.

'I'm very glad I saw the birth of my son,' said Simon unconvincingly. He delivered that line with the kind of conviction you expect from someone who has been under torture for twenty-four hours.

'I'm so glad he was able to be here with me,' said Melanie. She would probably never have sex with him again.

Crackle. Credits.

'And that's just about it,' said the course leader as she flicked on the lights. 'The miracle of birth. Any questions?'

Whoever said, 'Do we really have to go through this?' spoke for all of us.

I followed the white-faced men back to the room where the women were waiting for us, snarfing down chocolate Hobnobs with impunity while they could still get away with claiming they were eating for two. The boys all smiled happily enough and pronounced the video 'interesting', 'fascinating', 'better than ER', but I could tell that something had shifted irrevocably over the past half hour. While the men talked about how much easier it would be to be supportive now that they knew what they were in for, I could only hear the things they had said while still outside.

'I am never having sex again,' one of them had announced. 'At least, not with my wife.'

Prior to watching that video, birth had been such an abstract concept. Most of the guys had been very pleased with the idea of their wives being pregnant; it was proof that they weren't 'shooting blanks' as Ed would have put it. And then there was the happy side-effect of having a wife with bigger tits without paying for a boob job. After the video, the men looked at their wives as though they knew a terrible secret the poor cows weren't yet in on. We alone knew that these bountiful-looking creatures with their big, bouncy bosoms were about to subject us to the kind of entrail-popping display that only Sigourney Weaver could reasonably be expected to be prepared for.

Well, that was how I felt when I looked at Kara. God knows how much worse I might have felt if I knew that after this hideous experience I might be expected to continue to sleep with her. I made a pact with myself there and then that if I ever, ever, ever had to be the girl on the trolley, I would be there on my own. I didn't want *anyone* to see me poo on the delivery table. No spectators allowed unless they could offer drugs. Not even my mother. Ed would be banned from the hospital.

'How was the film really?' Kara asked me, sitting cross-legged on the floor like a Buddha. She reached up and took my hand to pull me down to her level. 'Look at their little faces,' she glanced around the room at the men. 'Terrified to a man. Thank God I've got you for my birthing partner. We girls are so much braver.'

'Absolutely,' I agreed.

Waiting for the final month of Kara's pregnancy to pass was like waiting for my A-level results. Most of the time I was happy. Most of the time I didn't really think about D-Day at all. But there were nights, far too many nights, when I stared up at the ceiling above my bed and prayed that the father of Kara's child would ride back into her life on his motorcycle and insist on taking my place in the delivery room.

How can you tell your best friend that you'd rather she experienced the Miracle of Life on her own?

Kara started having serious contractions while I was at the studio one Wednesday morning. Her waters broke all over her Habitat sofa while she was watching a home makeover programme. I got the call right in the middle of the show. Nelly scuttled across the room with the message scribbled on a piece of paper: 'Kara. Labour. Now.'

Eleanor glanced at the note first and knew exactly what it meant. 'You better get going,' she said.

'But we're in the middle of the show,' I replied hopefully.

'Forget that, stupid! We can cope without you. We'll get you a taxi.'

'I can take the Tube.'

'Nelly,' Eleanor ignored me. 'For God's sake call Heidi an account car.'

Eleanor thought she was being considerate. She had no idea how little I wanted to be at that hospital right then, that I wanted to take the Tube, to do anything that might buy me just a little extra time. How long did it take for someone to give birth once the contractions had started? If it took me an hour to get to the hospital and another fifteen minutes to navigate my way to the ward, perhaps I would miss the birth altogether.

'Charing Cross Hospital, right?' said the driver as I climbed into the car. 'Outpatients?'

'No,' I said. 'My best friend's giving birth. I'm supposed to be there with her.'

'Better put my foot down then.'

'Please don't hurry,' I begged. 'It's much more important that you don't get a ticket.'

The bastard covered three miles in seven minutes, going at speeds I had thought utterly impossible to achieve in London unless you were travelling by helicopter.

'My wife was in here six months ago,' he added helpfully as we pulled up outside the hospital doors. 'So I can tell you the quickest route to maternity. Through those doors there, turn left at the end of that corridor, up the stairs . . . Get your skates on.'

'All right,' I snapped, barely concealing my frustration.

The driver's instructions were spot on. And, contrary to the tradition of hospital receptionists, the girl on the maternity-unit desk was incredibly helpful. It didn't even matter that I had forgotten to bring photographic ID because Kara had helpfully left a picture of me (taken on our last girls' holiday in Majorca) with the receptionist for exactly such an emergency.

'Don't you need to see something more official?' I asked.

'I trust you,' the receptionist smiled. 'Follow me.'

She led me through a white corridor that reminded me of one of those documentaries about near-death experiences. People having near-death experiences always float along a brightly lit corridor, don't they? We had to walk past six other delivery rooms on our way to the one where Kara was waiting for me. I felt like Clarice Starling visiting Lecter in *The Silence of the Lambs*. From each room emanated the sounds of crying or moaning and at any moment I expected a bloodied face to smash up against one of the little windows criss-crossed with anti-shatter mesh.

I had never felt quite so scared.

As we neared Kara's room, the corridor grew ominously quiet.

'Has she had it?' I asked hopefully.

'Oh no. She's been waiting for you to get here,' said the girl with a smile.

And then I heard it: the most heart-stopping sound since Ed broke his left femur on the rugby pitch and I was near enough to hear the damm thing crack. It was the type of horror-movie noise that makes you wish they hadn't invented surround-sound. It was the wail of a soul in purgatory. The scream of the damned. It was the sound of my best friend in labour.

I stopped dead outside the door, having a sudden flashback to Melanie of the video, legs in stirrups, blood on the bed, passing a basketball. The agony of a camel squeezing through the eye of a bleeding needle. Sigourney Weaver splattered with gore as the thing rips through her comrade's bony chest. I grabbed the hospital receptionist by the arm as blackness crept in at the edges of my vision.

'You're not going to faint, are you?' she asked.

'I just don't think I can do this,' I told her.

And I vomited all over myself, the receptionist and the shiny tiled floor. Then I slipped in my own mess and fell over.

I went down as heavily as Ed being tackled from behind on the rugby pitch and cracked my head on the corner of a trolley. I was out cold. Within seconds, I was on that trolley and being checked for signs of concussion. The nurse who treated me smiled knowingly when the porter told her that he'd just wheeled me up from maternity.

So that was how I came to miss Forester's birth. I had a bump on my forehead pretty much the same size as the bump that Kara shed the same day. When he was satisfied that it was safe, my doctor allowed Ed, who had cancelled half his afternoon's appointments to race to my side, to take me in a wheelchair to visit Kara and her newborn.

'Always trying to upstage me,' Kara announced when we arrived at her room.

After a couple of minutes' obligatory baby admiration, Ed was sent out to get some sandwiches, leaving me and Kara alone. Considering she had just given birth, she was looking remarkably perky. With the red bump on my forehead, she said I resembled a toad.

A knock at the door and the midwife bustled in to check on the new baby's progress. 'Incredibly short labour,' she said in something like admiration as she placed Forester back in Kara's arms.

'Thank God,' said Kara. 'If you can call three hours of the most intense pain this side of having your nipples pierced with a blunt needle "short".'

'You must be sad that you didn't get to see your son being born though,' the midwife added.

To me.

Kara just about managed to hold in a guffaw until the midwife had left the room.

'*My* son?' I asked.

'This is London,' Kara reminded me. 'Lots of babies have two mums and two dads around here.'

'I am sorry I missed him being born,' I said then, almost sincerely. In truth, I knew I had been more frightened of the impending birth than Kara had been and weeks later, as Kara recounted her tale of pain and fear and impromptu diarrhoea in front of a simply *gorgeous* obstetrician, it got increasingly hard to say I was sorry to have missed the moment when Forester came into the world.

'So, what's he going to be called?' I asked as I sat in my wheelchair beside Kara's hospital bed and popped grapes into my mouth in quick succession. Jake and Jamie had been the two top contenders for boys' names in the weeks running up to the birth. If the baby had been a girl she would have been another Heidi, despite my protest that being called Heidi had caused me a whole world of unhappiness: first with the goatherd jokes (especially when my mother plaited my hair) and then 'Hi-de-hi', sung out in a Welsh accent every time I entered the class-room or put my hand up to answer a question. I think I was the only kid in my class at school who didn't love that sitcom.

'Forester,' Kara said suddenly.

'Is that his father's surname?'

'No. That's going to be his first name. Forester. Forester Knight.'

'Is Forester an actual name?' I blurted, and immediately felt guilty.

'Yes it is. It's in this book I've been reading.'

She nodded towards her overnight bag. I could see the corner of a romance novel sticking out of it. 'What is that? A Barbara Cartland novel?'

'Stephanie Ash, actually. I found it in the waiting room when I was in for a check-up last week. It's really rather good.'

'But naming your son after a Mills and Boon hero?'

'I don't care,' said Kara. 'I like it. It's unusual. And I really think it suits him.'

She tucked her finger into the blankets around the baby's head and gently pulled them away so that I could see his tiny face. 'Forester,' she whispered. 'Forester Knight. It's a very manly name. And he's going to be a hero.'

'Or a lumberjack,' said Ed, when Kara told him her decision on his return from the sandwich shop. 'How much gas and air did they give you?'

But it didn't take long for us to get used to it. And now, six months on, it seemed almost impossible that Forester might ever have been called anything else.

'Aren't you a handsome boy?' I murmured over his sleeping head when I checked on him about half an hour after Kara's departure for the restaurant. 'You're the handsomest boy in the world. In the whole wide world.'

'What about me?' Ed had crept in and was standing beside me. He wrapped his arms around my waist. 'Have you forgiven me for the eyebrows yet?' he asked.

'If you change the first nappy,' I told him. 'And the second one,' I added while I still had the upper hand.

'Anything you say, my dear. I just love changing nappies.'

I had a feeling this babysitting thing was going to be easy. As long as Ed was in charge.

14

We settled in for a quiet night. Forester didn't stir so we retired
to the sitting room and switched on the TV – volume turned
low, of course, at my insistence. I felt like an SAS man trying
not to alert enemy soldiers to my presence as I crept between
sitting room and bathroom. There was to be no loo-flushing
until Kara came back. The whole house was so quiet that when
Ed sneezed a little too loudly I almost hit the floor as though I
was under fire.

'For God's sake keep it down,' I said.

'Heidi,' Ed sighed, 'I was only sneezing.'

'You can sneeze far more quietly than that,' I complained.

'I fancy an Indian,' Ed announced at about nine o'clock.
'Where are the menus?'

'Stuck to the fridge,' I said. 'Where they normally are.'

Ed heaved himself out of his chair, the best chair in our
sitting room. You could feel the springs through the cushion in
the one that I was sitting on.

I quickly sat down in the warm space he left behind, while he
rang through our order. Always the same. Chicken tikka
masala for him. Vegetarian korma for me. One pilau rice
and a peshwari naan to share. It was probably the Indian
equivalent of always eating egg and chips. Whenever I called
our order through, I thought I heard the guy at the other end of
the phone line groan as he heard me chant the menu numbers I
knew by heart. I very much wanted to try something different,
just to prove that I wasn't completely unadventurous. But

when it came down to it, veggie korma was simply the dish I always fancied most. In any case, Ed never changed his order either.

It was while Ed was on the phone to the Delhi Diner that I felt a peculiar quiver in my left buttock. It took me a very interesting moment to work out that I must be sitting on his mobile phone switched to vibrate. I fished it out from underneath me, intending to hand it over to him, still ringing, so that he could answer it as he finished talking to the guy at the takeaway. But while I was fishing about between the cushions, I must have accidentally picked up the call.

'Whoops,' I said into the receiver. 'Didn't mean to press that button. Ed Gordon's phone.'

The caller cut me off. Or perhaps they had just given up after waiting so long and didn't notice that I had, at last, picked up.

'Bugger.'

I checked the last number dialled, hoping it wasn't Roberta expecting Ed to go into the surgery and attend to some dental emergency – I had very little patience for dental emergencies despite the good fortune my own little crisis had ushered into my life. But it wasn't Roberta. It was Scotty and Clare's number. Scotty was probably calling to make sure Ed was still alive after his sorry exit the previous night. I decided to ring him back and give him a hard time for failing to fight the case for Ed's eyebrows. But when I pressed redial it was Clare who picked up the call.

'Hello,' she said, sounding unsure, as though she was picking up the phone in someone else's house and wasn't convinced she should be doing it.

'Oh hi, Clare. It's Heidi. I think I just cut Scotty off. Is he there?'

A pause.

'Er. No. He's still at work. He'll probably be there till nine-ish. Saturday's a busy day for viewings.'

'I suppose it is. But Ed just got a call from . . .'

'Actually it was me who called,' Clare interrupted. 'And I was trying to speak to you.'

'Oh.'

'Yes. I, er, I couldn't find your home number and I don't think I've got your mobile number so I looked through Scotty's contact sheet and called Ed. I thought he could give me your number and . . .'

'Well, you've got me now. What's up?'

'Er, just, er . . .' Clare hesitated. 'Look, can I call you back in a second or two? I think I can hear *my* mobile ringing in the other room now. I'll call you back in a minute.'

She hung up, leaving me staring at the phone. She was a strange girl sometimes.

Ed had finished ordering the curry.

'Did my phone ring?' he asked.

'Yes,' I told him. 'But it was Clare. And she wanted me.'

'What did she want?'

'No idea.'

Ed's phone began to vibrate again. I still held it in my hand.

'This will be her.' I pressed connect.

'Right.' It was Clare. She sounded as though she had run up and down the stairs since I last spoke to her. 'Sorry about that. Now where was I? Oh, yes. I was calling to say that I think we should arrange a baby shower for Sophie.'

'She's not having the baby for another six months,' I pointed out.

'I know. But these things take some organising and I figured if we start planning now we'll have a better chance of getting everyone together at the same time.'

We? My heart sank. Since when had I become a member of the rugby widows' entertainment committee? Putting together my own wedding had been enough to make me swear off organising so much as coffee for three in the immediate future.

'I thought you might be able to help,' Clare explained. 'You know Sophie much better than I do, what with Zach being Ed's best man. You probably know more of the friends she has outside us rugby-club hangers-on. The only alternative is for me to come clean and ask Sophie herself for the names and numbers of the people she would like to be there. But that's boring. And it would be nice for the party to be a surprise, wouldn't it?'

'Yes,' I agreed. 'I suppose it would.'

'So,' said Clare brightly, 'I thought we might shoot for a Sunday afternoon in late September. Like the fifteenth. Do you have your diary there?'

'Hang on,' I sighed.

Clare kept me on the phone for another half hour brain-storming the baby shower. Where should we have the party? At one of our houses or at a hotel? She knew a great place in West Kensington with a sweet little conservatory that would be the perfect spot to have tea. How should the room be decorated? She knew a good party shop in Fulham where we could buy fab decorations in pink or blue or perhaps yellow, if Sophie had decided not to find out the sex of her baby before he or she was born, or simply didn't want to tell us. What kind of games could we play?

'Games?' I said.

'Yes, games. You know, like guess the celebrity from their baby pics. And we could have a sweepstake, where we all try to guess the baby's sex and weight.'

After that she wanted to talk about Valentine's Day. Were Ed and I going to do anything special?

'No chance. I think we had our big Valentine's Day last year.'

By the time I got off the phone, the Indian had arrived, Ed

had eaten all his share and made a start on mine. I snatched the plate away from him.

'I'm still hungry,' Ed complained.

'Welcome to the world of the happy bride-to-be,' I snarled at him. In the time it had taken me to shift six pounds to get into a wedding dress, Ed seemed to have put on another fourteen. But my barbed comment didn't pierce his new, cuddlier yet hair-free exterior. He just grinned.

'I think it's your turn to check on the baby,' I announced, slapping his hand away from my naan bread.

Ed had warned me that when it came to nappy-changing, after the initial two guilt changes he and I would be taking turns. Fortunately, Kara came back before my turn came up. After Ed had deftly swapped one damp nappy for a dry one, Forester slept all the way through the evening and was still asleep when Kara knocked quietly on the front door at ten minutes past eleven. Unfortunately, Forester did wake up the second he heard her voice. And then he filled his nappy.

'He's been saving it up for you,' I joked. 'Thank God.'

It was clear from Kara's face that the date had been fantastic and even the state of Forester's bowels, as she knelt down in her Donna Karan trousers to change him, couldn't stop her smiling.

'Honestly, Heidi, by the time we got to the restaurant I was so nervous I was ready to turn round and come straight back again. The taxi driver practically had to frogmarch me in there. But the second I saw Duncan, I knew everything was going to be fine. He was so good-looking! So much better than his picture.' He had sent one after a great deal of persuading. 'And so well dressed. I think I was expecting someone whose trousers stopped halfway down his legs or something equally awful. And thank God he is as tall as he claimed.'

'Thank God,' I agreed. 'What did you talk about?'

'Everything. Everything! London, life, love.' Kara's face was split by a grin at the thought. 'We talked about Chiswick – he's just bought a flat by the river. Will we vote Labour or Conservative at the next election? He's voting Green. Cats or dogs. Which do you prefer? We both prefer dogs. He used to have a mongrel called Berkeley . . . Bark-ley? Get it? Bark.'

'Ha ha,' I said. 'What else?'

'What limb you would sacrifice for cheese?'

'Eh?'

'You know: which of your limbs could you bear to have cut off in order to be allowed to keep eating cheese? That came up after we had the most amazing mozzarella in our tricolore salad – Heidi, you have never tasted anything like it; just like the stuff you get in Tuscany. Anyway, Duncan started this incredibly funny conversation about what you would give up in order to be able to keep eating cheese.' Kara laughed at the memory. 'He said he would give up all his limbs as long as his nurse would spoonfeed him Gorgonzola every day for breakfast. Hilarious.'

'Yes,' I said. 'Very funny.' It was clearly one of those occasions when you had to be there. 'You really did talk about everything.'

A shadow passed across Kara's face momentarily. Having refastened the poppers on Forester's baby-gro, she sat back on her heels and sighed as she watched him happily kicking his feet at the air.

'Ah. Everything *except* Forester,' I deduced.

'Except Forester,' Kara admitted. 'I just couldn't find the right moment. Not tonight. Things were flowing along so well and so fast. I couldn't just say, "By the way, I've got a baby." It would have brought things to a crashing halt.'

I gave a small, sympathetic smile of understanding.

'But I will tell him about Forester next time I see him. And

'I'm absolutely convinced he will be fine about the whole thing. He clearly loves children. He kept telling me funny little stories about his older sister's kids, and says he can't get enough of them. She's got a boy and two girls, all under seven. They make him laugh so much, he told me. He babysits them all the time. In fact, I think he might be getting a bit broody himself. My having a son isn't going to faze him at all.'

I nodded, though I wondered how Kara could have listened to a load of cute anecdotes about Duncan's nephew and nieces without interjecting with some cute story about her own son, who was, this sudden bout of diarrhoea notwithstanding, by far the cutest child on earth. Still, who was I to judge how and when Kara should tell her life story?

'So when is the next time?' I asked.

'Wednesday. If I can find a babysitter . . .'

The statement hung in the air. I knew it was a request.

'I know it's Valentine's Day. Even Mum and Dad are off on some romantic dinner date.'

'Don't think we're celebrating it this year . . .' I mused.

'And you did so well tonight. I really expected you to be on the phone every two minutes with some panic or other.'

'You did?'

'Face it, Heidi: sometimes you hold my baby as though he's a rat with bubonic plague. I'm really proud of you for getting over that.'

I didn't know whether to be flattered or angry. It was one thing for me to know I wasn't exactly comfortable around babies but another thing entirely that my discomfort had been noted. True, I didn't have to touch Forester at all between Kara dropping him off and picking him up again, but Kara didn't need to know that. Suddenly, I felt as though I had something to prove.

'If you think you can trust us,' I said, with heavy emphasis on 'trust'. 'Then I'm sure Ed won't mind if we babysit again.'

'Is that the sound of Heidi Savage volunteering?' Kara teased.

'It's not that bloody difficult, looking after a baby.'

Even as I said that, I was praying that I wouldn't come to regret my sudden confidence.

Kara grabbed my face in both her hands and planted a kiss on the end of my nose.

It was only when she let go of me that she noticed the muck on her hands and the nice fresh poo smudge on my cheek.

'I volunteered us to babysit again,' I told Ed when Kara left.

'You mean you volunteered me,' murmured Ed into my neck.

'You only had to change one nappy,' I snapped.

'Hey, calm down. I don't mind,' said Ed. 'It's good practice. Next time you can watch me do it. Unless you're intending me to give up work and be a stay-at-home dad when my first son is born.'

Ed's hands slowly slid up my sides from my waist to my breasts. He squeezed them together amorously and I had that feeling you get at the top of a rollercoaster, where gravity momentarily loses its hold on your body and your internal organs rise towards your mouth. But it wasn't a sensation of lust or desire.

'I don't think I've got enough energy to shag tonight,' I said.

'You haven't had enough energy for weeks,' Ed commented. Complained. It was true. I had been making excuses since the start of the year. 'Why do you feel so tired all of a sudden, Heidi? Are you sure you've been eating enough? Getting enough iron?'

'You were the one who said I needed to lose a few more pounds before the wedding last night,' I cried, pulling myself out of his hold.

'Hey, that was a joke!' Ed tried to pull me back to him.

'Some joke,' I said. 'You told me I looked like a whale in front of all your friends.'

'I did not. You know I think you look wonderful.'

'Do you?'

'Of course I bloody do. Whatever I said last night, you know I was only joking. And drunk.'

I did know he was joking. Ed would never have put any pressure on me to lose weight for the wedding. I knew he adored my body – my curves, my lumps, my bumps. He was the one man I had been truly happy to stand naked in front of. But for some reason that night I let him think that his goofy comment at the rugby dinner had made me angry. I stormed from the sitting room into the bathroom, closed the door behind me and let it slam shut in passive anger. No brushing teeth side by side that night. When I got into bed – wearing a nightdress – I turned my back on him, while he pleaded his case into my shoulder. I refused his kiss goodnight.

'Come on, Heidi. I'm trying to say I'm sorry. I'm an idiot. I know I am. What do I have to do to make it up to you? I hate it when I upset you. Sometimes I say such stupid things I don't know why you ever agreed to marry me in the first place. And then I go and get my eyebrows shaved off. You would be within your rights to call the wedding off. I can only tell you that no man will ever love you more . . .'

He sounded so contrite, so very sorry for himself. I hated myself for letting him think that I really thought he was an arsehole, even for half an hour. But for some reason I couldn't articulate even to myself, I wanted to hate him in that moment. I just didn't want him to touch me. I wanted him to walk away from me. I wanted him to *be* away from me.

'Heidi,' Ed pleaded.

Eventually, I turned to face him and kissed him on the forehead.

'Pax?' he asked.

'Pax,' I told him. 'I know you didn't mean it. I love you.'

But the moment for actually making love had definitely passed.

Next day I got my period. The single drop of blood swirled like ink against the white porcelain. It was as though I had bled poison out with it. Ed looked relieved too when I blamed my latest outburst on premenstrual tension.

'What can I say?' I laughed. 'It's my hormones.'

15

The following Wednesday morning – Valentine's Day – Ed left the house before me. I found a Valentine's card addressed to me on the breakfast table. Ed had already opened the card I had chosen for him and it had pride of place on the kitchen windowsill. Ed had signed his name inside my card – no point pretending any more – which had an arty print of a Parisian street scene on the front. It was a beautiful reminder of the events of twelve months earlier, of course. I immediately felt guilty that I had put so little thought into the rather crude card I had bought for him in return.

As I walked to the Tube station, the Interflora army were already out in full force, delighting lucky girls all over London with roses that had mysteriously doubled in price since the twelfth. Postmen limped under the weight of that day's declarations. Giggling schoolchildren examined each other's cards for clues as to the identity of mysterious senders. A white-haired gentleman smiled a secret smile to himself as he travelled into work that morning with a nice big red carnation for a buttonhole.

Love was in the air and it was definitely not a good day to be single. I was just surprised I didn't feel more smug that I wasn't.

On the airwaves above London too, it was a day of soppy requests and the old romantic standards. As I walked into the station, I was greeted by the sound of Celine Dion's theme song to the movie *Titanic*. Eleanor walked in just behind me.

'Oh, for fuck's sake,' she muttered. 'That's the third time I've heard that hateful song this morning.'

Eleanor was very much single. Unhappily so. She had recently lost the very last of her romantic optimism at a speed-dating event where no one ticked her box. 'I couldn't find a date on a bloody date plantation,' she assured me on a regular basis. And in order to get through the day without screaming she had declared that *Let's Talk London* would be a romance-free zone.

'Our little contribution towards keeping those suicide figures down,' she said when she announced her loveless plan to the team.

So, while every other station in London played Celine Dion and gave air space to declarations of undying devotion and marriage proposals, Flo's guests for the most romantic day of the year (according to the men at Hallmark) were an entrepreneur who had made a small fortune selling second-hand car parts over the Internet and a representative from a new charity that provided free counselling for couples in relationship crisis. Helena from The Good Relationship Trust came onto the show to explain why the charity was campaigning for government support for their work.

'We're going to have a segment on how to have a successful divorce on *Valentine's Day*?' breathed Flo.

'That's right.'

We all knew better than to mess with the boss.

At the time Eleanor had announced her plan, I had thought her the ultimate killjoy, but when Valentine's Day rolled round, I found myself curiously glad of the breathing space in a world that had gone hearts and flowers crazy overnight. Somebody needed to inject some reality back into proceedings.

'The cost to the nation of all these broken relationships is incalculable.' Helen began her case with the usual depressing statistic of the more than one in three marriages that fail. 'The trauma of divorce can lead to depression, problems at school for some children, increased childcare costs when both parents suddenly have to work . . . And statistics have shown that in many cases people soon regret getting that divorce after all. They realise that the grass isn't any greener and they might actually have been able to stay together if they had known how to start a proper dialogue about their problems. Our organisation provides support for that dialogue.'

'But what if talking through those problems just makes the couple more certain that they simply married the wrong one?' Flo asked.

Eleanor and I both leaned forward on our desk in concentration while we waited for the woman from The Good Relationship Trust to answer.

'That's why we'd like the government to look more closely at helping us to provide *pre*marital support as well. We also aim to offer counselling for those who are about to get married, to help them make sure they're ready for the next step.'

From the corner of my eye, I saw Eleanor turn towards me ever so slightly.

'Doesn't sound very romantic,' said Flo.

'It isn't. But romance can blind us to reality.'

Eleanor nodded wisely.

'And then there's the enormous societal pressure we put on couples to make their relationship official with a big white wedding. I frequently counsel couples who admit they had misgivings about getting married even as they stood at the altar taking their vows. But they went through with the marriage because the marquee had been paid for, the invitations had already gone out and they didn't want to disappoint people. Unbelievable as it sounds, these couples chose an unhappy marriage that can take years to unwind over just a few days or weeks of embarrassment and discomfort. Nobody ever died of embarrassment.'

'But don't you think premarital stress is inevitable?' Flo interrupted. 'I think I'd be pretty reluctant to plight my troth if I'd spent six months doing seating plans.'

'Yes. But sometimes what we think of as the usual pre-wedding nerves are actually the manifestation of reservations that go much, much deeper. Our subconscious minds cry out for us to take a proper look at the way we feel . . .'

'God, could that show have been any more depressing?' I groaned when we were finally off air and the guests were safely out of the way.

'Shall we see if we can get you and Ed a free premarital appointment?' Eleanor joked. The whole office had been extremely amused to hear about Ed's eyebrows. 'Or perhaps we don't need to after all.'

Having escorted that morning's guests out to the account cars, Robin was staggering back into the office under the weight of what looked like a hundred red roses. In the end, it turned out there were only three dozen, but they were beautiful. Red as blood and every one as big as a cabbage. And they were for me.

'Oh, how lovely!' said Flo, burying her face in the blooms to get their scent. 'Ed really is a treasure.'

'Or still feeling very guilty!' interjected Robin.

'Let's hope he keeps it up after you're married,' said Eleanor. 'Next year will be the big test. Ask the woman from The Good Relationship Trust.'

'They're great,' said Nelly, fingering a single bloom wistfully. 'Must have cost him a fortune.'

'Bit boring,' said Robin. 'Getting roses from your fiancé. Are you sure they're from him?'

'Quite sure,' I said quickly. 'The clue was in the card.'

Eleanor snatched the card from me and peered at the message. 'Remember Amsterdam' was all it said.

'Remember Amsterdam? What does that mean? I thought Ed proposed to you in Paris.'

'He did,' I agreed. 'But he took me to the Netherlands on our first Valentine's Day together. Before I started working here.'

'Oh. Okay.' Eleanor seemed happy with that.

'Wish someone would send me some roses,' said Nelly.

'Perhaps Jack has a Valentine's surprise up his sleeve,' Robin teased.

'You can have some of these,' I offered.

'Won't Ed be disappointed?' Nelly asked.

'A man pays for three dozen roses on Valentine's Day, he doesn't expect the girl to start giving them away,' said Robin.

'Ed's not like that. He really won't mind.'

'Don't be silly,' said Flo. 'Robin's right. He'll want to see them all when you get home. Though perhaps you could just leave them on my desk for a while. I'll make believe I've got a secret admirer until it's time to go home.'

'It would be lovely to have a secret admirer, wouldn't it?' sighed Nelly.

'Ridiculous commercial bullshit,' said Eleanor.

Flo winked at me as she passed my desk.

At home, on the kitchen table, Ed had placed a single pink rose in a bud vase. He stood at the hob making 'une omelette aux herbes fines'.

'Remember Paris?' he said.

16

Our romantic interlude wasn't going to last long that night. Kara arrived with Forester just after Ed and I finished eating our omelette. She was much less nervous about leaving her son with us for the evening this time. In fact, it seemed instead that she was obscenely keen to offload the baby and head off for her second rendezvous with the lovely Duncan.

Duncan had managed to wangle a table for two at one of the hottest new restaurants in town, despite the fact that it was Valentine's Day and he had given very little notice. 'Unless he booked the restaurant months ago and would have asked any old girl,' said a cynical Ed. Kara concluded more favourably that Duncan must have serious sway in the restaurant world as a result of his job. He was a fine-food importer. Olive oils, flavoured vinegars, truffles, that kind of thing. He spent much of his time travelling between organic farms in Italy, Spain and France in search of the perfect pecorino, amazing Manchego, the ultimate Brie. Hence the passionate conversation about which limb you would be willing to give up for the sake of fermented dairy, I suppose.

'Get any big Valentines' surprises?' Kara asked me while Ed washed up in the kitchen and Kara and I played Pee-po with Forester in front of the TV. I didn't have a chance to tell her before Ed popped his head round the door.

'Hey! It's my main man,' he said to Forester. 'What's the plan for this evening then? Watch a couple of nasty videos? Drink some beer? Shoot some pool?' He took Forester by his little hands and moved his pudgy baby arms through the motions of taking a shot at the black. Forester opened his mouth wide in delight. His silent movie laugh, as Kara called it. He couldn't seem to control himself after that: his eyes and mouth just got wider and wider as he looked up into Ed's face. Perhaps it was the lack of eyebrows that brought it on.

Kara repeated the sleeping, feeding and peeing schedule she had just outlined to me. Ed nodded and parroted the key elements back to her to signal that he'd listened and understood. 'I feel so much better knowing that a responsible adult is here,' Kara told him. She gave me a wink as she said it, but I suspected there was still more than a little element of truth in the joke.

'Have a great evening,' I told Kara as I showed her to the door. Ed had volunteered to make sure Forester went to sleep and Kara was happy to let him, having decided that my fiancé had the magic touch when it came to her son. 'I'm horribly jealous of you going out,' I added, while Kara had me check her teeth for lipstick and gave me one last twirl in her fabulous new dress.

'Even with such a handsome fiancé at home?' she teased.

Nearly five days after the ritual shaving, Ed still wasn't looking that great. The marker-pen eyebrows were still pretty visible, a pair of faint grey slugs that reminded me of Michael Jackson's tattooed-on make-up, while, underneath, gingery stubble was starting to show through. Itchy stubble. Ed had developed a new nervous tic over the past twenty-four hours – rubbing at the pathetic reddish growth.

'Stop it,' I told him when he had finished settling Forester down and walked back into the kitchen scratching like an ape.

'But they're driving me crazy,' Ed complained.

'And you're driving me crazy by scratching your face like that. You'll get brow dandruff,' I told him. His skin was already getting pretty dry from the constant friction.

'I'm sorry this Valentine's Day isn't quite like last year,' Ed told me as he poured me another glass of wine and we settled down in front of the television. 'Just think, this time twelve months ago I was absolutely bricking myself while we waited in the queue to go up the Eiffel Tower. Did you really not guess what I was going to do when we got up there?'

In truth, I had suspected that something was going on from the moment we got to our hotel and found a bottle of vintage champagne, but Ed had seemed so agitated and stressed out in a *bad* way, I wouldn't have been at all surprised if he had changed his mind and dumped me instead of proposed while we were surveying the view.

Ed picked up my left hand and began to stroke my fingers. 'You've got such beautiful hands,' he said. 'I just had to put a ring on them.'

I smoothed my right hand over his prickly bald head while he continued to murmur compliments. Ed could be such a softy at times. It was one of things that had surprised and delighted me about him when we first got together. Apart from the fact that he was sexy as hell. He was a man who spent his day pulling teeth and his weekends rolling in the mud with fourteen other men, yet he often said things that sounded like the beginning of a poem.

He lifted my fingers to his lips and kissed them one by one. He huffed on my engagement ring then pulled his shirt cuff up over his hand and used it to give the diamond a polish. 'Best investment I ever made,' he said. 'I don't know what I would have done if you hadn't said yes.'

'Thrown me off the top of the Tower?'

'If I hadn't been wearing a neck brace, I might have done.' He had almost broken his back the week before we went to Paris. At least once a season, someone in Ed's rugby club ended up in hospital.

Now he leaned over and started to kiss my neck. Soft, slow

kisses of the kind that could normally be guaranteed to drive me crazy.

Not any more. Not right then.

'I think I can hear Forester,' I said.

Ed momentarily lifted his head from my cleavage. 'I can't.'

'No, wait,' I insisted, actually holding Ed's head firmly away from me so that he couldn't start kissing me again. 'I can definitely hear him. There. He did it again. A little whimper. Didn't you hear it too?'

Ed sat right up and cocked his head towards the door. 'Nope. I can't hear anything.' He headed back down towards my chest. I blocked him.

'That's because your hearing is fucked from getting hit in the head on the rugby pitch all the time,' I told him. 'Forester is definitely crying. I'd better go.'

I started to get up but Ed gently pushed me back down into the chair.

'He'll go back to sleep if you leave him.'

'And what if he doesn't?'

'Give him a few seconds at least. I still can't even hear anything.'

'Well, I can. What if he's whimpering because he's got a blanket wrapped around his neck? What if we check on him in ten minutes' time and find out he's choked himself to death?'

'For God's sake. I'll go,' Ed sighed. 'Since I have the magic touch.'

Perhaps I had heard Forester crying; perhaps I hadn't. Whether he was awake or not before, he was definitely awake by the time Ed finished tripping over the vacuum cleaner I had left out in the hallway with the intention of taking it upstairs. Ed reached out to steady himself against the hall table, which was really just a gathering place for junk mail, and brought that crashing down after him too. Forester's cry went up like a fire siren.

'Ed!' I shouted irritably, though it clearly wasn't his fault. I was the one who had left the Dyson spilling cables all over the place, after all.

When I came out into the hallway to set the table right, Ed had already picked Forester up and was beginning the long process of getting him to go to sleep again. He paced the room with Forester against his chest, rubbing the baby's back and cooing 'Swing Low Sweet Chariot'. He could only fit in three paces before he had to turn.

It was quite a sight, these two men in my life. One so tall and broad, one so small and new. And yet Ed didn't seem nervous at all as he rocked from foot to foot with Forester's head on his shoulder. Since picking up Forester for the first time, Ed had quickly lost his 'baby terror'. That was the term Clare used for the look on Scotty's face when anyone passed him an infant.

'He acts like you've just handed him a grenade with the pin pulled out. Honestly, he'd much rather cuddle a rugby ball.'

Ed, on the other hand, was turning out to be a natural. Why didn't I feel more pleased and proud? Why did I find it such a turn-off?

'I'll put the table back when Forester's asleep again,' Ed assured me. 'You just sit back down and relax.'

I didn't need to be asked twice. By the time Ed came back to the sitting room however, I had dug out the wedding invitations and was busy writing out more addresses with the calligraphy pen I had learned to use especially.

'What are you doing?' Ed asked.

'Our wedding invitations.'

'Now?'

'When else am I supposed to get them done?'

I had put the box of unwritten invitations in Ed's place on the sofa. He sat down heavily in his chair and picked up the television remote control. 'At least this must mean you still want to get married,' he said.

Kara, like Cinderella, made sure she was back before midnight. By half eleven, actually. Ed and I were happy enough to stay in on Valentine's Day but Ed had insisted that he wanted to get a decent night's sleep and that meant being in bed before midnight.

Kara didn't seem unduly disgruntled by such an early curfew. When I opened the door she was standing on the top step, swinging her fake Kate Spade handbag and gazing off dreamily into the distance like some 1960s chick who had just managed to kiss Paul McCartney. When I asked her how the date went, she gave the kind of sigh I reserved for particularly fantastic ice-cream. She was feeling so full of the joys that she grabbed me round the waist and waltzed with me in the hall.

'Went well then,' I deduced.

'So well . . . I could have danced all night!!!' she sang.

'Sssssh!' I put a finger to my lips. 'The baby.'

'Was Forester good tonight?' she asked.

'With me in charge,' said Ed, bringing out the Moses basket with its snoozy cargo. 'He wouldn't dare not be.'

'You're getting pretty good at the baby thing,' said Kara admiringly.

'You should have seen him,' I told her. 'Cuddling, singing, changing nappies.'

'Changed him twice. I think he's got a touch of diarrhoea again.'

'Probably because he's teething. They swallow a lot of saliva.'

'Too much information,' I said.

'You're a hero, Ed.'

'I'm just a modern man. So, is there going to be a date three?' Ed asked.

'Oh yes,' Kara nodded enthusiastically. 'And a date four and a date five and date six and dates for ever! I hope. You know, I don't think I've ever met someone I felt so easy with. It's just so comfortable being with him. It really is as though we've known each other for years, not just two and a half weeks.'

'And this is the one you met on the Internet?' Ed mused.

'I know. Isn't it crazy? It's the last place I expected to find a man this good. If anyone had told me six months ago that I would go online and find someone who not only doesn't look like he's been living underground for twenty years but makes me feel as though I can say just about anything and he'll understand exactly what I'm trying to tell him and never judge me and . . .'

'Did you?' I began, assuming that this meant she had made the ultimate revelation.

Kara pulled a sorry sort of face. She knew exactly where my mind had leapt to. 'Heidi, it was Valentine's Day. The place was completely packed. I felt absolutely sure that if I said, "Oh, by the way, I've got a baby," the whole room would suddenly fall silent and stare at us. He was having such a great time. I was having such a great time. I didn't want to spoil things.' She shrugged her shoulders up to her ears.

'Isn't that the best time to broach a tricky subject?' said Ed. 'When things are going well?'

'Would *you* really want to have that heavy a conversation in a packed restaurant?' Kara responded. 'Honestly, Ed, the place was so busy we were practically rubbing elbows with the couple on the next table. I heard all about her repetitive strain injury from too much typing, and all about his bowels . . . I didn't want them to know my business too.'

'Fair enough,' said Ed. 'There might be a better moment.'

'Your call,' I agreed.

'Sometime soon though, eh?' said Ed.

'Of course,' she said, waving our concerns away. 'Of course I'll tell him as soon as I can.'

But the longer you keep a secret, the harder it gets to reveal it. Everybody knows that much. It's like trying to peel a sticking plaster off slowly. If you do it quickly, there's just the short sting. Do it slowly – the coward's way – and you will feel and hear every single tiny hair screaming in agony as it is ripped in slow motion from your pores. A secret kept for too long is like one of those old-fashioned fabric plasters that never come off in one piece and leave a sticky residue for weeks.

I'd decided at the beginning of my relationship with Ed that we would never keep secrets from each other, not even little ones (unless they were secrets of the surprise-birthday-trip-to-Prague variety). I had bitten my tongue on secrets both big and small in the past and it had always ended badly. What is the point of promising to spend the rest of your life with someone if there is still a part of you like a locked room they just don't have the key to? It was hard at first. Keeping secrets is a good way to avoid total intimacy and avoiding total intimacy is the best way to avoid pain. But I hadn't kept any secrets from Ed, and soon found I didn't want to.

Until now.

'Happy Valentine's Day,' Ed murmured into my neck as he turned out the bedside light. 'I'm sorry it was such a washout compared to last year. Omelette. Babysitting. Just the one very unspectacular rose.'

I closed my eyes tightly against the guilt.

And that might have been the end of it. I comforted myself with the thought that my mystery bouquet wasn't such a big deal if I didn't even say 'thank you' for it.

That night I hoped that someone nice found those beautiful roses where I left them on the bench next to the tube station and took them home to some other nice person who would really appreciate them. I just wanted to be rid of those flowers because they reminded me of a moment of betrayal: the moment when I didn't tell my ex-boyfriend that I was about to get married to Ed.

'Remember Amsterdam.'

Of course, I knew the second I opened the card that the roses weren't from Ed, because I've been to Amsterdam only once in my life and it was Steven Gabriel who took me there.

How many years ago was it now? I calculated almost ten. I'd just finished my final year at university. Steven had already been out in the real world working for a year and he surprised me with a weekend away to celebrate the end of my torturous exams.

Steven met me at my shared student flat in Leeds and we took a boat across the North Sea from Newcastle. We couldn't afford to fly back then. Steven had hardly any money, since the advertising agencies could take their pick from hundreds of students prepared to work for nothing to get in. I had minus five figures at the HSBC. The boat journey was terrible; I felt sick all the way. But Amsterdam more than made up for the agony of getting there, even though Steven had booked us into a bed and breakfast where the linen on the two single beds in our room was patterned with old cigarette burns and the bath drain was clogged with past guests' pubic hair. It was seedy, but that was part of the adventure. Amsterdam was meant to be a bit seedy, wasn't it?

When we finally finished reacquainting ourselves in that horrible room (in those early days, two weeks apart felt like for ever and required lots of catching-up time in bed), I held onto Steven's arm tightly as we wandered through the red light district, gawping at the girls in their windows. I nibbled a corner of a hash cake in a brown café and felt sure I was going to be smoking on a crack pipe by the time I got back to Heathrow.

Amsterdam was at once thrillingly dangerous and strangely Disney-like. Away from the call girls and cannabis, I loved the pretty painted barges on the canals, the crooked, narrow houses, even the hurdy-gurdy rise and fall of the Dutch accent. Eating chips and mayonnaise and apple pie and cream in Dam Square. Laughing at the paintings from Van Gogh's potato period. If I'm going to be honest, I preferred Amsterdam to Paris. No pressure to be chic for a start. The Dutch are the only European nation that dresses anywhere near as badly as the British.

During the course of the weekend, Steven bought me yellow tulips from the floating market and a pair of tiny wooden clogs that hung in the kitchen of the flat we shared until the day we broke up. They were the first things I threw into a bin bag.

What had he been thinking when he sent those roses? That even though Ed was my live-in 'boyfriend', the relationship couldn't possibly be so serious that I was off limits for a bit of floral flirtation? I felt a small twitch of indignation that Steven could have been so dismissive about my big relationship before I reminded myself that he only had his conversation with me on which to base his outrageous assumption.

Above and beyond that, he obviously also thought it was appropriate to flirt with me again. He must have thought – based on those three minutes of small-talk in the car park – that all was forgiven. We could be great friends again now, he thought. He could try to start things all over again without having to go through the irritating post-mortem of what went wrong the first time. Because he certainly hadn't bothered with a post-mortem back then. From the moment he announced that he didn't want to be with me any more until the moment his best friend's car pulled up in the drive to take him and his things God knew where, had taken little over two hours. Hardly long enough to explain the death of a relationship that had taken five years to grow.

Flattered? Insulted? What was I supposed to be?

I was supposed to be getting married to someone else. I wasn't supposed to be thinking about Steven at all, much less analysing his motives for sending me three dozen red roses accompanied by a card guaranteed to bring back the hottest of memories.

Ed was soon asleep. I could tell by the pattern of his breath, the way his big shoulder moved up and down with somnolent rhythm. I curled myself tight against his back and breathed in the smell of him. Imperial Leather shower gel. The only shower gel he could be persuaded to use. Deep Heat muscle rub. He was always faintly scented with that stuff – his shoulder had been giving him trouble again since the rugby club's trip to Gloucester. I let my nose rest against that bad shoulder and tried to suck Ed into me as though I was a diver inhaling oxygen.

This was the man I loved. Literally in front of my nose. Dependable, wonderful Ed. His presence should have obliterated any trace of my romantic past. He had. He did.

However, while I tried hard to convince myself that Steven's big romantic gesture hadn't worked and he was still firmly consigned to my past with those little wooden clogs, there were still several other women of my acquaintance who were determined that Steven would feature more prominently in their futures (and, by default, in mine).

17

After the dubious success of Eleanor's anti-romantic Valentine's show (the emails and calls we'd received in response were all very depressing), we decided that the subject of that Friday's programme should be altogether lighter. At the Thursday afternoon meeting, it came down to a toss-up between Morris-dancing or cheese-rolling (that other great British spring tradition). In the end, we decided to try to go with both – have a battle of the best of English country madness with representatives from each insane activity explaining why their particular brand of lunacy was the better one. Unfortunately, the cheese-rolling representative wouldn't be able to make it into the studio. He'd broken both his legs chasing a cheese down a very steep hill the previous weekend.

'Can I just bring something to everyone's attention for next week?' Nelly said at the end of the meeting.

'Not the LK Bennett shoe sale?' said Robin.

'Is it?' Flo perked up. She had been on the point of dozing off. We all had. There was something about the combination of heating turned too high, hot chocolate, the doughnuts Eleanor bought on her way into work . . .

Nelly gave Robin her sternest look. 'Actually, it's something that I thought might be a good basis for the whole of next Friday's show.'

'Go on,' said Eleanor, yawning. 'I'm intrigued.'

Flo put her finger to Robin's lips before he could say anything stupid again.

'Next Friday is National Single Parents' Day,' said Nelly.

'Is it really?' Flo asked. 'I didn't even know they had such a thing.'

'There have been a couple,' said Nelly. 'But this one is on a much bigger scale than before. They've got funding from the National Lottery this year.'

'Nelly,' said Eleanor, 'you are a superstar. How did you find out?'

'I made sure we were on a couple of mailing lists. You said that we should always make sure we stayed on the mailing lists of our guests' organisations.' That was true. Nelly logged the details of all our guests diligently and was the queen of the follow-up call. Robin could never be bothered, relying instead on picking his stories out of the tabloids.

'What a great idea,' said Flo. 'But how should we celebrate it?'

Flo looked at Eleanor. Eleanor smiled back.

Oh God. I knew at once exactly what Eleanor and Flo would suggest if Nelly hadn't already made the arrangements. Flo's eyes were actually sparkling.

'Well,' said Nelly. 'Obviously since it's official Single Parents' Day for the whole of the United Kingdom and Northern Ireland, the main charities have been inundated with requests for people willing to do interviews and the BBC have nabbed most of the single parent celebs. Which is why I circumvented the queues and went straight to that chap who came on the programme a few weeks ago. The one Heidi knows from university.'

I buried my face in my arms and groaned. I had been stitched up good and proper.

'What was his name again?' Eleanor asked disingenuously.

'Steven Gabriel,' said Nelly.

'Oh, yes,' said Flo, getting in on the joke. 'I *think* I remember the guy you're talking about.'

'What about the rule we're supposed to have about not having the same guests back on the show more than once a year unless there's a *really* good reason?' I began my case for the objection. 'Steven was on this show less than two weeks ago.'

'There is a really good reason to have him back on. It's National Single Parents' Day,' said Eleanor simply.

'And he was really good,' Flo agreed. 'After some of the guests we've had on the show lately, I deserve to work with someone who can actually handle breathing and talking into a microphone at the same time.' She looked at me pointedly. The previous week, Flo had interviewed her worst ever guest in the history of the show, a first-time novelist – one I had championed – who said next to nothing for the first ten minutes then burst into tears when Flo asked her to talk about her inspiration for the book, which was all about her dead mother. That show had been a salt-water washout.

'Mr Gabriel was certainly popular,' Nelly reminded everyone. She flipped through her notes for some figures. 'We had our highest ever listener call volume for that show. In the region of fifty per cent more calls than usual for a Monday afternoon.'

Damn Nelly and her statistics.

'And as far as I can remember,' she concluded, 'all the responses were positive.'

'Yeah,' I protested. 'But there were still plenty of listeners who didn't call, I'm sure. People who might find his second appearance boring. There must be someone else we can interview instead. What about my friend Kara? She's still a single mum with an interesting story; she's just started seeing a man she met online. She could talk about single parents and dating.'

'We had Kara on the show less than six months ago,' said Eleanor.

138

'Rules were made to be broken,' I said furiously. 'You just bloody well said so yourself.'

'Steven is an official representative of the Lone Parents Network,' said Flo. 'That gives him a bit more gravitas than Kara.'

'Gravitas is very important on *Let's Talk London*,' agreed Eleanor.

'Oh, rubbish,' I said. 'We've just spent half an hour discussing the possibility of doing a whole show about blinkin' cheese-rolling!'

'And Morris-dancing,' added Nelly.

'I don't care who comes on the show as long as I get to go outside and have a cigarette while you girls are scratching each other's eyes out over who can have him,' said Robin.

'Well, I don't want him!' I said. I don't know why I said that. It just burst out of me. My colleagues all stared at me again.

'Why aren't you happy about this?' Eleanor asked me as I stomped about the office that afternoon. 'He's the perfect guest for Flo that day.'

'Sure,' I replied.

'Did something happen between the pair of you that you haven't told me about?' Eleanor continued. 'If there's some big reason why you can't be in the same room as him, we won't have him back on the show. But it's been almost a decade since you guys split up, hasn't it?'

'Seven years.'

'That's still an awful lot of water under the bridge, Heidi. Bloody hell, I've almost forgiven my husband for being a complete twat and it's less than seven years since he moved in with my stepsister.'

I could hardly compete with that Jerry Springer-style revelation. I'd forgotten about Eleanor's particularly painful case of sibling rivalry.

'But if you still don't feel comfortable then I can tell Nelly and Robin that they've got to stay late and come up with something different. I'm sure Nelly won't mind missing her salsa class again . . .'

'Look, it's fine,' I said, crumbling in the face of her not terribly subtle emotional blackmail. 'The show is all set and you're right: I'm overreacting. I'm sure Steven will make Friday's show extremely interesting. It's just that he is my ex-boyfriend and I don't want Ed to think that I'm deliberately getting him back in the studio.'

'What did Ed say when you told him about the last time?'

'I didn't tell him,' I admitted.

'Then there you go.' Eleanor knew she had me. 'He doesn't need to know this time either. Don't go catching some terrible lurgy before next Friday, will you?'

The cow.

Steven's imminent return as Flo's Friday guest raised a whole host of questions for me, not least whether I should tell Ed.

Ed and I didn't often talk about work. When he got home from the surgery he wanted to switch off, and he was almost always able to. There were very few times when Ed couldn't be distracted from the fortunes of his patients by a bottle of beer and a repeat of *Friends* on the TV and, to be honest, I was happy enough with that. I wasn't overly keen to hear the details of other people's gum disease. Particularly not over a TV dinner. We didn't talk much about my job, either.

But this was different. Ed and I were getting married. And Steven wasn't just another guest on the show; he was my ex. He was my *significant* ex. Ed needed to know that he'd popped back up in my life.

Prior to getting together with me, Ed's longest relationship had lasted just six months and he freely admitted it had only lasted that long because the girl in question had been posted in

Hong Kong for most of that time. None of Ed's exes mattered that much anyway, he assured me. Some of them were still good friends. And one thing I've learned is that the only exes you can really be friends with are the ones you are thoroughly over. In fact, one of them was Sophie, now married to Ed's best friend.

Ed and Sophie had dated for just a couple of weeks before Ed made his excuses in an extremely cowardly telephone call (that was how he described it). Fortunately for Sophie, Zach, who shared a flat with Ed at the time, was only too happy to be a nice big shoulder to cry on when Sophie appeared on their doorstep with murder in mind. Zach managed to persuade her that she had had a lucky escape and after that destiny took over. Soon she was able to announce that Ed's brief appearance in her love life was one of the best things that ever happened to her. How else might a dental-equipment sales rep have ended up meeting and marrying a man who worked in the City and never ventured outside the Square Mile to socialise?

Yeah. Ed's exes were harmless. Ancient and occasionally quite amusing history. He had a good line in dinner-party anecdotes about the ones who had found him lacking and sent him packing. Half of them had ended up dating his friends. Certainly none of them had ever caused him to lose a couple of stone in weight and try to persuade medic friends to write a prescription for anti-depressants.

Seven years should have made Steven ancient history for me, too.

Why was I so worried about telling Ed that Steven was going to be on the show? For a second time. I don't know why I hadn't mentioned that first surprise encounter. I didn't think Ed would be jealous exactly – there was nothing to be jealous about. But what if I didn't bother to tell him and my discomfort at Steven's reappearance came out as an 'amusing' anecdote at the next *Let's Talk London* Christmas party? 'Did Heidi tell you about the mess she made of the desk the day she looked up and saw . . .' Or what if Kara spilled the beans one day, which was much more likely. If I hadn't forewarned Ed then it might suddenly appear as though I had a *reason* for not letting him know.

It seemed simple. A woman who was planning to get married should have no secrets from her beloved fiancé except the design of her wedding dress. Talking of which, Nelly had left a neat note on my desk saying my mother had called to remind me I had a fitting at four thirty that afternoon.

'You must be excited to see it,' Flo said when she noticed Nelly's Post-it.

'What?'

'The dress, of course. Will you bring in a Polaroid so we can have a look at you in all your glory?'

'Sure,' I groaned. It was the last thing I needed.

I got to the dressmaker at four thirty-five to find my mother already there. She had travelled up from Southampton to meet me for the fitting and then go for a bite to eat before she caught the train home again. It was a curious thing. Mum had never been one for dragging me round the shops trying to pretty me up, as Kara's mother did with her throughout her childhood, but she was playing the mother-of-the-bride role to its fullest. After Ed and I got engaged, Mum took the train up to London three Saturdays in a row to help me trawl the bridal departments of London's best stores until I found a wedding dress I didn't think made me look like I was on my way to one of Elton John's fancy dress birthday parties.

In my imagination, I got married in the Chelsea Registry Office wearing a white pant suit à la Bianca Jagger. In reality, I was going to be married in a sixteenth-century church in a full-length ivory silk gown. The bodice was strapless but a thin over-shirt of lace covered my arms and décolletage. It was tasteful and yet pretty. I wouldn't even have thought to try it on but the sales assistant coerced me into giving the dress a whirl and it turned out she was right. I was surprised at how enamoured I was of something so feminine when I finally put the dress on. That was six months ago. Now my very own version of the shop sample was ready to be tweaked into perfection.

The dressmaker was already getting impatient by the time I arrived; another bride was due at five. I tore off my jeans and lifted my arms like a ballerina so she could drop the dress over my head. A stray pin scratched at one of my thighs as the skirt settled around my feet.

'Don't bleed!' my mother shrieked when I shouted 'ouch'.

'I won't bleed deliberately,' I said.

I stepped up onto the podium so that the dressmaker and her assistant could move around me easily with their pinning guns. My mother pointed out that the hem looked a little crooked at the back. There was much tugging on the bottom of the skirt to prove that the left side did in fact match the right exactly – it must be my legs that were uneven. The bodice needed to be taken in a little tighter, however.

'You've lost weight,' the dressmaker said accusingly.

'Heidi, are you eating properly?' asked Mum.

'I'm eating like a bride.'

'Have you had any more thoughts about your headdress?' my mother asked while I lifted my arms obediently so the dressmaker could get to a dart.

'A helmet?' I suggested. The previous week, Mum had called in a panic to tell me that part of the plaster on the vaulted ceiling of the church had fallen down. They'd had to hang nets from the beams to stop any further chunks of masonry wiping out the faithful.

'Be serious,' she said now. 'I still think you would look lovely in my old veil. It would solve the something old and the something borrowed bit as well. If the moths haven't already got to it.'

Mum had kept her veil for thirty-two years. It had been her mother's veil before that. It was a heavy affair, real lace, not tulle. It reminded me of the crocheted doilies my grandmother would put over the milk jug to keep the flies off during the summer. I didn't see how it would be possible to wear that veil and get down to the altar without a guide dog. And there was the small fact that I wasn't sure I wanted to wear a veil anyway.

'We've got some veils you can try to get the look,' said the dressmaker's assistant.

'No, really. No need.' I didn't particularly want to mess my hair up – I was having one of those extremely rare good hair days – but I could tell that Mum wasn't going to let it go.

'Just to see,' she whispered.

'We've got some little coronets to fasten the veils in place,' the assistant continued. 'These just came in today.' She showed me two headdresses that looked as though they had been fashioned out of the gold foil that usually wrapped Galaxy chocolate. I let Mum choose the one she liked best, which was, of course, the one I thought most hideous.

The bodice pinning was finished now. I stepped down from the podium and let the assistant fasten the first veil to the back of my head with a hard plastic comb. Could plastic draw blood? In the right hands, it seemed.

'Your hair's a bit slippy,' she explained as she jabbed at me again and again.

Finally the damn thing stayed put. I heard the ethereal whisper of tulle as between them, the assistant and my mother lifted the top layer of the veil up and over my face. A moment's more fuss while the crown was placed on top of that.

'Come and take a look,' said the assistant, helpfully holding out her arm for me in my newly blinded state. I stepped back up onto the podium. The tulle in front of my eyes and the same tulle reflected in the mirror completely obscured my face from view. I realised the significance of hiding my features: as I stepped into the church I would be Heidi Savage, but as I stepped out I would be a different woman altogether. A wife. One half of a married couple. This veil was going to be my chrysalis, hiding the transformation.

I always preferred caterpillars to butterflies.

Weddings are so much about the bride, aren't they? The bride gets the best outfit and the most attendants. But I realised then that all this fuss was giftwrapping. I was giving myself to Ed. But would he be getting what he really wanted?

When we chose the church in which we were to be married, we had tea with the vicar and read through the wedding vows with him. Ed knew there was no way I was going to promise to obey him and he joked that it might be more appropriate for that phrase to come in his half of the vows anyway, since that was already the status quo. So we took out 'obey' but for the most part we left the rest of the vows as they appeared in the traditional prayer book. One of the parts we left in was about coming together to have children and, lately, that too had been worrying me. Was I in effect making a promise that I would be the mother of his child? What if I changed my mind?

They were just words. We could have a proper conversation after we were married and if I decided then that I didn't want to have children and Ed decided that having a family was more important than merely being with me, well, we could always get a divorce . . .

Behind me, I heard my mum sniff loudly. It happened every time we went into that damn shop. It had happened every time I put on a wedding dress when we were still just checking dresses out, before I chose the one I wanted.

But this time, I was tearing up too. I was standing in my wedding dress imagining Ed with another woman, a woman who definitely wanted the sort of life he had always hoped for. The life we had talked about when we were new and it all seemed such a long way off and therefore safe to speculate about the house and the garden and two point four children playing with a chocolate Labrador on the lawn. It hadn't seemed like such a bad scenario then, had it? I had listened to Ed talking about the future we could have together and been happy to join in, picking names for a boy and a girl. 'And what about the point four?' Ed asked.

'Minnie?' I suggested.

Ed still talked about that fantasy. He ran through a new set of children's names (specifically boys' names) every time someone he admired scored a try. I'd stopped. Had I stopped before Kara got pregnant? Before Forester was born? When had I started to find baby-scan pictures faintly menacing?

'My little girl,' Mum muttered, as she always did.

'Do you want me to lift the veil back so you can see what you'll look like with your face showing?' the assistant asked.

'Not quite yet,' I told her. 'Give me a moment longer like this.'

A moment to sniff back my tears. I could have got away with claiming that the sight of my dress had filled me with un-stoppable happiness that was manifesting itself as sobbing. But I didn't want to have to explain anything at all. Not then.

'For God's sake, Mum,' I muttered instead. 'There have been far too many tears from you considering I'm supposed to be getting ready for the happiest day of my life.'

I was glad to get back into my jeans. I forgot to take the Polaroid for the girls at work.

When the fitting was over, Mum and I jumped into a taxi and headed for Harvey Nichols. Mum wanted to catch the very tail end of their winter sale and perhaps find the perfect birthday present for James, my brother, who was turning twenty-six in a few days' time. I managed to persuade her against buying a Pringle jumper that I knew he was a long way off growing into. He may have been working in the City but my brother wasn't going to be taking up golf any time soon.

After that we trawled through the racks in the Max Mara concession. Mum tried to convince me that I needed a pair of brown trousers of the kind that only an Italian woman could make chic.

'Housewife trousers,' I muttered.

'Well, you're going to be a wife soon enough,' Mum joked.

'I'm not having my fashion sense removed as part of the ceremony.'

When we had finished shopping, we went upstairs to the restaurant. Mum tittered like a schoolgirl while the waiter, who was clearly gay, flirted with her over the menus. Once we had chosen, Mum continued to gossip about a bunch of people I had never met and probably never would. It was hardly my kind of gossip anyway. No surprise comings-out or hotly denied boob jobs, just a litany of hernia operations, recently diagnosed Type II diabetes, and people seen taking sneaky cuttings from prize plants in other people's flowerbeds.

'How's Kara getting on?' Mum asked when she'd finished telling me about an extension that didn't have planning permission.

'She's met a man.'

Mum's eyebrows dipped into a frown that she quickly ironed out. She knew she wasn't supposed to be disapproving: Kara may have been a single mum but these days that was no reason to shut yourself away in the poorhouse.

'She met him on the Internet.'

'He's not a serial killer, is he?'

'I don't think so. It's becoming quite the way to get a date.'

'And how is little Forester getting on?'

'Growing like a weed.'

'I heard. Ed said you'd been doing some babysitting.'

'When did he tell you that?'

'When I called the other evening. You weren't home.'

I remembered now. In fact, I had been home. When I saw Mum and Dad's number on the caller ID, I told Ed I didn't have the energy. I would have let the answer-machine pick up but Ed couldn't do that. He always picked up the phone to his mother and now he always picked up the phone to mine too. Not picking up when your parents called only happened in television dramas as far as Ed was concerned. Good people like us didn't find their families frustrating.

'Were you out somewhere nice?' Mum asked.

'Probably still at the office,' I lied.

'On a Sunday? You know, I wish we could get your show down in Southampton. I'd listen to it every morning. Had anybody interesting on lately?'

'Nobody interesting at all.'

Our food arrived. She told me about Dad's cholesterol level in more detail as she picked the coriander out of her salad. I really should be watching Ed's. Some girl I didn't remember had had a baby. Was I taking folic acid in preparation?

'Preparation for what?' I asked.

'For having a baby. To prevent spina bifida.'

'Who's having a baby?'

'Well, you. After the wedding. I know Ed wants to start a family as soon as possible. He told your dad.'

'Did he now?'

'You ought to start thinking about it soon. You can't start getting prepared too early. I overheard a girl in the hairdresser's who's started having IVF. She's only twenty-seven.'

'I don't think I'm ready just yet.'

'No one's ever ready. The day comes and you just get on with it.'

I paused with my fork halfway between my plate and my

mouth. Get on with it? Like you did? I wanted to say to her. I saw the woman sitting on the back step of the house, finishing her cigarette while the baby cried upstairs. It would have been the perfect moment to ask her about that day. The perfect moment to say, 'But you didn't find it came naturally, did you, Mum?'

It wasn't just that afternoon on the step that was coming back to me now. The last couple of days, I'd been trying to remember what life was like when I was four or five years old. Dad had a good job and came straight home every evening. He bought my mother flowers every payday. She had friends, too. Good friends. Auntie Alison who was training to be a hair-dresser and cut my hair using a Tupperware salad bowl as a style guide. Auntie Kath who made me a fabulous fairy outfit on her professional sewing machine. We saw a lot of Auntie Kath and Auntie Alison while James was still a baby. It seemed so obvious now that it was because Mum couldn't cope on her own.

'What if I turn out to have more in common with you than my mousey brown hair and my too-thin lips and my bloody childbearing hips? What if I have a baby and I hate it?' That's what I wanted to ask. But I didn't. I just let her carry on trying to put my mind at rest with an overlong anecdote about the woman in Dad's office who, having insisted that she would be sending her child to boarding school as soon as it was off the tit, ended up enjoying motherhood so much she quit her job and had two more children in the space of twenty-four months.

'Honestly, Heidi, nobody thought she would be happy to stay at home and be a mother. But even if you're not happy to do that, you can still work part-time.'

'Yeah,' I said listlessly, battling with the old sow image again. I let Mum continue with her theme until even she was bored.

'Don't forget to call James on his birthday,' she said when

she had run out of what she clearly thought was appropriate motherly advice.

'I won't. What does he have on his present list?'

James was still writing out a present list every year, even though he worked in the City and had enough cash to buy himself the whole toy shop these days. It was part of his role. Little brother, youngest son. Most *cherished* son. At least since he was out of nappies. Had Mum's overcompensation for ignoring him when he was a baby made him the brat he'd become? 'They fuck you up,' Larkin's poem began on my internal radio station.

'Perhaps you could get him some of the CDs he's asked for.' Mum searched in her handbag for the little Smythson notepad my brother had given her for Christmas the previous year. 'There's an album called *Strays* by someone called Jane Addiction.'

'Jane's Addiction,' I corrected her.

'Yes, that's right.'

After supper, Mum and I took another cab to Waterloo. I waited with her until her train pulled into the station and walked down the carriages until we spotted one that was occupied by another woman about her age and a 'nice young man in a suit' who looked as if he might at least have a go at defending his fellow passengers if the train was rushed by hoodlums at Clapham Junction.

We stood on the platform until the guard started walking the length of the train closing the last few open doors. Mum pressed my cheeks between her hands.

'I love you, darling.'

'I love you too.'

We kissed goodbye.

And I walked away feeling miserable. Every time I arranged to see Mum, I told myself it would be different. I told myself that I wouldn't regress to a surly teenager, that we would talk about lots of serious mother/daughter subjects and I would happily take advantage of the wisdom of her years and ask for her advice. But we'd never had that kind of relationship. Never. I was too scared to tell her I was unhappy and I think she was too scared to notice. Every time I put Mum back on the train I felt the distance between us more keenly than ever, as though I'd just waved off a childless actress who was acting my mother for the day. As though we didn't know each other at all.

On the way home that night, I decided that I had to tell Ed what was coming. I would broach the subject as soon as I got into the house.

'Eddy, I've got something to tell you.'

'What?' he said.

'Next Friday is National Single Parents' Day, we're doing a show on the subject and the man we've got coming in to talk to Flo is my ex-boyfriend.' That seemed the best way to say it. One sentence. All of a rush.

Ed was quiet.

'My ex-boyfriend Steven,' I clarified. 'The one I went out with at university and when I first arrived in London.'

'Mmm-hm.'

'Well, I just thought you should know. That's all. You don't mind, do you?'

'Mind what?'

'That I'm going to be working with my ex.'

'No, no. You go ahead.'

I suppose it was the answer I wanted. But I wasn't altogether convinced that Ed had even understood the question. He hadn't looked up from his newspaper once while I talked to him and I remembered a statistic I once heard. I think it was on a show we did on the differences between the sexes. The guests were a couple who had made a fortune out of books explaining the science behind those niggling things your other half can't help doing. He explained that women can't park because their eyes are too far apart, like a rabbit's: a huge field of vision to spot predators from all sides, but we've got no depth perception. She explained that her man never listens to anything she says because he sometimes quite literally can't. When a man is reading, he is practically deaf. It's the perfect time to tell him how much those shoes really cost you.

I considered telling Ed about Steven one more time, just in case. But I didn't.

18

Meanwhile, Kara's romance continued to blossom. The following week she had date number three with Mr Wonderful and, yes, we were babysitting again. It seemed to have become Ed's new favourite pastime.

Forester was asleep when Kara dropped him off this time. She put the Moses basket down in the spare room as though it was full of Fabergé eggs, then crept out of the room backwards like a princess who has just stolen a jewelled crown from beneath the smoking nose of a dragon.

'How has he been?' I asked.

'Fine. Fine. Poo not particularly runny today,' said Kara, getting straight to the point. 'And I changed his nappy just before he went to sleep. You may get away with it altogether. I'll be back at half eleven. Or, um, midnight?' she ventured.

Forester squawked his indignation before I could voice mine.

'Okay. Half eleven it is. Shit, he's waking up. Just, er, just bounce him for a bit, will you?' Kara suggested. 'Or get Ed to do it. He seems to have the knack. He'll go back to sleep in a minute.'

Whatever happened, she wasn't hanging around. The Kara who was too nervous to leave her baby in our care was a very distant memory.

I waved her off, then closed the door on the chilly street outside and headed back into my warm house where Ed was already sitting on the sofa with Forester in the crook of his arm.

'Who's my favourite baby?' Ed asked him. 'Who's going to play rugby with his Uncle Eddy when he grows up?'

Looking in from the outside, it was a very cosy start to a particularly cosy and low-key evening. Exactly the kind of evening I was happy to be settling down to, I thought as I warmed the first of the bottles Kara had prepared. In a couple of years' time, things could be exactly, comfortingly, the same as this. My husband in the sitting room, perhaps a baby of our own in the crook of his arm. I didn't really envy Kara heading out into the night on her date, I told myself. I didn't envy anybody still out there in the wilderness, looking for love, spending their weekends trawling the smoky bars or bungee jumping their way around the world in an attempt to convince themselves that they were having fun when all they really wanted was to *stay in* with someone special.

I myself had never done a bungee jump. But flinging yourself off Chelsea Bridge on a piece of elastic was hardly the kind of life experience sadly missed that Marianne Faithfull sang about in her famous song 'The Ballad of Lucy Jordan', was it? I'd done everything I really wanted to do.

Except fly on Concorde. But it was too late for that now and I'd heard it wasn't very comfortable anyway.

Or climb Uluru. But that wasn't politically correct now that no one called it Ayers Rock any more. I should be glad I hadn't ever done that and enraged the Aboriginal gods.

Or sleep with the Red Hot Chili Peppers . . . hmm.

A moment of guilty fantasy about the lead singer's magnificent tattooed chest was cut short by the pinging of the microwave, announcing that Forester's supper was ready.

In any case, there was no reason whatsoever why I couldn't still do the few things I hadn't ticked off my list *after* Ed and I got married. Except the Red Hot Chili Peppers thing of course. I was sure Ed wouldn't mind too much if I decided that I still had to paint our bedroom hot pink. Or learn to speak

Spanish. Or see the Taj Mahal. Or get my motorbike licence . . .

I glanced through the open door towards the sitting room where Ed was still engaged in one-sided conversation with the baby. 'And in 2004, the England team rousted the French and . . .' Forester was transfixed. Then I heard the phone ring. Ed's mobile. He dug down the side of his armchair to find it.

'Hello,' I heard him grunt. 'Oh, hi.' His voice immediately softened. 'Wait a second.'

He got up from the chair with Forester still tucked under one arm, and closed the living-room door to take the call.

What was going on? I paused halfway between microwave and kitchen door and found myself straining to hear. Not only had Ed closed the door, he had lowered his voice as well. But from the few noises that escaped the sitting room and the distinct lack of hearty exclamations, I guessed he was talking to a woman.

I waited until I heard the volume on the television turned up again before I strolled into the sitting room oh-so-casually with Forester's milk.

'Hey,' I said. 'What's up? Was I too noisy for you?'

'Uh?'

'You closed the door while you were on the phone. Was I making too much noise?'

'No. No, not really.'

He couldn't seem to understand why I was asking. 'Is that for my main man?' He took the milk from my hand. Forester beamed. Ed didn't have any trouble getting him into the right position for a feed this time. 'I'll just give him his bottle, yeah? What a guzzle-guts!' Ed exclaimed as Forester sucked the milk down. 'You're going to grow up to be big enough to lead the England rugby team, you are.'

I sat down in my chair and looked askance at my fiancé playing 'Dad'. Who had he been talking to? I decided that it was probably just one of those irritating marketing calls. Ed never put the phone down on a marketer. He had worked in telesales while he put himself through dental college and knew how tough the job was.

'Do you want to wind him?' Ed asked me when Forester finished his milk.

'That's okay,' I said. 'You seem to be doing just fine.'

Kara's third date with Duncan was equally dreamy. They'd been ice-skating on the outdoor rink at Somerset House. It was something I'd always wanted to do but Ed and I never got around to it.

'So, what did you talk about this time?' I asked her, as she gathered up Forester's things and prepared to load him into the back of her Ford Fiesta.

'Heidi,' she jumped straight down my throat. 'Give me a chance for God's sake. I will tell him about Forester. Of course I will. But tonight just wasn't the right time either. We were ice-skating. We were too busy trying not to fall over to talk about anything faintly serious. When on earth did I have the opportunity?'

'But . . .'

'I know. I'm not a moron. I do realise that if this is going to go anywhere, it's best that I tell him sooner rather than later. I don't want him to think that I'm the kind of girl who would deliberately mislead someone. And if this isn't going to go anywhere, then best detonate the time bomb sitting underneath us as soon as possible, right?'

'He'll be fine about it,' I said as confidently as I could.

'Sure.' But the beatific expression that seemed to have become a permanent fixture on Kara's face since that first date with dream-boy was gone. 'I hope so . . .' She chewed her lip and admitted, 'Heidi, I just can't think how to bring it up.'

'Why don't you send him an email?' I suggested, as we strapped Forester into his car seat.

'But that's so impersonal.'

'Not really. It's the way your relationship started. You've got a history of sharing things that way.'

'Our favourite colours and animals and pop bands. Not the secret history of our lives. You can't get really serious in an email.'

'I don't agree,' I pushed on. 'It's more acceptable these days. Job applications, wedding invitations, birth announcements. Everything is done by email now. Like writing a letter, only faster. And he might actually be grateful to hear the news that way rather than face to face. It will give him a chance to react honestly and really think about his response.'

Kara nodded thoughtfully. 'Perhaps you're right.'

'But you need to do it soon. Really soon,' I stressed. 'Before you see him again.'

'I'll do it before I see him again,' she agreed.

'Which is?'

'Friday night. Don't worry. Mum and Dad are in town that day so I can commandeer them to babysit. Don't want you to think I just see you as the unpaid help these days.'

'Ed seems to rather enjoy it,' I said.

'Will you help me write the email?' Kara asked.

'Of course. You can forward it to me at the office before you send it.'

Kara must have written the email the moment she got home. It was at the top of my inbox first thing the following morning.

From: KaraKarma@hotmail.com
To: DuncanStevenson@earthlink.net
Re: Three things you don't know about me.

Dear Duncan,

It was so great to see you last night. I don't think I've had so much fun in ages, though my knees are both completely black

157

and blue with bruises and I suspect I may have broken my back; I hadn't been ice-skating for years. Can you walk properly again yet? Anyway, I'm looking forward to seeing you on Friday but before we make arrangements, there are just a few things I need to tell you.

1. I really have never done Internet dating before. I know you can't believe it but you're my first!
2. I hate Chinese food.
3. I have a son.

That's right. You really did just see that last sentence. I have a child. Feel free to stop reading right now. But if you haven't snorted coffee all over your keyboard in horror and already pressed delete, please let me tell you something about him. His name is Forester. He's just six months old. His father and I are not in contact at the moment – we broke up before he was born – but I hope that he will show an interest in his son in the future. After all, Forester is the most wonderful baby on earth.

Duncan, I'm so sorry I didn't tell you all this face to face. I hope you'll believe that I haven't had very much practice at dating as a single mum – in fact I've had none – so I've never had to broach the subject before. And I hope you'll be flattered to know that I have been having such a wonderful time with you I simply didn't want reality to intrude. I didn't want anything to put the brakes on. I hope that whatever happens, you'll be able to forgive me for that.

I look forward to hearing what you think.

Lots of love,

Kara. x

It was a lovely email, I thought. Flo, who had trained as a relationship counsellor to help any listeners who might call in to the show, agreed that it was pretty well written. Just the right combination of humour, flattery and seriousness.

'Perfect. I hope he realises what a great woman he's got there,' said Flo.

'I hope so too,' I said.

That day, my entire office waited on tenterhooks for the next email from Kara; Flo and Eleanor had me check my inbox once every ten minutes. There was a collective sigh of relief when news finally did arrive, just as we were getting ready to leave for the night.

'He says that it doesn't matter to him one bit. He loves children. He still wants to see Kara on Friday night and he wants to meet Forester as soon as he possibly can.'

Eleanor started the round of applause.

'Thank God,' said Flo. 'Viva romance.'

19

Viva romance, indeed. I wasn't feeling very romantic. When Flo said those words, my thoughts immediately flew to Ed's eyebrows. Somehow, Ed's losing all his body hair had made me really focus on how I felt about him physically. Since the first time he kissed me, I'd been nuts about Ed on a physical level. For at least six months, we were one of those embarrassing couples who can't stop necking, not even in the supermarket queue. After that, things calmed down a bit but until the beginning of that year, we definitely shagged more than average. Would we be able to get that back? Now that Ed was bald, it was suddenly easier to picture him as an old man, having lost his hair permanently. He didn't have a particularly great head-shape. From a certain angle, it looked as though he had a double dome. It shouldn't have mattered, I know. But I found myself being disgusted with him half the time and disgusted with myself for being so shallow the rest.

It was in this context that I tried to be glad for Kara, but overall I was in a bad mood and couldn't shake it off. When my mum called to talk about the wedding yet again – could she invite the daughter of a couple she and Dad knew from their Ceroc class – I found myself getting irritable within seconds, smashing her previous record for taking me from 'hello' to carpet-biting rage. I cut the conversation short in case she heard me sighing and thought that it had more to do with her than usual. I still hadn't mentioned Ed's frightful appearance to Mum.

The thought that Steven would be back in my studio so soon didn't help. Every time the phone in the office rang I hoped it would be him calling to say that he couldn't make it after all. That there had been some kind of emergency. Parents were always having child-related emergencies. The rest of the time I spent berating myself for hoping that so much as a snuffle should afflict poor little Isabelle and keep her daddy from going on air.

The night before he was due on the show, Nelly phoned him to confirm the time we would expect to see him.

'Can he still come in?' I asked.

'Of course.'

After supper that night, Ed went next door to play cards with Mrs H.

Ed had cooked. It was my turn to do the washing up. I took off my engagement ring and placed it in the misshapen pottery dish on the kitchen windowsill where it sat every time I did the dishes. Which wasn't often. I pulled on the big pink Marigolds Ed always wore when he did any housework – he was very careful about his hands, a good habit he had picked up from the dental nurse who worked alongside him – and ran hot water into the sink until the bubbles were as high as my nose.

Scrub, scrub, scrub. I scrubbed as if each pass of the scourer would erase some of the lunatic chatter from inside my mind as well. I had gone over that one conversation I'd had with Steven so many times, trying to remember the exact tone of his voice, checking each sentence for nuance. He had obviously been flirting with me. And I had flirted back. Why else would he have sent the flowers? Now I was working on another scenario. What was I going to say when I saw him again? Should I mention the flowers? Did he want me even more because I hadn't responded? I scrubbed harder, penance for even thinking that last thought. It didn't matter whether he wanted me or not. I absolutely didn't want him. I had someone better now. Better suited to me. A better person. Ed was next door, bringing a little bit of happiness to the life of our neighbour.

When I saw Steven again I would be civil. That was all.

Steven represented a single parents' charity. Fatherhood had mellowed him and he took his responsibilities seriously these days.

I was comparing Ed and Steven and Steven was coming out on top.

I looked into the kitchen sink like a fortune teller looking into a glass. As the bubbles popped and disappeared, I could foresee nothing but danger. I couldn't meet Steven again. The way I was feeling, it was too big a risk. I had to go sick the following morning. So what if Eleanor knew what I was really doing? How would she ever prove that I had lied to stay at home and stop myself from potentially making a terrible mistake?

I took off my rubber gloves, rinsed the rubber smell off and smeared hand cream all over my fingers. As I reached for the little ceramic bowl, it seemed to leap out of my slippery reach. Next thing, the extremely handmade-looking gift from one of Ed's grateful child patients was in four pieces on the tiled kitchen floor. And my engagement ring was in two.

'Shit,' I murmured as I picked up the platinum band in my left hand and the diamond between my right thumb and forefinger. 'How the hell did that happen?' I looked at the setting. The shiny prongs that had held the diamond in place didn't seem to have shifted and yet here was the stone, loose of its moorings and looking faintly small and unremarkable against the pink skin of my palm. 'Shit.'

I walked slowly to the bedroom, carrying the two pieces of the ring like the body of a dying bird with its tiny heart still fluttering. As I walked, I realised that part of me felt guilty, as though I had deliberately dropped the ring on the floor. I tucked the band into the slot in the velvet cushion of the ring box and placed the diamond beside it. My empty left hand felt peculiar, as though the ring was still there. I wasn't given to believing in signs but this looked like a big one.

Ed came back home just as I was closing the ring box, and knew something was wrong the second he looked at me.

He wasn't angry. The ring could be mended, of course. It was clearly the case that the ring was faulty rather than me being particularly clumsy. Ed would take it back to the jeweller's on his way to the surgery the following morning.

As long as the ring was back in time for the wedding, I said. But later, when Ed popped to the corner shop to buy a pint of milk for the following morning, he came back with a jewellery box.

I opened it to find another ring. It wasn't real of course, but a child's dressing-up toy.

'They had some left over from Christmas,' Ed explained.

'You shouldn't have bothered,' I said, I looking at the chip of glass set in gold lacquer-covered plastic. 'I mean that.'

'It's cubic zirconia,' he said in a Ferrero Rocher voice. 'Lasts longer than diamonds.'

I gave a little snort of amusement.

'I hate the idea of you not having a ring at all.' Ed was quite serious when he said that.

'I could have lasted a week, you fool,' I said.

'Yes. But I don't think I could get through a week without knowing that all you have to do is glance down at your hand to be reminded that I love you. It feels strange seeing you without my ring after all this time. It's as though I'm leaving you unprotected.'

'You mean un*marked*,' I said.

'I mean unprotected,' Ed repeated. 'Try it on.'

But this romantic equivalent of the Post-it note or a nametag didn't fit my engagement finger. Or even my thumb. Perhaps it would have looked delicate on the ring finger of a nightclub singer who went by the name of Dave in broad daylight. I could almost have worn it as a bracelet.

'You could wear it on a chain around your neck,' Ed suggested.

'It might make my throat go green. I'll keep it in my purse,' I said.

Ed nodded a little sadly. As I watched him walk into the other room with his shoulders slumped forward, I knew that I had done it again. He had gone out of his way to make me smile and I had stuck another cocktail stick into his heart. I don't know why I did it but I seemed to be doing it all the time these days. The words just popped out of my mouth like a hiccup. Not so long ago, I would have happily worn that stupid fake ring until my real one was ready again. By acting so prissy now, I wasn't refusing to wear a symbol of 'ownership', I was refusing to wear our team colours. *Our* team.

'I'll wear it round my neck,' I called after him.

'No,' said Ed. 'I don't want you to get an allergic reaction.'

I didn't push it, and told him I was going to have a bath. He didn't offer to join me. But later in bed he rubbed his nose against my hair and told me he loved how silky it was. And I felt guilty because I knew exactly why I'd given myself a deep conditioning rinse that night for the first time in months.

20

It seemed I wasn't the only girl in the office who had pulled out the sartorial stops for Steven's arrival. Flo looked magnificent, dressed from head to toe in black that made her signature red lipstick look brighter than ever: obscenely bright and glossy like the mouth on a rock album cover. Eleanor meanwhile had gone for a more casual look than usual: her long brown hair hung loose over her shoulders and her white blouse was unbuttoned to the top of a lacy camisole with a pendant necklace pointing the way to her best assets in case nobody thought to look without a prompt.

'Aren't you cold?' I asked.

'Of course I am,' she admitted. 'But I couldn't find the right cardigan to put over the top.'

Oh, the agony of being a girl out to impress.

Even Nelly seemed to have made something of an effort. She had her contact lenses in instead of her glasses, though she insisted it was only because she'd lost a screw in her specs the previous night and they had to be sent away to be mended. Robin was the only one of us unmoved by Steven's imminent arrival.

Was it possible that Steven had made an effort too? He was wearing a suit, cut close to emphasise how slender he still looked when years of beer-drinking were starting to catch up with most men his age. The dark pinstripe was offset by a bright green lining, like the flash of a kingfisher's wing. He'd had his hair cut since we saw him last as well. He looked less tired.

'Meeting first thing this morning,' he explained when Eleanor cooed over the line of his jacket. 'Wasn't sure I was going to get away in time.'

'We're very glad you did,' said Flo.

'Morning, Heidi,' he said as he walked past me into the studio. 'Doing okay?'

I nodded my reply, trying not to look at him any more closely than I would have looked at other guests. Trying hard not to breathe in his aftershave. But I couldn't hold my breath for ever. When the door to the studio swung quietly shut behind Steven and Flo, there was still just the faintest trace in the air. It wasn't that he had sprayed too much on that morning. I would have recognised Steven's aftershave anywhere. Creed. A taste he inherited from his father. I'd blown half my term's grant on a bottle for his birthday during the second year we went out. When we were no longer together, I could at least be thankful that every neck I buried my face in to hide my tears didn't smell exactly the same.

'Heidi?' Eleanor broke into my thoughts. 'Where were you just then?'

'Just wondering whether I asked Ed to put carpet freshener on the shopping list,' I lied.

'Can you speak into the green microphone for me?' Jack asked Steven.

'One, two, three. Hello, hello.'

Flo had her headphones on, one covering her right ear, the other slightly back from her left so that she could still hear Steven talking to her naturally.

'You're looking lovely today,' he told her. 'New dress?'

'This old thing?' she lied.

'News in forty seconds,' Eleanor interrupted her. I could tell she would have swapped places with Flo in a heartbeat.

Flo clicked back into professional mode. 'It's just going to be more of the same,' Flo assured her guest. 'We'll talk a bit about the special events your organisation is running over the weekend, then I'm sure the listeners would like to hear more about your personal story.'

'I imagine you would as well, wouldn't you, Heidi?' Eleanor whispered to me.

Flo opened on the usual statistics. The number of children being raised in single-parent homes. The lack of support for people doing it on their own. Now onto the cheerier news: single parents didn't have to struggle alone any longer. There were lots of organisations out there, and today they were celebrating their achievement.

'In the *Let's Talk London* studio today, we're thrilled to welcome back Steven Gabriel. After he came on the show a couple of weeks ago, we had hundreds of calls from people in his position, particularly single fathers, asking how they could find support groups in their area. Steven is a representative of the Lone Parents Network. How are they going to be marking this first National Single Parents' Day?'

'Well, Flo, my particular group is going to be having a party this evening. We've got entertainers for the kids and lots of booze for the adults.'

'Sounds good.'

'There's lots to celebrate. We've been lobbying the government for more financial support to help lone parents get back to work, pursue further education or to be able to stay home and be a mum or dad . . .'

Eleanor leaned forward on the desk, hanging on his every word. Whenever he glanced her way, she gave him a little wave. I sat back, trying to convey disinterest with my body language, but I couldn't wait for him to stray from the official line.

It seemed an age before Flo got onto the personal questions. Steven reiterated his own situation. Four-year-old daughter. The short marriage. Sarah.

'Why do you think she left?' Flo took the words out of my mouth.

'Because having a child changes your life irrevocably. I don't think Sarah was ready for just how different things would be: it simply didn't fit with the way she wanted to move forward. But the wonderful thing I've found is that while I have more to do and need to work harder than before to support my little family of two, the things that used to really stress me out seem to have melted away. When you have a child, it's as if you can see what's really important again. I used to spend hours obsessing over office politics. Now, I just don't care. I used to be something of a workaholic. Now that I have Isabelle there are times when I just have to be at home. I have to sit down with her and look at a picture book. Prior to having a child, I thought that I would find being a father boring, but I don't; I get as much out of it as Isabelle does. Reading a book to my daughter is far more relaxing than any yoga class or a weekend in the country or a couple of pints after work. She has forced me to slow down and look at the view and I'm telling you that view is lovely.'

Once again, as soon as Flo invited calls, the phone lines lit up like Oxford Street in December. And once again, the callers were not the regular nutters who would call every day in to give their opinion on anything if they thought it might give them a small platform to espouse their dreadful views on immigration or peculiar sex. There were even some guys.

'I feel like you understand my life,' said one man. 'My wife left me last year. We had two kids together. Jack is six now and Marie is just three and a half. I felt like my life was over when she went, but now I feel like she did me a massive favour – I don't think I would have got to know my children properly if she hadn't walked out when she did.'

'You've made me feel like I can carry on,' said another woman. 'Since I ended up on my own with my son Thomas, there have been moments when I thought that I would just walk out of the house and throw myself in front of the next passing car. But listening to you this morning reminded me of the good times. I'm going to give your society a call.'

Then came a call that Eleanor put through. 'Steven,' said a familiar voice, 'I just want to say good for you. You're the last person I would have expected to make a good single father but it sounds as though you're doing a great job.'

'Thank you,' said Steven. 'Who is this?'

'It's Kara. Kara Knight.'

'Kara! How are you?'

'I'm well. I'm a single parent too these days. I've got a six-month-old. His name's Forester.'

'How lovely,' said Steven without missing a beat.

'His father and I broke up before he was born.'

'That's a shame.'

'Have to admit I didn't know him well enough to decide whether it's any great loss or not,' said Kara with typical candour.

'But you're doing okay?'

'I'm doing wonderfully. Forester is an absolute dream. The best mistake I ever made. But there is something I want to ask you.'

'Fire away.'

'What about dating again now that you've got a child? How do you tell someone you're a single parent without scaring them away?'

It was an odd question, given that Kara seemed to have found the perfect answer already. But I thought perhaps she just wanted to share her experience for the benefit of the other listeners.

'Well,' Steven paused. 'I have to be honest with you and say that I don't have a clue. I haven't exactly thrown myself into the dating scene since Sarah left. In fact, I haven't dated at all. So, "I don't know," would have to be my answer.'

'Why haven't you dated?' Flo jumped in. 'A good-looking guy like you? There must be hundreds of women out there ready to take you and your daughter on.'

'But having Isabelle makes it all the more important that I don't mess around. The last thing I want to do is have a string of women traipsing through my daughter's life. I think it's emotionally disrupting. I'd rather wait until someone special comes along.'

'I understand,' said Kara.

'I can't take romantic decisions lightly any more. When I start dating again, believe me, it will be because I've met someone I think could be around for a very long time. Someone amazing.'

'They don't come around very often, do they?' Flo commented.

'Maybe only once in a lifetime,' said Steven.

And then he looked straight at me. And I dropped a pencil on the floor.

'Next time you dive under the desk I'm going to hand you a dustpan and brush while you're down there,' commented Eleanor.

'Sorry I can't help you there, Kara,' said Steven. 'But I don't think I'll be too far wrong if I say that the right guy is going to be able to take in his stride the fact that you have a child.'

'Thanks for the support,' said Kara.

'I can't believe this man is not dating!' Flo exclaimed. 'Ladies, this is one morning when I wish this show was on TV.'

*   *   *

Afterwards, Eleanor insisted that Steven join us all for lunch – well, me, Eleanor and Flo. Robin and Nelly, as juniors, were left to man the office. And since Friday was one of the days when Isabelle spent more of the day at her preschool, Steven agreed.

'I want you to tell me all about the young Heidi Savage,' Eleanor said, linking her arm through his as we strolled towards the Italian where we always had lunch on a Friday, provided some huge newsworthy scandal we needed to cover wasn't breaking out and changing the face of history minute by minute.

'You should think very carefully before you do that,' I warned him.

'I'm the boss,' said Eleanor. 'You've got far more to lose by upsetting me than her. Think of all those future commissions. I could get you paid the next time you come on.'

'Don't start looking for a yacht,' Flo sighed, referring to London Talk Live's woeful fees.

'Well,' Steven began, 'I don't think she's changed very much at all. Certainly not looks-wise.'

'After all those years!' Eleanor exclaimed. 'That's pretty unbelievable. I wish someone would say that about me.'

'I wish someone would *mean* that about me,' I replied.

'I do,' said Steven.

'Yeah, right.' I carefully avoided his eyes.

'In fact,' Steven continued, 'I'd say she actually looks rather better than I remember.'

We had reached the Italian. I pushed the door open and pretended I hadn't heard.

'In actual physical terms or just the way she dresses?' Flo probed.

I turned around and glared at her. 'Do you mind?' I asked.

'Not at all,' Flo teased me.

Over lunch, Steven proceeded to regale Eleanor and Flo

with an inventory of the contents of my wardrobe circa the early Nineties. 'Horrible,' was his summing up. It was fair to say that I was a little late to give up on the leggings/big shirt combo that had been so popular when I was in the sixth form but I had thought that the bottle-green velvet ball-dress I bought to attend the black-tie ball at the end of my first year was rather flattering.

'She looked as though she'd borrowed the dress from Fergie. Before Weight Watchers. It was awful.'

'That dress almost bankrupted me.'

'You should have sued.'

'I thought it looked nice.'

'You looked like a womble.'

'And if you don't watch it,' I piped up, 'I will have to dig out some photos of you with your mullet.'

'Mullet? I never had a mullet.'

'Oh, but you did,' I insisted. 'And way before it was fashionable.'

'Have you got photos?' Eleanor asked.

'Don't make me use them.'

Truth was, I knew I didn't have any photographic evidence of Steven's fashion misdemeanours any more. At one time, I had a shoebox full of photos of Steven Gabriel. Then he chucked me. Later that evening I had a pile of photo pieces. And still later the same night, a pile of ash in the bottom of my dustbin – my plastic dustbin – and half a dozen firemen in the kitchen. I was lucky I didn't die from the fumes.

'Bring the photos into the office next week,' Flo begged me.

'I'll see if I can find them,' I lied.

And that's pretty much how lunch continued. Eleanor and Flo managed to wheedle all sorts of stories out of Steven. Snippets from my past life that I hadn't heard in years. Snapshots of drunken evenings and student silliness. Bad behaviour and more bad outfits.

'This isn't fair,' I piped up occasionally, but always to no avail.

'I only tease her because I know she likes it.'

And I blushed because I did like it. Though I protested at each new revelation, I was enjoying the attention. His attention. And loving the banter. We were like a comedy double-act getting back together for a tribute show. Whatever Ed and I had, it was fair to say that we had never quite bantered as easily as Steven and I did. Ed and I finished each other's sentences from time to time but he never surprised me with the way he did it. He never took what I was saying and turned it round, made it funnier and fed me my next line all at the same time.

Steven made me glitter, and he could still do it.

'Get these two,' laughed Flo. 'Bickering like an old married couple.'

I clammed up after that.

'Three o'clock,' Steven announced suddenly. 'I really do have to go. If you're not there to pick the kids up at three thirty on the dot, you get fined for every ten minutes you're late. Five pounds.'

'Five pounds for ten minutes. That's steep.'

'Yeah, but some of the parents I've met are so desperate for the childcare they'll pay it. Thirty quid for an extra hour in the office? It's worth it if you're some big cheese in the City.'

'I had no idea that having children was such an expensive business,' Eleanor sighed. 'Think I'm going to stick to pedigree Labradors. Another coffee, Heidi?'

'I'll have a non-parents' privilege latte,' I told her.

'Have two,' said Flo. 'You'll be in Steven's position soon enough.'

Steven smiled at me. I blushed and felt a contraction in my stomach. If it hadn't been for Eleanor's last comment, I would have put it straight down to having a flashback to a time when Steven Gabriel's smile was the reason for my existence.

'Well, thanks for lunch.' Steven reached out to shake Eleanor's hand. I counted down the seconds left until I could really say that I would never have to see his face again and know it. It would be for the best. 'I'll see you all again soon, I hope.'

'You bet,' said Flo. 'In fact . . .' I could almost see the idea lightbulb come on in her eyes. 'What are you doing tomorrow night?'

'Tomorrow night? Saturday?' Steven paused. 'Nothing that I know of.'

Shit, shit, shit. I knew exactly what was coming.

'Then why don't you come to Eleanor's birthday party?'

Eleanor enthusiastically nodded her agreement. 'What a great idea. I can't believe I didn't ask you myself. The whole team will be there. You'll know Heidi, of course. Heidi will definitely be there. If she knows what's good for her. I think I've got a spare invitation in my handbag.'

She pulled one out. Robin had designed the invitations on the office computer, transposing Eleanor's head onto a picture of Barbie's body.

'You're turning forty?' Steven breathed. 'Unbelievable. Eleanor, can I just say you most definitely do not look your age.'

'You can.' Eleanor blushed. 'Even though I know you're just pulling my leg.'

'Not at all. You put the youngsters in your office to shame. Swanky venue to celebrate in.'

'I know the owner,' Flo crowed. 'I sorted everything out.'

'So you'll come?' Eleanor asked.

'I'd love to. I don't know how I'll ever get to see the inside of this place otherwise.'

'Brilliant.' Eleanor clapped her hands together. 'I'm so glad you can make it. It's going to be so much fun. Isn't it, Heidi?'

'See you tomorrow evening,' he said to me.

Oh yes, it was going to be so much fun.

Ed had already left for a couple of rugby matches in Hereford when I got back home that night. I found a note on the kitchen table telling me that my newly repaired engagement ring would be ready for collection the following morning.

21

I forgot all about that note when Saturday morning rolled around again and, before any working girl could reasonably be expected to surface, Kara was on the doorstep with Forester in his buggy.

'Rough night?' she asked when she saw my scarecrow hairdo.

'For heaven's sake, Kara. It's eight thirty in the morning. On a Saturday!'

'Time to start the weekend,' she said. 'I've been waiting to come over since five.'

'Thank you for sharing your misery.'

'I'll buy you a full-fat latte at Starbucks. And two muffins.'

And then she smiled so broadly I couldn't help smiling back.

Half an hour later, we were ensconced in our usual sofa.

'This Duncan man seems to be having a magical effect on your mummy,' I told Forester, who was more interested in chewing one of the straps on my handbag than eating one of the spoonfuls of puree of indeterminate origin I had been offering him. I could hardly blame him. All baby food, whether it was supposed to be beef and potatoes or apples and custard, looked exactly like mucus to me. I sneaked a taste of the spoonful he had been refusing.

Exactly like mucus.

Kara was at the counter, making it up to me with coffee and muffins.

I looked around the room. The place was packed even at nine on a Saturday morning. There was a new branch of Holmes Place gym just down the street and this was clearly the coffee bar where many people chose to reward themselves and undo all the good work they had done at body jam or 'legs, bums and mums', as Ed mockingly referred to it. 'A class for kept women, the unemployed and new mothers.' At least it meant that I wasn't the only girl in the place wearing a tracksuit. But I wrestled my handbag from Forester, to much protest, and slicked some lip-gloss on in any case.

With Forester placated by a rubberised teddy bear that reminded me of a dog toy, I flicked through a newspaper someone had left on the table. It was one of the tabloids so I went straight to the horoscopes, reading Ed's first, then mine, then Kara's. Kara's promised her 'unexpected encounters' again. It was clearly a hazard of being a Scorpio. Mine, unfortunately, promised nothing so exciting. Something about needing to check my tax return.

Kara was taking her time. When I looked up, she was near the front of the queue. She had a cardboard tray with both our coffees and a couple of those fun-free muffins. She was staring into space rather dreamily as she waited for the queue to shuffle forward. As I watched, a man joined it beside her. A very good-looking man dressed in tracksuit bottoms, with a yoga mat tucked under one arm. He leaned forward, tapped Kara on the shoulder and whispered something in her ear. My God, I thought. That girl is on fire. She's pulled again.

But she didn't look all that happy about it.

She had clearly been surprised by whatever the stranger whispered. I saw her face register shock. A slight jerk in her shoulders. She turned towards him but soon had her free arm wrapped around her body in a classic defensive pose. She was swaying a little agitatedly from foot to foot and looked as though she might break into a run.

Who was he?

I watched the exchange for a moment, wondering whether I was going to have to wade in to the rescue. He didn't look like a nutter but she was clearly uncomfortable in his presence. What had he said? I wondered. Perhaps he was some guy she'd dated before Forester was born. If I hadn't been in charge of holding our place on the sofa and guarding the baby at that moment, I would have gone across on the pretence of looking for some sugar and found out more.

After a little while, Kara noticed I was watching her. I gave a wave. She raised her eyebrows and gestured towards me with her head. The man she was talking to turned in my direction and nodded. He gave me a little wave of his own, and a mega-watt smile that almost made me put my hands to my cheeks to cool them down. Then he turned his attention back to Kara. They said a little more and she giggled shyly, seeming a little more relaxed. The guy's coffee arrived. He picked up the cardboard cup and, giving Kara a kiss on both cheeks that was necessarily awkward thanks to their various accoutrements, he left at a jog.

Juggling our twin lattes, Kara struggled back towards me. Her encounter seemed to have left her more than slightly flustered.

'Who was that?' I asked, as she handed me my mug. 'Did you get me some sugar? No.'

'Yes.' She handed me two sachets.

'So?' I persisted. 'What happened there? Who was he? Were you being chatted up?'

'Not exactly,' she said.

'But he looked pretty keen. Did you already know him?'

She nodded.

'Then how come you didn't introduce me to him before I got engaged to Ed? He's like George Clooney's better-looking brother. Yoga though. Not sure what I think about men doing yoga. On the one hand it suggests sensitivity. On the other hand, who ever had great sex with a really sensitive man?'

I expected Kara to join in. Ragging on sensitive men was one of our favourite pastimes, when we weren't ragging on those men who weren't sensitive at all. But that morning Kara was quiet. She picked a corner from her muffin and offered a teeny piece to Forester. He opened his mouth like a little baby bird and took the muffin from her fingers, chewed for just a second or two with his single tooth, then spat the resulting soggy mess out over his bib with a frown.

'The sugar-free ones aren't very good,' she agreed with him.

'Come on, Kara. Who was that man?'

Kara took a mouthful of scalding coffee before she answered. 'It was mumf-mumf . . .' she muttered without opening her mouth.

'Mumf-mumf?'

She swallowed and winced at the heat. 'It was Duncan,' she said more clearly. But not much more clearly. Certainly not very loudly.

'What? Not *the* Duncan?'

'*The* Duncan,' she nodded.

I swivelled in my chair to see if I could perhaps get another look at him walking down the street, but he was long gone.

'Bloody hell, Kara. Now I understand why you're so excited about him. Why on earth does a man who looks like that feel he has to advertise for a date?' I realised too late how that might have sounded to a woman who did feel as though she had to advertise for a date. 'I mean . . . Sorry.'

'No, you're right. He's not exactly what I expected to find on the Internet either. He's . . . he's gorgeous.'

'You took the words right out of my mouth. Why didn't you introduce us?'

'I did.'

'Hardly. You just nodded at me from across the room.'

'I would have brought him over but he said he had to go.'

'Without even saying hello?'

'He left his car on double yellow lines. Besides, I was a bit . . . you know, I was a bit flustered. I didn't have a chance to think properly. I didn't expect to see him this morning. Certainly not here. Not when I'm looking like this . . .'

'Looking less like the mummy than I am,' I reminded her of a dig she had made at me that morning. 'Don't worry about it. He was looking a bit casual himself. And his body language told me he was pretty damn pleased to see you even if you are looking like a dog. Would have thought he would have come across and said hello to Forester though.'

'He had to rush,' Kara said again. 'Besides, Forester isn't such a stickler for manners as you are.'

As if to underline the statement, Forester belched. Then he smiled as if he were very pleased at the knowledge that he, Forester Knight, had made that big noise all by himself.

'But he's never actually seen Forester, has he? I would have thought he would have wanted to see the baby he's heard so—'

'He met Forester last night,' Kara interrupted. 'When he dropped me off after our date he came in and saw Forester then.'

'What? And your parents?' I remembered that they had been babysitting.

'And my parents.'

'Talk about a baptism of fire. Poor man! How did he cope with that?'

'He coped fine.'

'And your Mum and Dad?'

'They loved him.'

'Did they really?' I raised my eyebrows in surprise. Kara's parents had never approved of any of the guys she introduced them to before.

'They did. At the moment they'd be happy if I shacked up

with just about anybody so long as they can tell everyone at the Conservative club I'm not a single parent any more.'

'I can't believe you didn't tell me Duncan met the entire family last night . . .'

'Perhaps I was going to tell you,' Kara almost snapped. 'Perhaps it was the next thing I was going to say but you've hardly let me get a word in all morning.'

'Right.' I sank back into my chair, more than a little stung. And surprised. Kara wasn't usually too shy to interrupt me with her stories.

'I'm sorry.' She immediately reached across the table and touched my arm in a gesture of appeasement. 'That wasn't fair of me. I don't know why I said that at all. God, that man just makes me so nervous. In a good way,' she added, fanning her face with the newspaper I had been reading. 'And last night. Well, I guess I'm still shaking from the stress of introducing him to Forester and my parents all in one go.'

'It doesn't matter. At least I can put a face to the name when you talk about him now. And I approve. We've got to do something with you guys. You and him and me and Ed.'

'A foursome?'

'Yeah. Doesn't have to be cheesy, though. I could cook. Or Ed could. Or we could get a takeaway if you don't want to be poisoned.'

'I think I'll wait a little bit longer before I introduce him to you guys, if that's okay with you.'

'Do you think we'd frighten him off?'

'Frankly, yes. You know, he didn't really have to go and move the car. He just said that he really couldn't be seen with anyone dressed in such a terrible tracksuit.'

Forester flicked some soggy muffin at me as the punchline.

22

About half an hour after I got home from having coffee with Kara, my mother telephoned. I was in the middle of washing up at the time, so I didn't rush to pick up, knowing that the only people who called our landline were telemarketers. Everyone I might have actually wanted to talk to knew to go straight to the mobile. Back when I first got a mobile, I only ever switched it on when I was outside the house. These days it was never turned off. Having said that, Mum and Dad still called the landline first too, under the impression that dialling a mobile was as expensive as using a SAT phone to dial Washington from Kabul.

I knew it was Mum the second the answer-machine beeped. That familiar hesitation. 'Hello, Heidi. It's Mum here. Nothing to worry about; just calling to see how you're getting on.'

I listened guiltily, hands still in the sink, as she told the answer-machine that Dad's cholesterol test had shown a real improvement. It must be to do with that butter-replacement spread that the newsreader who is probably a lesbian had been advertising. And I wouldn't forget to call James, would I? His birthday was coming up in a week.

'He didn't call me on my birthday,' I muttered, wondering whether siblings ever stopped keeping score.

'Okay then, darling. Give our love to Eddy, sweetheart. Bye. Bye.'

I heard Dad mutter something in the second it took her to put down the phone.

I stood at the basin for a moment longer, looking out across the fence, freshly painted by Ed on both sides last year, that separated our garden from Mrs H's. As I watched, she emerged from the house to pin two tea-towels on the washing line whose pulley system Ed had carefully cleaned of rust and oiled so that Mrs H could pull the uppermost of the two lines up and down more easily. She glanced towards our kitchen window and waved at me. I waved back a soapy hand. But the sight of Mrs H had intensified the guilt I felt at not having picked up the phone to my mother. It suddenly occurred to me that perhaps she had picked up something from the way I was after the dress fitting. I dried my hands off and keyed in the familiar digits.

'Hamble three-six-seven,' said my mother.

'It's Heidi.'

I could ask her. I could ask her right then.

But instead I asked her to tell me about Dad's cholesterol count and whether she could let me have the name of that spread that was supposed to be able to lower it.

Silently, I begged her to ask me what was wrong. Couldn't she hear from the tone of my voice that I wanted to talk about more than bloody Benecol?

'I'd better go,' I said. 'I've got to get a few things from the supermarket.'

'Okay, love,' she said. 'Bye bye.'

'Bye, Mum.'

I had the phone halfway back to the cradle.

'Wait, Heidi.' Her voice squeaked out from the earpiece.

'Mum?'

I waited for her to say the magic words that would allow it all to spill out.

'Don't forget your brother wants that CD.'

Jane's Addiction. I scribbled it down at the bottom of my shopping list. There were lots of early March birthdays in my diary; it was one of those boom birthday times in the year. A result of June honeymoons, early summer holidays, a definite rise in the sap. As well as James, I had to buy a gift for Eleanor, my boss. Something I could give her at her fortieth birthday party that night.

We had already had a whip-round in the office: Nelly had collected forty pounds from each of us towards a birthday present – a rather beautiful vase from Heal's. But I had no doubt that fabulous gift would not really excuse us from making personal gestures of our devotion to the woman who held our careers in the palm of her hand. Or so she claimed when things weren't going her way.

I went straight to Boots and bought a small vial of 'personal lubricant'. That was the funny part done. Then I crossed the road to a chi-chi gift shop and bought a ridiculously expensive leatherbound notebook. In her more wistful moments, Eleanor claimed that she would love to give up her job and become a writer. Forty was one of those milestone birthdays where you make lots of plans for the future and do your best to change the bad patterns in your life before they become permanent. If Eleanor didn't manage to write her novel this year, she could at least write a list of things she wanted to get done she could look back on a year later – and weep for another twelve months gone without ever once using her gym membership, if last year's birthday tears were anything to go by.

Kara had tried to persuade me to babysit for her again that night. I was relieved to be able to say that this time there was absolutely no way I could help her out – that evening had been earmarked for Eleanor's birthday celebrations for a very long while. There was to be no skiving off, even if it was a Saturday. Non-attendance at Eleanor's birthday party would be viewed as dimly as taking an unscheduled day off work to recover from a hangover. Celebrations had started the previous evening, as soon as the day's work ended, with two bottles of champagne courtesy of the station boss, who joined us to raise a glass. That evening, we were to meet up again in the VIP room of a nightclub Flo had hired months previously, when we her workmates, but especially me, insisted that she shouldn't let the big day pass unmarked.

As I waited for yet another unwanted encounter with Steven Gabriel, I wished I had kept my big mouth shut or insisted on an extremely intimate gathering with a fixed and immovable number of guests that wouldn't allow for last-minute invites.

Would he take Eleanor up on her invitation? At lunch he had said that he would. He had told her that he had a free evening. But was his enthusiastic acceptance just for show, out of politeness? Free evenings were pretty rare for a single parent. Why would he want to waste one with a bunch of people he had only met twice? Myself excepted.

He wouldn't come. I was pretty sure of that as I watched the shop assistant giftwrap Eleanor's notebook (knowing even as she did it that I would have to unwrap the thing again as soon as I got home to make sure she had taken off the price). Steven would not come to Eleanor's birthday party. He had friends of his own to see. But after I had bought James's birthday CD in the Virgin Megastore, I found myself drifting into a little boutique. And though I wasn't supposed to be buying anything too extravagant while Ed and I were about to lay out so much money on the wedding, I found myself fingering the fabric of a little silk dress with spaghetti straps. Utterly frivolous. The dress was layered, a fluttering millefeuille of delicate whisps of pink and orange and red that looked as though someone had cut a piece of sunset sky down to make it. I normally wore black – I had a dozen dresses shaped exactly like this in various shades of charcoal – but the deep pink that dominated the dress was actually one of the few bright colours that flattered my shell-pale skin.

'Would you like to try that on?' an assistant asked.

I followed her into the changing room – no harm in trying anything on.

As soon as the hem settled around my knees like the petals of a tulip turned upside down, I knew I was going to have it. And I knew I was going to wear it that night.

Eleanor had a lot of friends. The bouncer on the door of the club had me right down at the bottom of a guest list that covered four whole sheets of A4. As he looked for my name, I scanned the list too, reading upside down, looking for only one name to see whether it already had a tick beside it.

It didn't. Steven Gabriel had yet to arrive, and perhaps he never would. I realised I had been holding my breath, but I wasn't sure whether I was relieved or disappointed. I had taken as long to get ready to go out that night as I had back in the beginning of Ed and me. I told myself that it was just for fun; I hadn't been clubbing for a long time. I wanted to look the best I could possibly look to feel comfortable in a club full of kids who were still at primary school when I last went dancing, but the freshly made-up face that had looked back at me from the bathroom mirror knew there was only one person I really wanted to impress.

I wondered what had happened. Perhaps, as I had thought earlier, he only said he would come to the party to appease Eleanor and wasn't going to bother, assuming that she wouldn't actually notice whether he was there or not. Or perhaps he had intended to come but his babysitter let him down at the last minute.

Or perhaps he was standing right behind me.

'Hey.'

Zip. My shoulders were up by my ears.

'I'm glad I bumped into you out here,' he said. 'I hate going into these places on my own. You look nice,' he added. 'New dress?'

'Not really,' I lied. He put his hands on his hips and looked me up and down like a horse-buyer making an appraisal. I felt so hot, he might as well have put his hands on *my* hips and turned me round to get a better view. 'Some old thing I had in the back of my wardrobe,' I elaborated.

'Suits you.'

'You're looking pretty sharp yourself.' He was wearing the kind of jeans Ed wouldn't be seen dead in: dirt-washed Diesel that hung from his slim hips. Ed favoured Sandhurst chic – disgusting red or mustard-yellow 'casual' trousers worn slightly too tight that added years as well as inches. The only advantage was that he wouldn't have to change his look when he hit fifty.

'Shall we go in?' Steven asked me.

He offered me his arm. I didn't take it, using the coat I had draped over one arm and the handbag in my other hand as my excuse. Steven took my coat and offered me his arm again. I couldn't refuse it this time.

'I thought perhaps you wouldn't be able to get a babysitter,' I said conversationally as we walked across a glass bridge from the lobby into the club itself.

'Isabelle's with her grandparents tonight. In fact, she's there tomorrow night too. I've got all weekend to misbehave.' He smiled like a wolf.

'Well, I won't be misbehaving,' I shot back. 'This is my boss's birthday party after all.'

'It's pretty dark in here. And I won't tell a soul.'

If there was a double meaning there, I pretended not to get it.

*   *   *

The VIP room at Shades was already packed with partygoers. I recognised lots of faces from the station and saw plenty of eyebrows raised in surprise as I walked in with someone who definitely wasn't Ed.

I stopped to say 'hi' to Jack, the studio manager, who hovered by the cloakroom looking as bewildered as if he had fallen through a hole in Middle Earth and come out in Studio Fifty-four in his beard and ancient camouflage jacket. He would rather have been at the dentist having gum surgery, I'm sure, but he had a huge crush on Eleanor and would have followed her anywhere. I noticed a fleeting expression of anguish cross his face when he saw Steven – Jack had put on a brave face while Eleanor swooned all over the studio – which disappeared when he saw Steven was with me.

'You came together,' he said, as though it was a statement of fact he could cling on to.

'We met at the door,' I said. 'Great party.'

'No real ale,' said Jack, indicating his bottle of Mexican lager with disdain.

'You're a real-ale man?' said Steven.

'Yes,' said Jack. End of conversation.

'Where's Eleanor?' I asked.

Jack jerked his thumb towards a tight knot of people standing close to the bar. Floating up from the centre was a helium-filled silver balloon emblazoned with the legend, 'Still naughty at forty.' It was like a buoy indicating Eleanor's whereabouts in her sea of friends.

'Perhaps you could give her this if you get to her,' said Jack. He handed me a beautifully wrapped box that suggested something Jack had thought long and hard about was hidden inside.

'Will do,' I promised him.

'I'll follow you,' said Steven.

When Steven and I managed to push our way through the crowd, Eleanor's facial expressions were the exact opposite of Jack's. Her eyebrows raised in delight when she saw Steven and dipped ever so slightly when she saw he was with me.

'You came together?' was her first loaded question too.

'We bumped into each other just outside.'

She beamed at that. 'I'm really glad you could make it,' she said to Steven. 'But don't let this girl hog you all night.'

'No need to worry about that . . .' I began.

'You and I have got to have a dance,' Eleanor continued. 'Don't forget.' She was swallowed up by a new wave of people bearing gifts. Jack's small box and my book and vaginal lubricant were placed in a pile on the table beside her.

'Your boss is a really lovely woman,' said Steven as we waited side by side at the bar. 'It's very friendly of her to invite me to her party.'

'I think she may have an ulterior motive for wanting you here tonight,' I told him.

'So might I.'

I said nothing, trying to catch the barman's eye as an excuse for my lack of response.

'Heidi! Steven!' Flo insinuated her way between us and wrapped her arms around us both. She was already pretty drunk, having spent all day on a shopping spree with Eleanor, taking a limo from shop to shop and necking Moët all the way. 'It's really good to see you here,' she said, addressing her comment to Steven, of course. 'The show went really well last week; we got loads of phone calls asking about you and your charity. In fact, you were so popular, I wouldn't be surprised if my boss ends up giving you a regular slot.'

'Or your slot,' I warned.

'That would be great,' said Steven.

'We're in the corner over there,' Flo continued. 'Me, Robin,

Nelly and Jack. We've got a kitty for alcohol. Want to come in on it? Steven, you're one of us tonight. Come and help us suss out all Eleanor's weird friends. Apparently, Eleanor's ex-husband and the sister who stole him away from her are both coming along later on.'

'Sister?' Steven echoed.

'Yes,' said Flo. 'And I mean her sister. Not her sis*tah*.' She kissed her teeth. 'Barman!' Flo caught his attention immediately. She was a woman with presence and a pair of breasts like 'chocolate-covered footballs'. I'd heard Robin describe them as such while talking to a friend on the phone when he thought no one was listening.

We squeezed around the table where Robin and Jack were nursing their beers distractedly while Nelly tried to interest them in some new government policy on dividing up the airwaves.

'Boy, girl, boy, girl,' Flo bossed and situated herself between Robin and Steven. I had the choice of sitting next to Steven or Jack. It wasn't really a choice. Jack seemed to have spread out most of his belongings on the bench next to him, as though he was setting up camp. It was a defensive manoeuvre he employed at the studio as well.

I sat down next to Steven, making sure that my leg didn't touch his – pretty hard, given the space we were left to work with. I actually had to hang on to the edge of the table to be completely sure I wouldn't tip off onto the floor. With my free hand I arranged the floaty skirt of my new dress over my knees, crossed my legs demurely at the ankle. Steven glanced down, smiled.

'You ever been to Barbados?' Flo asked Steven. 'I grew up there. Not quite sure how I ended up here. It's like paradise, Barbados: just like England only sunnier.'

'I haven't been.'

'I'll show you around any time you want to go.'

It was clear that while Flo had invited us both to join the table, she wasn't actually interested in talking to anyone but my ex. The horseshoe configuration of the table left me too far away from Nelly and Robin to easily strike up a conversation with them. Jack just nursed his bottle of beer, watching the dance-floor anxiously as though someone might dart out at any moment like a crocodile from a swamp and try to drag him over there against his will. Surreptitiously hanging on to the edge of the table, I felt as uncomfortable as I had done on my first visit to a nightclub, aged fifteen. At least this time I could drink.

I sipped at a glass of champagne and tried to interest myself in the dancers. A small group of girls I recognised as receptionists from the London Talk Live building had positioned themselves just in front of us. One of them clearly fancied herself as some kind of MTV diva. She gyrated herself through 360 degrees, then, catching sight of Steven, looked back over her shoulder, oh-so-casually, before lifting her hands to the nape of her neck and unfastening her long blonde hair so that it tumbled over her shoulders. I couldn't help glancing at Steven to see his reaction. He was watching the dance-floor in an unfocused sort of way as Flo chatted on in his ear. When the girl flicked her long hair in his direction, I thought I saw him hesitate mid-sentence while his brain registered the blonde girl's presence. Then he took a sip of his drink and carried on talking. The rollercoaster lurched in my stomach again. I was ashamed to find I felt relieved when another gang of revellers blocked the blonde girl from his view.

'I need to go and powder my nose,' Flo announced after a while.

The only way out was through me.

Steven immediately leaned back to make way and in doing so, leaned his body firmly against mine. Apart from a handshake at the radio station, this was the first physical contact we'd had since he hugged me to sleep the night before we broke up.

'Sorry,' he said. 'I didn't mean to squash you.'

'I'm okay,' I said, though I was blushing like an Austen heroine in the wake of an improper glance from her hero.

Flo sashayed away and Steven scooted into her place. 'Slide in a bit more,' he said.

On the dance-floor, the blonde was back. Steven glanced up again, attracted by the toss of her hair like a bird of prey spotting the silver flash of a fish in the water. But then his eyes were on me.

'Flo can't half talk.' He rolled his eyes in mock despair. 'Are you having fun? Bit different from that club we used to go to in Leeds, isn't it? What was it called?'

'The Dungeon,' I said with a smile.

'That's the place.'

'With all the Goths and the death-metallers.'

'And the dirt-cheap beer. I haven't thought about that place in ages.'

He looked at me and smiled somewhat furtively. His eyes flickered. I wondered whether he was having the same memory as me.

'Remember the night we . . .'

He definitely was. He was thinking of the night when he pulled me behind a big velvet curtain at the side of the stage and made love to me there and then while five hundred students slammed to Love Removal Machine. He held my gaze, waiting for me to finish his sentence.

'Out of my place, girlfriend,' interrupted Flo. That same sensation washed over me. Three parts relief, two parts disappointment.

'I've got a better idea,' said Steven when I got up to let Flo slide back into the banquette. 'Let's dance.'

He took me by one hand and Flo by the other and dragged us both on the floor, both protesting, though Flo rather less so than me. She knew she had the advantage; she loved to dance. As soon as she stepped onto the floor, she stepped into the music, turning herself beneath Steven's arm until she was close up against him. I stood as far away from him as our joined hands would allow and shuffled from foot to foot. Flo spun out from him again. It was clear I was just in the way. I dropped Steven's hand and let them carry on dancing à deux.

But I couldn't slip easily back into my seat. Robin was on his feet now and took over where Steven left off. I wasn't quite so outclassed this time. Robin grabbed both my hands and we shuffled back and forth together. He was biting his lower lip in concentration as he tried not to step on my feet.

Beside us, Steven and Flo moved to an altogether different beat – the one that was actually playing. Steven lifted his arm again, Flo turned underneath it, slowly, slinkily, maintaining eye contact until the last possible moment like a ballet dancer keeping her eyes fixed on an imaginary point to keep her balance in a pirouette. Steven gave a little hip swing in response. He stepped backwards to give Flo room to step towards him once more. They danced like a pair of Cuban lovers. I wondered where Steven had learned to dance like that; he certainly hadn't been able to do it when I knew him. I felt a rush of heat, imagining myself in Flo's place as he curved an arm around her waist and she melted into his side.

The music got a little slower. The lights dimmed suggestively. All around us, people moved a little closer, reached out to take hands, wrap arms around waists, lay heads on shoulders.

Robin pulled hard on my left hand so that I had no choice but to step towards him. I could tell that he was intending to do this dance with me.

'I hate this song,' I said. 'And I need the loo.'

I headed straight for the girls' room and ran my wrists under the cold tap.

When I came back, Steven was nowhere to be seen. Flo was still dancing, with Robin crushed against her breasts. I suspect he thought he'd died and gone to heaven. Nelly was in deep conversation with Jack. Eleanor, the birthday girl, sat on her own to the side of them, a party hat dropping on her head. She looked as though her party was over, or should be. It was a good moment for me to make an unobtrusive exit, except that my handbag was still wedged between Eleanor and Nelly. Foiled again. I had no choice but to sit down next to my boss.

'Heidi,' said Eleanor, 'I've got to tell you a secret. A really big secret.'

'Oh dear,' I said, 'you look serious. Am I going to regret being made party to this knowledge?'

Eleanor took a fortifying sip of champagne. Or rather, a glug. 'It's not really my fortieth birthday,' she said. 'That was three years ago! I made a decision to take three years off my age when I hit thirty and I've been keeping it a secret ever since.'

'You're joking.'

'I don't know why I did it. Thirty sounded so old back then.'

'Well, you had us all fooled.'

'Did I? Did I really? Perhaps when I first did it. But now I'm starting to wonder if the only person I'm fooling is myself.'

'Oh come on,' I said. 'Whether you're forty or forty-three, it's your birthday and you're looking wonderful. I hope I look as good as you do when I really hit the big four-oh. Age is just a number, anyway. Or an attitude,' I added.

'You're a good girl,' said Eleanor. 'Don't tell Robin and Nelly, will you?'

'Of course not.'

'Flo already knows. She thinks it's funny. She's been knocking seven years off her age since she hit fifty.'

I snorted some champagne onto the table. 'Fifty!'

'That was two years ago. Don't tell Steven about either of us, will you?'

'God, not you as well.'

'What?'

'Falling for Steven Gabriel?'

'He is quite unfeasibly lovely,' Eleanor sighed.

I chose not to make any comment on that.

'Look, Heidi,' Eleanor said then, 'I've been honest with you and I want you to know that you can be honest with me too. I know it's not really my place to say.'

'Then perhaps whatever it is, you shouldn't say it.'

'You know how much we all like Eddy. He's a really great bloke. A top bloke. The kind of man you want to have as a friend. The kind of man you could rely on in a crisis. Which is a good job, considering he is a dentist. But just lately, you haven't seemed all that excited about getting married to him. Used to be we couldn't get you to shut up about the wedding. These days you seem positively pissed off if anyone asks about it, and you forgot to take a picture of the dress. Is everything okay?'

'Of course it is.'

'Are you sure? Like that woman who came on the programme said, if you're having second thoughts then the best thing you can do for both you and Eddy is tell him about it.'

'Eleanor, I'm not having second thoughts.'

'You're right. I mean, you should know. God, I don't know why I started this . . .'

'You can stop any time you like,' I assured her.

But she wasn't going to.

'Next to Steven, Eddy seems so, well . . . I don't know, Heidi. I'm drunk. I'm drunker than I've ever been. But I can't help thinking what a good couple you and Steven must have made. There's something about the way you *are* around him. Somehow you just look right together.'

'So did Liza Minnelli and David Gest. Or Michael Jackson and Lisa Marie Presley,' I replied. 'And look how that lot turned out. The way people look together is no indication of how well they get along. Believe me.'

'I've made you angry, haven't I?'

'Of course not,' I lied. Eleanor was still my boss, after all. 'Of course not. You can say whatever you want. It's your birthday. Your fortieth birthday.'

'You going to shake your stuff on the dance-floor, Eleanor?' Robin shimmied up to our table. 'I've asked for some tunes from the Eighties to get everyone going again. You were young in the Eighties weren't you, Heidi?'

'I certainly was, you little shit.'

'Then come and show me how to do the "Thriller" dance.' He did a moonwalk for my benefit.

'I've got to get home,' I said. I reached for my bag and shrugged my coat on. It was slightly damp from spilled champagne and I congratulated myself for having left my knock-down Prada at home that evening.

'Leaving already?' Steven asked. 'After the blood, sweat and tears I lost getting to the bar for this?' He held out another bottle of champagne. 'I think it was my round,' he said.

'Oh no.' Flo, who had collapsed onto the sofa the second Robin let her go, saw the bottle and went into a decline again. 'I'm not touching any of that.'

'And I can't finish another bottle on my own. One more before you go,' said Eleanor to me.

'I really should be going now.'

'One more glass of champagne,' Eleanor insisted. 'I haven't seen you guys properly all evening and I want to raise a toast to my team.'

'One more glass before you go,' Flo joined the chorus.

'Then I'll leave with you,' Steven told me. 'You heading in my direction?'

'I don't think so. I live in Chiswick and you live in East London, don't you?'

'It's all within the M25. I'll get the taxi to drop you off and take me on.'

My conscious colleagues awaited my answer with thoroughly inappropriate interest, looking from me to Steven like spectators at a tennis game as we batted the proposal back and forth.

'Really, I'm sure it would be much easier for a cabby to take you east on the flyover. Taking me home is a ridiculous detour.'

'It'll take five minutes.'

'And the rest.'

'There'll be no traffic.'

'It's a good idea,' interrupted Nelly, the one person who probably didn't want my relationship with Steven to turn into the office soap opera. At least not consciously. 'You're very unlikely to get a black cab this far out at this time of night and I would never get into a minicab on my own.'

'Nelly,' said Eleanor, 'you are so sensible. You are always so bloody sensible. Did you come out of the womb being sensible?' That last question was more like an accusation.

Nelly looked aghast.

'It's not a bad thing,' I assured her. 'This lot could learn something about self-control.'

'Stop fannying about and drink more booze,' said Robin, popping open the new bottle of champers and topping up Nelly's glass first. She sipped at it with a very worried look on her face. Now I felt obliged to join in one last time, if only to keep poor Nelly company with all this bad influence around her.

'Then we'll take a taxi back to yours,' said Steven.

'And you'll drop me off and go straight home,' said I.

'To *Let's Talk London*.' Eleanor raised her glass. 'To Robin and Nelly and Flo and Jack. And Heidi and Steven.'

He chinked his glass against mine and held my gaze while he drank.

23

Nelly was right about the taxis. There wasn't a black cab to be seen when we emerged from the club. Not even at the taxi rank outside the Tube station, where a hopeful queue of late night partygoers snaked all the way back towards Heathrow. Night bus after night bus sailed past the stops, too full to take any more passengers, no matter how much they cursed and gave the driver the finger. It was too cold to stand and wait comfortably. Steven offered me his coat. I refused.

'You'll be cold too.'

'You know I run far hotter than you. You always had the heating in your room turned up way too high at college,' he reminded me.

'Taxi?'

The guy approached us sideways, like a crab. 'Taxi?' he hissed out of the side of his mouth. 'Where you going?'

I ignored him. I had a knee-jerk reaction to unlicensed minicabs. It just wasn't safe for a girl to get in one.

'Chiswick and then Hackney,' said Steven. 'How much?'

'Sixty pounds,' said the driver.

'You must be joking.'

'Fifty-five.'

'Forget it,' said Steven. 'We could fly to Barcelona for that. How far away is your place from here?' he asked me. 'Think you could walk it?'

I frequently did. On a summer's evening while it was still light and busy I wouldn't have thought twice about striking out for home on foot if I had male company to keep the muggers at bay. But not in freezing drizzle.

'It's too cold,' I said.

'We'll get even colder if we just stand here with the rest of the lemons. Let's start walking and see if we can flag an empty cab down before it gets to the rank.'

'It's the wrong direction for you.'

'Well, if we get as far as your house before a car comes, you can make me a cup of tea and call me a cab from there. If you don't think Ed will mind,' he added.

I blushed at the sound of my fiancé's name. It was the first time either of us had mentioned Ed since that afternoon standing outside the studio. Even over lunch after Steven's second appearance on the show, Ed's name hadn't come up. Now it did. Steven had remembered.

'Why would he mind?' I asked.

'Then it's sorted. Lead the way. If you can in those ultra-glam shoes.'

He was taking the mickey. Ever practical, I had worn a pair of trainers to the club and changed into my party shoes just around the corner. Now I was back in the trainers again. You never knew when you might need to run away.

'This way,' I said.

He offered me his arm.

'It's okay,' I told him, stuffing my hands deep in my pockets. 'I'm pretty steady on my feet.'

'You've obviously forgotten that time you tripped over your shoelaces after Kara's twenty-first.'

'I'm still trying to,' I said.

'I don't think I've ever seen you that drunk. I had to put you to bed, remember?'

'I don't remember very much after the blackout,' I replied.

That was a lie. In fact I remembered rallying enough to feel him kissing me to sleep. But I didn't say that, and Steven didn't push it. Instead he said something about the insanity of house prices in West London and how much more reasonable East London seemed in comparison. If you thought a quarter of a million for a converted pigeon coop on a busy main road was reasonable. I gratefully joined in with the traditional Londoners' lament.

Steven was pretty good at small-talk. He chatted easily about his week. How nervous he had been, coming onto the show again. How easy everyone had made it for him to feel part of the team. But the mundanity of our conversation didn't quite go far enough to diffuse the tension building between us. When I swayed from my side of the pavement to avoid an overhanging branch and accidentally knocked into him, I half expected to see sparks fly up where our shoulders touched. He reached out to steady me, still chatting, and didn't let go of my arm quickly enough. My cheeks burned up and I was grateful for the dark.

Eventually, we arrived at the street where I lived with Ed.
'This is it.'
'Very nice,' Steven commented. 'Very, er, leafy.'
'It's quiet,' I said. 'Near a Tube station. And there are lots of young professionals. Newly married. That sort of thing.'
'You sound like an estate agent.'
It was a far cry from the street where Steven and I had lived together. Opposite the flat we had shared in East London was a house that we suspected was being used as a brothel. An ever-changing parade of men drifted in and out of the doors while an equally changeable group of beautiful girls occasionally sat on the front steps smoking and waved to Steven when he left the house for work in the mornings.

I hadn't particularly liked living on that street. I wasn't one of those people who needed to live in edgy surroundings to feel more alive. Neither, thank goodness, was Ed. But I still felt the need to defend my retreat to suburbia.

'It's easy to get to work from here.'

We stopped outside number eight, with the navy-blue front door that Ed had repainted after I read a magazine article that said a blue door suggested affluence and might improve the value of our property. Not that we were going to be selling it any time soon. We'd bought the house specifically because it would be big enough for the pair of us and a child.

I opened my handbag to look for my keys. Stupid bag. It was voluminous and I could never find anything inside it.

'Which floor are you on?' Steven asked, while I hunted.

'The whole house,' I said.

Steven whistled to show he was impressed.

'No lights on,' he commented. 'Perhaps Ed's gone to bed.'

'Ed isn't home,' I answered without thinking. 'He's playing rugby all weekend.'

A pause.

'And Isabelle is with her grandparents until Sunday night.'

The suggestion was implicit. And, when I dared to look at him again, it was echoed in Steven's face, in the slow smile currently spreading across it. The cats were away. It was clear that Steven thought that's what I had meant, too. Though I had been complaining about the cold for weeks – spring still seemed a very long way off – I was suddenly sweltering hot and starting to sweat.

'I'd better call you that cab,' I said, as the front door swung open and we stepped into the hall.

I picked up the phone before I put the kettle on, desperate to minimise the amount of time that Steven spent in my flat. What had I been thinking, letting him walk me back from the club? I should have just made him wait with me at the taxi rank. Of course he didn't think I was going to send him home right away. But I had sobered up on the walk back home. It was as though I didn't want him to see where I lived. This place was completely uncontaminated by memories of him and the things that had happened between us. It was my place. Ed's place. I needed to keep it that way.

As it was, I didn't even manage to keep Steven in the kitchen. While I was being told that there would be no cabs available for an hour and I really ought to book ahead on a Friday night if I wanted to get anywhere after midnight, Steven wandered out of his containment in the kitchen in search of the bathroom. And when he had finished in the bathroom, he didn't come back to the kitchen but made straight for the sitting room, opening the door and walking in there as casually as if he were in his own home.

I felt horribly exposed. As though by seeing the inside of my flat, Steven could see what was inside my head. I put down the phone and followed after him at once.

'We haven't really done much to this place,' I said defensively. 'We haven't been here that long and Ed's been setting up his own business for most of that time. He's a dentist. He's set up his own surgery.'

Steven nodded. 'That must be hard work.'

He was standing by the fireplace now, casting his eye over the framed photographs on the mantelpiece. He must have recognised some of them: the photograph of my family outside the bungalow; a picture of James and me as children – I was six, he was two, and we were both dressed as miniature Beefeaters at a fancy dress party for the Queen's silver jubilee; a photograph of Kara and me all dressed up for our graduation ball. Steven had been at that ball. And all these pictures had once lived in the sitting room of the flat I shared with Steven.

'I think I've still got a copy of that photo somewhere,' he said, fingering the one of me and Kara.

He picked just one of the pictures up: a silver-framed snap of Ed and me on the beach at Holkham in Norfolk. It was taken exactly a year after we first met, on a weekend away that was sort of an anniversary celebration. I had wanted to go to Holkham ever since I found out that the wide, white beach Gwyneth Paltrow wanders down at the end of *Shakespeare in Love* is in England and not some exclusive private cove in the Caribbean. Ed had some friends who lived in a big farmhouse up there and arranged for us to stay with them. I had been so nervous about meeting them, desperate to pass muster with the people who were so important to a man who had, over the space of twelve months, become so important to me. As it was, they were just as keen to make an impression on me. Ed had already told them that he thought I might be The One.

It was a goofy sort of photo. Neither of us looked like we had just stepped out of the pages of *Vogue*. But we looked delighted. Completely thrilled to be with each other. As we were.

'Is this Ed?' Steven asked.

I nodded.

'Good-looking bloke. And I have to say you look very happy.'

'That was two years ago,' I said.

Steven turned to look at me, photo still in his hand.

'I mean the picture was taken two years ago, not that I haven't been happy since then,' I burbled.

'Of course,' said Steven. 'That was what I thought you meant.'

Steven put the photo back down very carefully. Then he picked up the smooth grey pebble that had been sitting in front of it.

'Ed gave me that stone when we walked on the beach,' I explained.

'I did wonder why you had such an interesting-looking piece of rock on your mantelpiece. Doesn't exactly go with the rest of the décor.'

He flipped the pebble up the air and caught it in one easy move. 'I've still got that rock you gave me somewhere. The one you pinched from that site of enormous archaeological importance. At the stone ring. Do you remember?'

Did I remember? We had made love right in the middle of it. At night, of course, when there weren't any tourists. Steven had spread out a picnic blanket underneath the stars. The moonlight had turned our skin silver. It really did feel as though something magical might happen that evening. Perhaps it had. But I didn't want to start reminiscing about that. Only two months afterwards, Steven and I broke up.

Instead I said, 'I called the cab firm I usually use but they haven't got anything for an hour or so.'

'I can wait,' said Steven. 'Haven't got to get up early tomorrow.'

'I'm going to call round a few other places to see if they can get you home before then.' I picked up the Yellow Pages and began to flick through. 'And the kettle's boiled. What do you want to drink?'

'Coffee. Instant if you've got it,' he added with a smile. 'It's faster.'

'How do you have it?'

'Same as I always did.'

'I don't remember.'

'I'll make it,' he said. 'While you call round and see if you can get rid of me a little more quickly.'

'I'm not trying to get rid of you.'

No such luck. It soon became clear that Chequers Cars were having a slow night compared to the rest of the minicab firms in West London. 'We have people who book a week in advance for a Friday night,' said one firm helpfully.

'Honestly, an hour will just fly by,' said Steven as he plonked a mug of camomile tea in front of me while I was dialling yet another number. 'And then you can get on with enjoying having the house all to yourself. Off on a rugby tour, eh? Never had you down for the sort of girl who would end up a sports widow. Especially not to a rugby player.'

'It's the season. He doesn't go away that often.'

'What must your father think?'

My father and Steven had bonded over the football. They both dismissed rugby as a game for toffs.

'Dad thinks that Ed is a truly decent guy,' I said.

'Despite his girlish inability to be interested in the offside rule?'

'I think Ed understands football as well,' I replied.

'How is your dad?'

'He's fine.'

'And your mum?'

'She's fine too.'

'And your brother?'

'Making a fortune in the City. Too busy to talk to any of us.'

'He'll get over it. You must give them my regards.'

I nodded into my tea. As if I would even tell them I had seen him. 'Well, wish your mum my best, too.'

'She always liked you.'

'I always liked her.' That was true. She would have been a dream mother-in-law. I loved going round to her house for Sunday lunch – long afternoons spent laughing over bottles of red wine. She cried when I called her to tell her that Steven had left me. I wondered how well she got on with Sarah.

'Well, I never thought I'd be sitting here,' Steven said after a moment's silence.

'Can't say it's a moment I envisaged either.'

He cocked his head to one side and let his eyes drift down my face towards my lips. 'It's nice, though. Being here with you.'

'You did a really great job on the show last week,' I said to change the subject. 'I'm sure Eleanor will be calling you to have you come on the show again. Perhaps when Flo's on holiday.'

'I'd like that. But I hope I'll see you before then. I'm not letting you get away again that easily.'

I brought my cup up to my mouth and took a gulp of tea. It was too hot. I coughed. Steven patted me on the back to stop me choking. His hand remained there, sliding down towards my waist slowly. Slowly. With intent.

'Biscuit?' I asked, jumping up and breaking the contact.

'No. No thanks . . .' I sensed a little amusement in Steven's eyes as he watched me dash to the kitchen again anyway.

'I've got Hobnobs,' I said.

'I don't want a biscuit. Not even a Hobnob.'

Neither did I. I put the tin on the coffee table.

'Chill out,' said Steven. 'You don't have to play hostess. I'm happy just to sit here and wait for that taxi. I suppose.'

His eyes drifted about the room again.

'Is that you on the Eiffel Tower?' he asked.

I grinned down on us both from a black and white photo on the bookshelf. If Steven had cared to get up and take a closer look, he might have seen my brand-new engagement ring glittering on my hand as I held my windblown fringe out of my face. It was Ed's favourite photograph of me. He had wanted it to be the picture on our wedding invitation. I had insisted on going for something plain.

I should have told Steven then. It would have been so easy to say, 'Yes. That picture was taken the weekend we got engaged.' But I let another moment pass. Confirmed the location and left it at that. I let him continue to think that there was little more between me and the man I had promised to marry than shared utility bills.

'You look beautiful,' he said.

'Thank you,' I managed.

'I can't tell you the number of times I've thought about that smile these past seven years.'

I didn't know what to say. I looked down at my hands. My

left hand still bare. My engagement ring still waiting at the jeweller's.

'You have the most beautiful smile I have ever seen, you know that? The way your eyes crinkle up when you beam. Your fantastic teeth. The way you throw your head back when you laugh.'

I continued to concentrate on my fingers. Steven's hand was on my back again, and this time he slid it up towards the base of my neck. I felt him caress the stray wisps of hair that had escaped from my inexpertly tied French knot.

'I can remember when you smiled at me like that. It's a bit like your orgasm face from what I remember,' he added with a laugh.

With the gentlest of pressure, he started to turn my head towards him. My body prickled as heat spread throughout my limbs. I kept my eyes downcast until my face was level with his, then I opened my eyes to see his blue-greys gazing back at me. He licked his lips. He stopped telling me how beautiful my mouth looked and I knew he was about to kiss me.

'Steven, I . . .'

He put his finger to my lips. Moved closer.

Then came the sound of a car coming to a halt in the street outside my house and the distinctly impatient beep of a horn.

'There's your cab.' I leapt up, grabbed Steven's coat from the back of the sofa and thrust it towards him. 'They quoted twenty quid to Hackney.'

'Heidi,' Steven tried, 'I don't have to . . .'

'You'd better go before he drives off,' I said, making it clear that he did have to leave and I was not going to take the conversation further.

'Fine. Fine,' said Steven, shrugging his jacket on as he too stood up. 'I'm going. Thanks for the coffee.' He hadn't managed to drink even half and I was already carrying his mug out to the kitchen.

I opened the front door for him on my way. 'It was nice to see you,' I forced myself to say.

'It was nice to see you too. Much too brief,' he added, eyes pleading. 'Much too brief.' He hesitated on the step.

'Bye,' I said. 'I'm going to close the door so I don't let the heat out.'

He sighed. 'Okay, Heidi. You do that.'

But I practically slammed the door behind him, as though slamming the door closed on a vampire.

My heart pounded as though I had run all the way home from the nightclub. I leaned against the front door until I heard the taxi pull away. What had I done? My own home suddenly looked different to me, as though I had somehow altered the composition of the air within those walls by inviting my ex-boyfriend inside. The home that Ed and I had created together had been reduced by my actions to any old house.

But I hadn't really done anything bad, had I? I hadn't kissed him. But I had let him think that he could kiss me. And I knew that, for just one second, I had wanted him to. I wanted him to overpower me. I wanted him to step over the barriers I had erected and take me in his arms, take the decision out of my hands.

I found myself in the kitchen, staring into the sink like a zombie. Then I caught sight of the mug Steven had been drinking from. As though it was carrying some radioactive trace of him, I flung it into the sink and doused it with hot water and suds. When it was safely out of sight and soaking, I picked up my phone and went straight to the bedroom, which was a scene of carnage.

The boxer shorts and socks Ed had been wearing in bed the night before he left lay where he had kicked them off. His chest of drawers looked as though it had been ransacked by a burglar. I imagined him filling his kit bag for the weekend, grabbing blindly for a handful of contents from each drawer like a crazed grandmother on the three-minute scramble in *Supermarket Sweep*. Then I imagined him turning up at his rugby tour without a single matching pair of socks. He hadn't even bothered to close the drawers again before he left. I kicked one shut with my foot.

Sitting on the bed, I pushed a mug containing the dregs of a week-old cup of coffee to the edge of Ed's bedside table so that I had somewhere to put my glass of water, then buried my face in his pillow. I had a sudden urge to breathe him in, as though the scent of my fiancé would put the face of my ex-boyfriend out of my mind. But I took just half a lungful before I recoiled in horror. The pillow smelled less of Ed than of hair-grease and cigarette smoke. And then I remembered that he had also promised to change the bed linen before he left for his rugby weekend. It was his turn. It had been Ed's turn for the past two weeks. The white cotton sheets were so filthy they were actually starting to shine. Jaw clenched with annoyance, I ripped the slip from Ed's special back-care pillow and hurled it in the direction of his boxer shorts. I got halfway through removing the duvet cover before I gave up – why should I bother? – and moved myself, my glass and my mobile phone into the spare room, where the sheets had only been slept in for one night. By Ed, while he was covered in sick. I took my duvet to the sofa.

I toyed with the idea of phoning Kara. It was as though my fingers were itching to dial someone and, if I didn't watch out, that someone would be Steven. But Kara would be fast asleep now. In the past, I wouldn't have hesitated to wake her up at such a crisis point, but sleep had become insanely precious to her since Forester was born.

Perhaps I should just phone Ed. The smell of him hadn't done anything to cheer me up, but his voice might and it was highly likely that he was still awake, if not sober. I pressed speed-dial number one. Ed's number was, of course, the one I phoned most often. But he didn't pick up. I left a message.

'Hello, darling. Just calling to say good night. And thanks for changing the sheets. Not.'

Almost as soon as I hung up on Ed, the phone chirruped to tell me I had a text message.

'Are you sure you don't want me to come back? Steven. X'

I wasn't sure at all.

I imagined him still sitting in the back of the taxi, waiting for my reply. How far had they gone? I wondered. Perhaps he was just waiting at the end of the street. Would I reply? Should I reply? What should I reply if I did? I could see him in my mind's eye, looking at the little screen expectantly, wondering whether I would be able to resist.

It took me a quarter of an hour to think of the appropriate response.

In the end, I texted just one word. 'No.'

He texted back within seconds.

'Is that "no" as in you're not sure?'

'Simply no,' I texted back.

And I vowed there and then that those would be the last words Steven Gabriel *ever* heard from me.

24

I always thought I would make a hopeless poker player. I've never found it particularly easy to hide what I'm feeling with an inscrutable face. I didn't sleep well that night after Steven left. Though I told myself I didn't ever want to hear from him again, I kept my mobile phone next to the bed and waited for the text message sound. When nothing more came, I admit I was disappointed that he'd given up so easily. When I looked at my face in the mirror the following morning, I thought I could see guilt around my eyes. But if I could see it, Ed couldn't.

Ed got home at about six o'clock, carrying a bunch of flowers I guessed he had bought at a service station. He swept me into his arms when he found me in the bedroom putting away that sunset dress.

'That's pretty,' he said. 'Going to put it on and seduce me?'

I hadn't tried to seduce Ed in a long while.

But when he kissed me this time, I forced myself to kiss him back. Properly. We hadn't made love in almost a month. I felt that if I didn't go along with it this time, Ed would be perfectly entitled to complain. We weren't even married yet. Surely we were still supposed to be at it every spare moment we had.

I didn't feel like it. Not in the least. But I told myself that if I just went along with it, everything would be okay. I'd got myself worked up about nothing. The more I avoided sex the more I thought I didn't want it. He'd touch me in the right place at some point, start a chain reaction.

I let Ed back me onto the bed, lift my T-shirt up and kiss his way from my breastbone to my belly. I let him run his hands along the length of my legs, stopping at the place where my thighs meet to massage me gently through the cotton of my bikini pants.

In turn, I automatically reached down between his legs. He was already hard. He had been hard since the second he pressed himself up against me by the wardrobe. He gave a soft, happy moan when I slipped my hand inside his boxers, but I was far from ready. I didn't feel aroused at all.

I tried to think of my favourite fantasies. I remembered a time back at the beginning of our relationship when Ed started to make love to me the second I stepped through his front door.

I had been dressed to go out to dinner. Ed told me on the phone as I made my way over to his house that I needed to hurry up. He had a seven thirty reservation at his favourite restaurant and didn't want us to miss it. All that went straight out of his mind when he opened the front door and saw me. I had made an effort. I thought that perhaps it would be obvious from my smile that underneath the black silk jersey dress, I was wearing hold-up stockings. I had never worn hold-ups around Ed before. In case it wasn't obvious, I inched up the hem of my skirt.

He gave a low whistle and pulled me straight to him. He ran his hands over my body in that dress as though he was a sailor who hadn't seen a woman in years. He kicked the front door shut behind me just as he edged the skirt of my dress up over my hips. Moments later I was wearing only my underwear and those stockings, still standing in the hall. He pushed me up against the wall and entered me there. Afterwards, we managed to slink as far as the sofa. We didn't get to the restaurant at all.

It was my favourite way to start feeling hot, remembering

that evening two summers ago. Just thinking about the look on his face could usually send blood to all the right places. But it didn't work that night. I couldn't seem to keep my focus on that memory while Ed did his best with his hands and his mouth.

Instead another image flickered briefly on the screen inside my mind. I saw Steven putting his hand on my leg as he moved out of the way at the nightclub, his eyes on mine as he acknowledged that briefest of contacts between our bodies. I felt his hand on the back of my neck in the moment before he tried to kiss me. And I felt the involuntary contraction of the muscles in my pelvic floor. A loosening. I gave a little moan of my own.

Ed looked up into my face and smiled with relief that we were getting somewhere at last.

'That okay?' he asked.

I closed my eyes against him.

And then I saw Steven's body on top of mine. His narrow waist. The flex in his pectoral muscles as he moved to lie on top of me. I was replaying an old movie I hadn't seen in years but I remembered exactly how it went from frame to frame. I remembered the look of concentration Steven would get. That first moment of connection as he eased himself inside me. The slow way he would start, moving his hips in a very slight circle as well as in and out. The breathtaking instant when he reached his full erectness and touched lightly but so effectively against my g-spot.

Faster and faster. I met the increase in pace by swaying my hips up to meet his. I tensed my feet against the mattress, brought my knees up higher, opening myself wider and wider as though I wanted the whole of him inside. I wrapped my arms around his back, clutching him to me, leaving fingermarks in his shoulders that would take an hour to fade. Faster, faster, deeper, deeper. His penis stiffened against the soft walls of my vagina and I knew that he was about to come.

I felt Steven's body as Ed pushed against me.

I saw his face.

An orgasm tore through me.

For the first time since Ed and I had got together, I had thought about another man while he was inside me. I had thought about Steven until the fantasy was so real to me I could almost smell his skin. It's no understatement to say that it made me depressed.

'Did I imagine it or was that amazing?' Ed breathed. He squeezed me tight.

I loosened his grip and lifted his hand to my mouth. Kissed his palm. 'It was fantastic,' I agreed.

Patient, loving Ed smiled as though he had just won the lottery. 'I love you,' he told me.

Did I deserve him?

25

Monday morning came much too quickly, and this time I was dreading it. I knew I would face an inquisition when I stepped into the office. I had, after all, left the party with the man it seemed everybody wanted. Including me.

Eleanor fetched my coffee but I knew it came with a high price tag.

'So you got home all right on Saturday night?' she began.

'I spent the whole weekend under the Hammersmith fly-over,' I said facetiously.

'Did you manage to find a cab that would take Steven all the way back east after he dropped you off?'

I nodded.

'Come on, Heidi,' Eleanor groaned. 'What happened?'

'I'd really appreciate it if you stopped going on about that man,' I said.

'Why are you so sensitive about this Steven Gabriel?' Flo tutted. 'We've all been dumped before, girl. The man's obviously trying to make amends. Even an elephant doesn't hold grudges as long as you do.'

I took a deep breath and began the sentence that I hoped would silence them on the subject once and for all. 'I'm sensitive about Steven Gabriel because we were going to get married.'

Nelly almost dropped her clipboard. Flo and Eleanor were red-faced at the thought of the embarrassment they might have inflicted upon me. Even Robin was sensible enough not to snigger.

'You are joking,' said Eleanor.

'If only.'

'You were really going to get married? Engagement ring and all?'

'Engagement ring and all,' I nodded.

'Oh, Heidi,' said Flo. 'We are all so sorry.'

'Would make a great segment for the show though,' Robin interrupted. 'We could get him in again. Two sides of a jilting.'

The women all glared at him. His attack of sensitivity hadn't lasted long.

'Sorry,' he muttered.

'It's okay,' I assured him. 'That is a good idea. But I certainly don't want to be one of the two sides of the live debate. In fact, I don't even want to talk about it in the privacy of this office, if that's all the same with you.'

'Of course,' said Eleanor. The others murmured their agreement, but for the rest of the morning I was painfully conscious that they were all desperate for me to pop to the bathroom or out to the coffee shop so they could discuss my revelation in full.

What do you do with an old engagement ring? I'm not the kind of girl who finds herself dripping in diamonds and platinum gifts bought by slavish admirers, but I've been given the odd bit of jewellery in my time. Some of it very odd indeed. Like the bumblebee earrings bought for me by Darren Cook back in 1987. Big, fat, golden bumblebees with black stripes picked out in enamel. I thought they were real gold until they made my ears go green. There were a couple of other bits in my jewellery box that had outlived the relationship they came from. I had a silver rope bracelet from India that I liked much better than the man who gave it to me. I still wore that from time to time. Another old flame had given me a pair of simple gold hoops that were too tasteful to throw away and too boring to wear.

But an engagement ring? What can you do with that when the engagement comes to an end other than marriage? I think, strictly speaking, etiquette demands that you give the symbol of a love lost back. If you haven't already hurled it at him in the heat of the moment. Or sold it. Not that my secret diamonds would have been worth selling. Hell, who even knew if they were real diamonds.

That Saturday night, after receiving Steven's last text message, I had looked at that ring for the first time in a very long time. I was taking off my earrings and, as I went to put them away, I found myself searching through a knot of tangled necklaces I never got round to wearing, for a circle of nine carat gold studded with nine very small and flat-looking diamonds.

It was Steven who had put the ring on my engagement finger. It was he who said that when we had been married for twenty-five years, he would replace the ring he had bought out of a catalogue with an obscenely big sparkler from Tiffany. At the time I said I wouldn't want another engagement ring. The sentiment made it worth far more than a Tiffany solitaire.

'With this ring,' Steven had said as he slipped it on my finger.

We were sitting on a clifftop in Cornwall when he did it. August bank holiday weekend. We had been camping near Land's End.

'Does this mean we're engaged?' I asked.

Steven held my hand between his. 'It means that I can think of no one I would rather be engaged to.' But we were still very young, he told me solemnly. If we went back to London and announced our engagement, people would want to know when the wedding was and we were a long way off being ready to afford a decent wedding.

'Let's just say that it's a promise ring,' Steven suggested. 'We can announce our engagement this time next year.'

Of course, we didn't last that long.

Less than a year later, on a Saturday morning in June, Steven told me that he didn't think we should be together any more. At first, I thought he was joking; it was so unexpected. He was sitting at the kitchen table. I was standing by the swing bin, sorting through that morning's post, throwing the junk mail away. I had just opened a wedding invitation from one of the girls I worked with. I asked Steven whether he would be free to come along. And that's when he said it.

'Heidi, I'm moving out.'

It was already arranged. He was going to stay with friends for a while. He'd carry on paying his share of the rent until I was able to find someone to move into the spare bedroom or get a smaller place on my own. I could keep the few bits of furniture we'd bought together. He would be back for his CDs and things in a couple of days.

It was all so clinical. Not at all how I had imagined. I didn't have an opportunity to argue my case. Looking back, I can see that Steven had already left the house in all but the physical sense.

'Why are you doing this?' I asked him.

'I don't know,' he said.

'Is there someone else?'

There wasn't.

'Is it something I've done?'

He told me no.

'Don't you love me any more?'

He said he would always love me.

But he was going and he couldn't tell me why. He couldn't tell me why the ring on my finger would never be replaced by a chunk of ice from Tiffany. He couldn't tell me why I was no longer the girl he wanted to spend the rest of his life with. He couldn't tell me why I was no longer the girl he even wanted to spend the weekend with.

'It's for the best,' he told me.

'How is it for the best? How? How?'

He couldn't give me the answers and eventually I ran out of strength to keep asking the questions. I sat on the edge of our bed and sobbed while he pulled a ready-packed suitcase out from beneath the bed. Kara arrived not long after. Steven had called to tell her that I might need a friend.

I had comforted myself with the thought that Steven simply wasn't the marrying kind. There would never be a Mrs Steven Gabriel. He simply wasn't capable of that kind of selfless commitment. My mother agreed with me. My father agreed with me (when he had to. He really didn't like to talk about the man who broke his little girl's heart). Kara definitely agreed with me. But how wrong we had been! Steven Gabriel walked another woman up the aisle less than two years after he left me.

What had been different about her? What was it about Sarah that had made Steven stay the course this time? Perhaps it was the fact that she was less suited to commitment than he was, bolting so soon after the baby was born.

Did I love Ed now more than I had loved Steven then? I must do. I was going to marry him. It was just that Ed and I had a different kind of love. A more mature love. Ed had never written me a love poem. Ed had never climbed three storeys to my balcony with a rose between his teeth. Ed had certainly never suggested that we each cut a nick in our thumbs and mingle our blood in the moonlight. But that didn't mean what we had was any less than the love Steven and I shared. It simply meant that we were grown-ups. It's easy to be passionate when you've got nothing to worry about except getting the odd essay in on time. Ed and I had a steady, comforting kind of love. The kind of love that would endure.

Not the kind of love that could be interrupted by a text message.

Hiding in the loos while my colleagues gasped at my revelation, I read Steven's messages one more time before I pressed 'delete'.

26

The following Friday was Kara's birthday. She had, as I had feared, requested babysitting privileges when I asked her what she wanted as a gift. All the same, I still dashed out at lunchtime to buy her present: a couple of Diptyque candles – Baies and Figuier, her favourite scents. Not very exciting, but I knew she would appreciate the little touch of luxury for her bedroom, especially now she almost had a love life again. Like Joan Collins, Kara believed in the power of appropriate lighting as a very effective adjunct to any beauty routine.

She arrived with Forester at seven o'clock, ready to dash off and meet Duncan at seven thirty. He had told her he was taking her somewhere special and she needed to 'scrub up'. Her birthday date outfit had been the subject of several frantic calls that week. This time, she had managed to find something new.

'You look like a goddess,' I assured her when she gave me a twirl in the little black dress with its kicky hem swirling around her knees. 'Would look even better without the changing bag.'

'Exactly what I was thinking.'

She swapped the wipe-clean holdall for the black Prada clutch I had bought in the sales and never found an occasion to use. That bag definitely wasn't big enough for an emergency pack of Pampers. Kara had thoughtfully provided two emergency packs of Pampers for Forester's brief stay with me and Ed.

'Have a wonderful evening,' I said. 'And if you end up being a little bit late because . . . you know . . .'

'Don't say that,' said Kara. 'I might take you up on it now I know what good babysitters you and Ed are.' She kissed me on both cheeks then kissed her finger and pressed it gently to Forester's forehead, not wanting to wake him with a real smacker. 'How's my lipstick?'

'Perfect.'

'Teeth?'

'Clean.'

'Hair?'

'Divine.'

'Personality?'

'Still lacking,' I joked in reply.

'I will see you by one in the morning. Unless, you know . . .' She winked.

'Where's he taking her?' Ed asked when I carried Forester into the house.

'It's a surprise,' I said. 'Very romantic.'

'Thank God I don't have to do that any more.'

I was about to rebuke him.

'I was joking,' he said. 'I got you these on the way back from work.' He pulled a packet of Maltesers out of his jacket pocket. There were about four left.

'A mouse must have got at them,' Ed told me.

'Thanks.'

'Want to shoot some pool?' Ed asked Forester. Forester beamed at him. 'Hand him over, H.' Ed took Forester from me and carried him into the sitting room. He had a newspaper spread out on the coffee table and on the back page was a picture of England's World Cup team.

'Right, young man. Let's continue your education. That's Johnny Wilkinson. That's . . .' Ed named each member of the team for Forester's benefit. 'Won't be long till we have you out there kicking a ball.'

It was about nine o'clock when the telephone rang.

'Heidi.' It was Kara.

'Hey. How's it going? Are you calling to check we haven't lost your baby? He's asleep right now. Ed gave him the first of his bottles about an hour after you left. He drank the lot. Ed winded him and had him in his cot in half an hour.'

'Good,' she said. At least, I thought that was what she said. It was very hard to hear. Firstly, because she was whispering and secondly, because she sounded as though she was calling from inside a wind tunnel.

'Everything's okay. Better get back to your date,' I told her. 'Where are you, by the way? Sounds like you're calling from the middle of the motorway. Has he taken you to Mirabelle like you hoped?'

'No. No, he hasn't.'

'Somewhere better?'

'Heidi,' Kara hissed, 'something terrible has happened.'

'Oh God. Have you gone off him already?' Kara was always going off people. 'Has he got a wife?'

'No. No. It's much worse than that,' she swallowed. 'It's my birthday present.'

'He got you Marks and Spencer's vouchers?' I joked. 'Red lingerie from Ann Summers? A strap-on dildo,' I warmed to my theme. Ed, idly eavesdropping from the sofa, raised an eyebrow at the last one.

'Much worse.'

'I shudder to think.'

'He got me first-class Eurostar tickets to Paris.'

'But, Kara, that's not terrible. That's fantastic!'

'For tonight.'

'Oh. Not so fantastic. That was a bit silly, wasn't it? Not asking you first.'

'He is the king of surprises,' Kara sighed.

'He certainly is. But tickets to Paris . . . What are you supposed to do with Forester? Are you coming back here to collect him? But you don't have a passport for him yet, do you?'

'Of course I don't.'

'How stupid of Duncan not to check,' I said. 'Can he exchange the tickets for another day?'

Kara mumbled something. I couldn't hear what she said at all that time. Then the signal on her mobile cut out.

'Would you believe he got her tickets to Paris?' I said to Ed while I waited for Kara to call back. 'For tonight?'

'Doesn't he know about Forester?' Ed asked, just as the realisation hit me.

He didn't know. Duncan didn't know about Forester. That explained why Kara hadn't dragged her new man across Starbucks to be introduced to me that morning a week before. He wasn't in a hurry to move his car off double yellow lines. She didn't want to have to tell him the truth. Perhaps she had even told him that Forester was *my* baby!

Oh, Kara, I thought. You've really done it now. She must have told him when he gave her his gift. No wonder she sounded so unhappy. I wondered if he had given her a chance to explain or just stormed off into the night.

The phone rang.

'Kara, he didn't know, did he . . .' I began.

'He *doesn't* know about Forester,' she said before I could finish.

'Doesn't know as in still doesn't know?' I asked her. Kara mumbled an affirmation. 'Then what the *fuck* are you going to do?'

'I can't tell him now.'

'But you have to. What are you going to do otherwise? Say you can't go to Paris because your parents want you home before midnight?'

'I can't tell him tonight.'

'Well, you can't go to Paris tonight either.'

'Heidi,' Kara almost sobbed, 'it's too late. I'm already on the train.'

More precisely, she was already on the other side of the Channel.

Duncan had announced his intention to take Kara to Paris for dinner when she met him at the Tube station and, for reasons known only to herself, Kara had allowed him to drive her straight back to her flat, where she rushed inside, packed a couple of things in her overnight bag and got her passport while he waited outside in the taxi.

'I thought he was literally going to take me for dinner there,' she said by way of feeble explanation. 'After all, Paris is only a couple of hours away since the high-speed link opened. I thought we would be back in London in the early hours. But he's booked us into a hotel.'

'Of course he booked you into a hotel, you idiot. Nobody ever goes to Paris for less than a night.'

'For two nights.'

'What?'

'He's booked a hotel for two nights. Oh, Heidi. What am I going to do?'

Cradling the wireless phone between my shoulder and my ear, I looked in on Forester, sleeping in his Moses basket in the spare room. He was utterly oblivious to the kind of nut he had for a mother.

'Help me out here, Heidi. What can I do?'

'Well,' I told her, 'it seems to me that you have a number of choices. You could get on a train straight back to London as

226

soon as you get to Lille and be back here by one o'clock as promised. Maybe a little bit later.'

'This train doesn't stop in Lille,' she said forlornly.

'Paris then. But that necessitates telling Duncan the truth about Forester right now. Or you could pretend he has said something that offends you, fabricate a row and flounce off back to London without explaining yourself at all.'

'God, I think I might have to go for option two. It's the only way.'

'It's a bit bloody cruel.'

'What other choice do I have?'

'Oh God,' I hesitated, knowing that what I was about to do might let Kara off the hook and be one of the most generous gestures known to womankind but would also simultaneously be a nightmare for me and Ed. 'There is just one more option.'

'Make it a good one,' Kara pleaded.

'You could prevail upon your very best friend to look after your baby for a further two nights. And owe her more favours than you can ever imagine possible. You may even owe her a great big present from Galeries Lafayette. A handbag-shaped one. Expensive.'

'Heidi, are you saying what I think you're saying?'

I took a deep breath. 'I'm saying you could ask me and Ed to babysit for the whole weekend.'

'Are you kidding?'

'I'm probably going mad, but I don't think I'm kidding. What do you think?'

'I think that would save my life. You know that would save my life right now, don't you? It would be the kindest, most wonderful thing you could ever do for me. Ever.'

'There's one very big condition.'

'What?'

'What do you think? You've got to tell him, Kara. You've got to tell him that you've got a child. You've got to tell him tonight. I still can't believe you got on a fucking train to Paris without telling him about your son. You are insane. You know that? You're a bloody unfit mother. When will you be back?'

'Sunday night. About eight o'clock.'

'Then I'll see you on Sunday night. With Duncan. So that I can be sure he really knows all about your darling son. That's my only condition.'

'Oh Heidi, I love you. I love you more than you will ever know.'

'And you love your son, too. So make sure you say so.'

'I will. I will. I promise. By the time I get back to London everything will be sorted out.'

She cut out again. This time she didn't call back.

I put down the phone with a little warm glow.

'Has he given her the elbow?' Ed asked when I walked back into the sitting room. 'What kind of idiot is your best friend? Bit of a bloody shock, planning a weekend away only to find out that the girl you're out to impress needs notice to arrange a babysitter.'

'She doesn't,' I said simply.

'What?'

'She doesn't need to arrange a babysitter. I told her we would look after Forester until she comes back.'

'*What?*'

'It's only till Sunday, Ed. Besides, you're always saying it's good practice, looking after other people's kids.'

I sank down onto the sofa next to him and nibbled at his neck. Ordinarily, this would have melted my huge hunk of a fiancé in a second, but this time he shifted away from me and stabbed irritably at the buttons on the remote control.

'Practice for what? Practice at being a bloody mug? You said we'd babysit for the whole fucking weekend? I don't believe it.'

'What else was I supposed to do?'

'I don't know. Tell her to be here at one o'clock like she said she would when we agreed to babysit for tonight. It's her problem she hasn't told this bloke about Forester, Heidi, not yours.'

'Look, I couldn't ask her to do that. She was already on the train.'

'Then phone the bloody police, have them stop the train and bring her back in handcuffs.'

'She'll make up for it. You know she will. And Forester is no trouble at all. He sleeps nearly all the time.'

Ed just looked at me and pulled the lid off another bottle of beer.

'We'll get through it,' I added.

'What's all this "we", Heidi? I'm assuming you mean "we" as in you and I. You seem to have forgotten that the past three times "we" have been babysitters for Kara, you haven't actually been anywhere near the baby at all. You just shove the cot in the spare room and shout for me every time you think you hear him crying. I'm the one who does all the feeds.'

'You like giving him his bottle.'

'. . . changes all the nappies.'

'You've only had to change his nappy three times.'

'Which is three hundred per cent more practice at nappy-changing than you've had. In your entire life,' he added.

'Okay,' I said. 'I admit I haven't exactly been hands-on, but I'll do my share this time. I promise I will. I'm sorry I offered your services without asking. I'll never do that again. But it's just for a weekend.'

'This is going to be a very long weekend,' said Ed.

27

Ed would soon come round to the idea, I told myself. It wasn't as though we had anything planned for the weekend. Having Forester around was hardly going to disrupt our busy social lives.

Besides, it was going to be a piece of cake. Ed and I had coped really well the three times we had been babysitters. Once again Kara had practically given us a timetable for her son and so far that evening he was sticking to it far more reliably than any of the British train companies stuck to theirs. He slept when she said he would, woke when she said he would, ate, burped and pooed exactly as per the instructions. He was used to me and Ed by now – especially Ed – and, I figured, he was still much too young to be unduly bothered if he didn't see his mother for forty-eight hours instead of the five-hour absence originally planned, despite Ed's gloomy prognosis that this single weekend of maternal abandonment would see Forester in therapy in twenty years' time.

Added to that, I think I was still a little bit high on my own fabulousness. How fantastic a friend was I? I had saved the day for my best pal and that made me feel very good indeed.

It was a shame that altruistic high didn't seem to have rubbed off on Ed, who maintained, loudly and often, that Kara was a stupid, irresponsible moral mess of a woman who wasn't fit to be back in the dating pool if she couldn't master the basic importance of being honest about such crucial facts as *having a baby* at such an early stage.

'Kara has been misrepresenting herself as someone who is free to go off and weekend in Paris on a whim. Well, she's not. She's the mother of a six-month-old baby. She's also a manipulator and a liar. She is basically every man's worst nightmare,' Ed concluded.

'That's a bit harsh. Who's to say we wouldn't have done exactly the same thing under the circumstances?'

Ed just snorted at that.

'Well,' I muttered, in an attempt to make things more cordial. 'Obviously, you wouldn't have done. And neither would I.'

'You know I'm playing rugby in Bristol tomorrow, don't you?' he said then.

'Yes,' I said. 'You told me three weeks ago. But it's not an important game, is it?'

'Every game's important. That's what being in a team is all about.'

'Scotty is always missing matches,' I pointed out.

'Scotty could soon find himself on the reserves.'

'But what about the baby?'

'What about him?'

'We're supposed to be looking after him.'

'There's that mythical "we" again.'

'You're actually still thinking of going to Bristol, aren't you?'

'You want me to let the lads down just because you volunteered us as unpaid slaves?'

'I'm sorry, Ed,' I said, for what felt like the hundredth time. 'I'll tell Kara she owes you, too. I'll get her to pick up a nice bottle of wine or something for you and I'll make it clear that we're never going to do this again. It's just this one time. I shouldn't have volunteered on your behalf but—'

'I don't want a bottle of wine. I just want you to see that your best friend is a selfish flake. Always has been. And as for you—'

'Don't take it out on me. I was just trying to be a good friend. The lads will understand.'

'Heidi, I'm not cancelling my match.'

'You're going to Bristol?'

'Of course I'm going to Bristol. As of ten o'clock tomorrow morning, you're on your own.'

'You don't really mean that,' I said.

'Oh, but I do.'

He was just showing off, I told myself. Ed's blustering insistence that he would be playing rugby the following afternoon, whether or not we were supposed to be babysitting, was the human equivalent of a male gorilla beating his chest. He just wanted to scare me into contrition. Or, more likely, into giving him an apologetic blow-job.

In all the time we'd been together, Ed had never sustained a frosty mood with me for very long. First thing in the morning he would call Richard, the club captain, and tell him he had to find a substitute. There was no way Ed would really go to Bristol and leave me home alone with a six-month-old baby. Especially since he thought so little of my baby-wrangling abilities. With that certainty in my heart, I let Ed rumble on about responsibility and commitment all the way over to Kara's house, where I let us in with the spare key and we gathered together all the things we thought Forester would need for a weekend with his substitute parents. More nappies. Hundreds of nappies. Clothes. A couple of teddy bears.

Kara's bedroom bore the signs of frantic packing. Three evening dresses still lay out on the bed where she must have flung them while she picked her clothes for the weekend. By a process of deduction I worked out that she'd taken one I always coveted. I felt a little pang of jealousy at the thought of her out there in France, embarking on her passionate affair.

'So she said she thought they were just going to Paris for the evening?' Ed tutted when he saw the mess. 'She knew damn well she was going to be away all weekend. Where is her bloody sense of responsibility? If she wasn't your best friend, I would call the social services.' He was holding Forester as he said this, and cuddled the baby more closely to him as though just the thought of the little poppet being taken into care had given him the chills. Ed loved Forester. That much was plain. I took it as another sign that by morning his rage would have thawed and I would not be left to babysit alone.

He was keeping up the grumpiness for a record duration though.

When it was time to go to bed, I carried Forester into our bedroom and placed him on his changing mat on the floor on my side of the room while I set up his travelling cot. At least, while I tried to set up the travelling cot. I couldn't quite understand how something that should basically resemble a netted cube seemed to have quite so many sides that didn't obviously fit together.

'What are you doing?' Ed asked when he had finished in the bathroom.

'I'm trying to put the cot up.'

'Well, that's part of something else entirely.' Ed discarded the rogue piece that had been foxing me and made swift work of the assembly. 'Why is the cot in here anyway?'

'Forester has to sleep in here, in case he wakes up. I won't be able to hear him if he's in the other room.'

'But I'll be able to hear him if he's in here,' said Ed.

'So?'

'So, you're the one who volunteered to cover the night-feeds, not me. My babysitting shift finishes at midnight as per my original agreement with your friend. I don't see why I should have to wake up when he cries too.'

'Don't be an arse, Ed.' I handed him some baby blankets,

which he neatly folded over Forester's mattress with hospital corners that would have made his mother proud. 'I've already said I'm going to get up. You'll sleep through it. You can sleep through anything.'

That was true. Ed had slept through a minor earthquake on a holiday to San Francisco we'd taken at the beginning of our relationship. He had been quite pissed off about it at the time and actually complained I hadn't woken him up to fully experience what might have been the only earthquake he'd ever get to participate in.

'Well, if you're going to get up when he cries, I'll sleep in the spare room,' he announced now.

'What?'

'I think it's best. That way one of us will be able to get some sleep. I've had a difficult week.'

'And I haven't?'

'Your best friend. Her baby. Your responsibility.'

I was beginning to get tired of that particular mantra.

'Your future wife. Her best friend's baby. Your husbandly duty to help out,' I countered.

'I am.'

With incredible delicacy, Ed lifted Forester up from the changing mat without waking him and laid him back down inside the cot. That done, Ed pulled a spare blanket for himself out of the top of the wardrobe and took his special foam-filled neck-ache pillow from our bed.

'Oh, Ed. Don't sleep in the spare room,' I pleaded. 'You're being ridiculous.'

'I'll see you in the morning,' he insisted.

He tripped over Forester's changing bag on the way out.

'Shit.'

And woke Forester up.

'Waaaah!'

'Ed,' I groaned.

'For God's sake!' He stormed on to the spare bedroom without looking back.

I jiggled the sides of Forester's cot in an attempt to convince him that it really wasn't worth keeping his eyes open to see me and Ed row. It didn't work.

Seconds later Ed reappeared at the bedroom door and tutted just like his mother when he saw what I was doing.

'Just make me a cup of hot chocolate,' he barked before he took over the baby. I didn't argue with him. I was only too happy to swap childcare for kitchen duty. Fifteen more minutes of Ed grumbling was a price worth paying if it meant that all three of us got to sleep before dawn. And by the time I finished making Ed's drink – slowly, I admit it – Forester was ready for bed again. Ed lay him down on his back once more, making sure his feet were right at the bottom of the cot and the blankets were tightly tucked in so that they couldn't ride up over his face during the night.

'How did you know he has to sleep like that?' I asked in wonder.

'Your best friend told us. Remember?'

'I don't.'

'I think you were too busy panicking to pay attention at the time.'

'Probably.' I nodded in embarrassed agreement. 'Thank you,' I said.

'I'm doing this for the baby,' said Ed. 'Not you. I'll see you in the morning.'

Then he kissed me perfunctorily on the forehead and went off to sleep on his own exactly as he'd threatened.

So, I was to share my bedroom with Forester alone that night. He didn't stir again but I found it impossible to fall asleep. Instead, I lay with my eyes wide open, straining to hear the slightest noise from his cot, praying that he wouldn't wake up and, at the same time, worrying that he had stopped breathing instead.

I would have felt much better if Ed were by my side, I knew. Then I could have nudged him in the ribs and said, 'Listen, can you hear that noise?' when I couldn't hear the baby sounds I wanted. He would have reassured me that everything was completely as it should be.

How did new mothers ever get any sleep? Between the noise and the worry, I couldn't see how it would be possible. Not alone. Every couple of silent minutes I had to get up and stare into the cot until I had convinced myself that Forester's tiny chest was still rising and falling.

After about an hour, I decided that the only thing was to call a truce and demand that Ed come back to his side of our big double bed. I was ready to promise anything just to be able to share the responsibility of the vigil I had taken on. Blow-jobs were the least of it. I would wax the car. I would even wash his rugby kit. I tiptoed out onto the landing, careful not to rouse Forester as I went.

'Ed.' I knocked tentatively at the spare room door. 'Ed? Are you awake?'

The only response was a snore.

'Ed?' I knocked a little more loudly in case he was just pretending to be asleep because he was still angry.

Another snore.

'Ed?'

I pushed open the door. Ed was on his back, sheets flung all over the place, mouth wide open, and definitely out for the count. I decided I had better let this particular sleeping bulldog lie.

So Ed and Forester slept on and I continued my vigil over the pair of them alone.

That night passed like the symbolic passing of twelve hours in a single movie scene. Having given up on sleeping altogether, I sat in the chair by the bedroom window, tired eyes on Forester in his cot, only the street outside changing as the movie cut from hour to hour.

At the darkest moment, drunken revellers on their way back from the pub were replaced by the urban fox whose patrol included our dustbin. The fox was chased away by the milk van, delivering milk to the only two houses in our street who didn't buy their semi-skimmed from the mini-supermarket at the garage. Pensioners both. The milk round was literally dying out. The milk van was followed by the post van. No post for us that day. Then an early morning jogger with his excited dog. A man dressed in a London Underground uniform headed out for the first Saturday shift. I saw them all. If I slept at all that night, it was for mere seconds.

At six thirty a.m., I heard Ed bumbling across the landing to the bathroom, just as Forester awoke with a squeak of surprise.

28

'Did you sleep okay?' I asked Ed over breakfast.

'Great, thanks,' he said, quite sincerely. 'And you?'

I just looked at him over the top of my tea-cup, imagining my raised eyebrows would say it all. Had he deliberately missed the sarcasm in my question?

'That fox knocked over our dustbin again,' I told him. 'I saw him do it this time. So there's no need to kill next door's cat after all.'

'There's still every need to kill next door's cat,' said Ed, without looking up from his paper.

'What are we going to do today?' I asked him brightly as he turned straight from the headlines to the sport pages. I had decided that the best approach to the rest of the weekend was to assume that Ed would be around to help me.

'Well, I don't know what you're going to be doing but I'm driving to Bristol, like I told you. We're playing the Spartans at one.'

'So you're still going?'

'Mmm-hmm.'

I had assumed wrong. A pause.

'You're joking.'

Ed glanced up and to the side as though checking his plans for the day with a voice from on high. 'Nope.' He shook his head. 'I don't think I am.'

'I see.'

Ed put down his newspaper and looked at me at last. 'Look,

Heidi. I told you I was going to be in Bristol this afternoon three weeks ago. It's written on the calendar in big red letters.'

'But I didn't know we'd have Forester with us for the whole weekend then. I didn't get any sleep at all.'

'I didn't really get all that much myself. The walls in this place aren't that thick, you know. I could hear you stumbling about all night.'

'Then you're probably too tired to play rugby anyway,' I suggested.

'Heidi,' Ed sighed, 'I'm playing.'

I switched from belligerent to pleading. 'I'm asking you to miss one match, Ed. One match in a lifetime.'

'Thin end of the wedge,' said Ed.

'You're a selfish, thoughtless bastard,' I told my fiancé. 'And ugly. Even with your eyebrows.'

Ed shrugged his shoulders. Even as I railed at him, he was putting down his paper and unfurling the changing mat on the kitchen floor. He lifted Forester out of his seat and began unbuttoning his baby-gro with the intention of changing his nappy. 'I bet Zach wouldn't play rugby if Sophie wanted him to stay at home,' I continued. 'I bet even Scotty would cancel a game if Clare had some kind of emergency. Jack is always crying off to stay home with the triplets.'

'Exactly. With the *triplets*.'

We both wrinkled our noses at the smell that assailed us when Ed took Forester's nappy off.

'Hand me the wet wipes.'

'Not until you tell me you're not going to Bristol,' I said, pinching my nostrils with my fingers.

Forester grabbed both sets of his own toes and started trying to fit them in his mouth, giving us a wonderful view of his extremely pooey bottom.

'Oh, for God's sake. Excuse me.' Ed leaned across me for the wipes.

'Is this what it's going to be like if we have kids?' I asked, still holding onto my nose as he cleaned the baby's bum with two deft wipes. 'One sleepless night and you have to go and relax with your friends? What am I supposed to do? I spent the night sitting up with him.'

'You didn't have to. You could have slept. Forester did.'

'I couldn't sleep. What if he had died? He was breathing really quietly. I kept having to check he was still alive. I really need to relax.'

'Heidi,' Ed sat back on his heels, wet wipe still in hand, 'this isn't my baby. Of course I wouldn't leave you to look after *our* baby on your own if you needed me. But you've had one sleepless night. Big deal. How many sleepless nights do you think I've had since I opened the surgery?'

'I don't know. How many sleepless nights have you really had lately? You always seem to be snoring to me. I listened to you snore all bloody night last night. No sleep, my arse.'

'Would you really rather we had both been awake?'

'I can't believe you're actually going to go to Bristol.'

'What do you want me to do? Let the lads down?'

'Or let me down? Well,' I sneered, 'I suppose there are fourteen of them. Majority rules.'

'It's for *half a day*.' Ed's voice came as close as it ever came to shouting. 'You can cope on your own for a few hours, can't you? I've got to go. I said I'd be at Scotty's for half ten. The baby's changed – you just need to give him a bottle. I'll put it in the microwave for you right now and I'll tidy up the rubbish on my way out. And I'll be back before you know it.' He said this last almost tenderly. Then he wrapped the wet-wipe and the used nappy inside a peach-coloured disposal bag that arguably smelled worse than its contents and started fastening Forester's poppers back up. 'It's so easy, even a girl can do it. Isn't that what Kara's always saying?'

'Don't do this to me, Ed.' Angry hadn't worked. Appeasing

hadn't worked. The only approach left to try was 'pathetic'. 'I'm scared.'

'Of what? Of this little blighter?' Ed picked Forester up and held him out towards me. Forester kicked his legs in delight as Ed held him in the air and I hesitated to take over. 'Come on, Heidi. Do me a favour. Take the baby. I've got to go.'

Forester let out a little squeal of joy.

I allowed the handover, but not before Ed threatened to drop the baby if I didn't. As he found himself in my hands, Forester's face instantly darkened and he looked back over his shoulder towards Ed in what could only be described as anguish. Him and me both.

'I'll see you tonight.'

Ed tried to kiss me. I turned my face away in anger.

'Fine,' he said. 'I'll give you a call later on.'

'Don't bother,' I snarled.

'I'll call you later,' he insisted. 'Bye, Forester.' He blew a raspberry against the back of Forester's chubby neck. Forester twisted in my arms and tried to reach out for Ed as he walked away. I heard Ed use the bathroom then head out of the house without looking in on us again. I remained in the same spot, staring at the kitchen door in disbelief.

As I heard the front door close behind Ed and watched the top of his head as he bounced off down the road, I finally shouted after him, 'You're supposed to be the one who likes children. Maybe I don't even want them at all!'

29

I felt shaky after Ed went out that morning. For quite a while I just stood there like a child, as though by not moving I could somehow reverse time so that Ed would come hurtling backwards through the door and change his mind about the rugby.

What a time to have a row. And what a bloody failure it had been; we hadn't really sorted anything out. I'd hurled a few verbal missiles and Ed hadn't bothered to duck them. Nothing had been talked through and resolved using the caring language suggested by all those bloody relationship counsellors who came to spout their wisdom on *Let's Talk London*. Instead, Ed and I had ended up having the kind of half-hearted spat that would haunt me for ever if he got caught in some motorway pile-up on the way back from Bristol and didn't come home that night.

With Forester still in my arms, I looked at a photo of Ed, in more handsome times, stuck to the fridge door with a Big Apple fridge magnet from New York, and felt a momentary twinge of shame. But that was soon gone when Forester gave a shriek of rage. Right in my ear.

'Believe me, I wish he'd taken you with him too,' I assured my best friend's son.

Once again I was furious that Ed would walk out like that. Sure, he almost certainly had told me weeks before that he would be spending that afternoon driving to the match with Scotty, but that was also weeks before Kara fucked off to Paris and left me holding the baby. Circumstances had changed, big time. Would Ed still have gone to watch the match if, rather than being stuck with Forester, I had come down with some hideous virus that kept me pinned to the sofa? Would he have been happy to see me sod off to the shops if he had so much as a sniffle? No way. I had no doubt that had the need for company and support been reversed, I would have spent my Saturday afternoon on Lemsip duty. When Ed got a cold I had to act as though he had meningitis. Once he had been such a big baby while recovering from a bout of the flu, I suggested he might like to write his will while he could still hold a pen.

There was the rub. Ed was a man. A sniffle equals tuberculosis for most men. He simply didn't see things the same way as I did. As far as he was concerned, by carrying on regardless of the sudden change to our plans, he wasn't leaving me to anything I couldn't handle on my own. After all, Kara looked after Forester on her own twenty-four seven. And if Kara could manage it – Kara, who had hardly had to pick up after herself her entire life – then surely a practical old plodder like me could manage five or so hours alone in the company of a six-month-old baby. Let's face it, if Ed and I ever had children of our own, he was hardly going to stop wanting to watch the rugby.

I could do this, I told myself. I could look after a baby on my own. Thousands of women raised children alone. Women who couldn't write a cheque or change a light bulb or produce a live radio show without assistance. I could do all of those things without any help from anyone with gonads. I could damn well give a baby a bottle and change a nappy. If I really had to. What was the longest you could reasonably expect a baby to wear a wet nappy for, I wondered? Didn't these modern nappies wick all the moisture away from their bums anyway? The TV ads were always claiming how comfortable modern nappies were. Could you safely leave a baby in the same nappy for five hours?

'If you get diarrhoea I am just going to put you outside until your mother comes to fetch you,' I warned Forester.

I didn't mean that, of course. I was going to look after Forester just as well as Kara or Ed ever could. I just had to get up and get on with it.

The trick was not to let Forester impose too much change on my life. I was sure I had heard that somewhere. My observations of the women I knew who had given birth seemed to show that there were two distinct types of new mother: there were those who went into self-imposed purdah at the birth of the first child, never venturing more than ten metres from the perpetually whirring bottle steriliser, brain wiped of all conversational material but the rights and wrongs of the MMR vaccine. And then there were those who simply treated baby like a slightly cumbersome new accessory, albeit, one hoped, an accessory as precious as a five-thousand-pound ostrich-skin holdall from Prada (which was the most expensive accessory I'd ever seen). Kara was, for the most part, one of the latter class of mothers and that was the kind of mother I was going to pretend to be.

Forester would fit into my life, not vice versa.

I could do this.

Ed had been gone for half an hour already and I still hadn't moved out of the kitchen.

'Right,' I said as though I meant business. 'You and I are going to start our day.'

I needed to go into town. I was going to go into town. And Forester was coming with me.

'We're going on a little shopping spree,' I told him. 'Don't look so excited.'

I stepped out of the kitchen and managed not to panic when I caught sight of the folded pram in the hallway. I briefly cursed Ed for not having unfolded it before he left, but then I remembered my new approach: I was a woman who could deal with baby accoutrements. No folding pram was going to phase me.

In any case, there was a major hurdle to jump before I even got to the pram: to get Forester dressed. And myself.

Outside, a sugar-dusting of frost still decorated the cars parked on the shady side of the street. One thing I had noticed was that Kara was obsessed with Forester's temperature. Letting your baby get too hot or cold was one of the worst things you could do, apparently. So I decided I didn't need to take Forester's baby-gro off before I put him in the bright red all-in-one padded jumpsuit Ed had picked out of Forester's wardrobe the previous night. You can't imagine what a relief it was to only have to consider putting something on rather than taking something off and then replacing it. It was one fewer thing with the potential to go wrong.

I picked Forester's jumpsuit out of his overnight bag and was fairly strutting as I got into the bedroom to choose my own outfit.

'Shall I wear red too?' I asked him, picking out one of my favourite sweaters. I laid it alongside the jumpsuit on the bed. If Forester was going to be my accessory for the day, it was important that we didn't clash, at the very least.

Forester seemed slightly less impressed by the matching ensembles I picked out for us. His bottom lip showed a dangerous hint of wobble.

'Just distract him,' was something Kara had said to me many times, forcing him upon me while she searched in her bag for her credit card, or fixed her hair or did something else that required both hands. I whirled Forester around in front of the mirror then carried him up close to it.

'Who's that baby?' I asked, pointing at his reflection's nose.

Forester failed the basic reflection recognition test – something I was pretty certain most chimpanzees can pass by the age of six months – but I seemed to have averted a grizzle. Forester stared at my mouth instead. Perhaps it was the funny voice I'd been putting on. I tried it again. French this time.

'Ooo's zat babee?'

Forester gave me a grudging smile.

I gave my reflection a half-smile of relief too. And then I noticed that I didn't look half as uncomfortable as I felt right then. I straightened up and stood side on to the mirror, with Forester riding high in my arms. Not bad at all. The girl in the mirror looked as though she was always holding babies. Couldn't get enough of them. Madonna and child. Twenty-first century. Chiswick. I imagined an avant-garde photographer trying to recreate a classic painting of the Renaissance using me and Forester as his models.

And then Forester poked me in the eye with his little chubby finger.

'Ow!'

I gave up posing and got back to the business of getting dressed. It would be nice to get out of the house before lunchtime. But I had reckoned without the fact that the padded jumpsuit had no immediately obvious opening and that Forester, who was by now lying on his back in the middle of the big double bed, was not about to offer his cooperation.

Dressing Forester Knight was like dressing an octopus. Legs into the jumpsuit first seemed the best way to start, but every time I touched one of Forester's chubby feet and tried to direct it into a leg-hole, he evaded my grasp and instead stuck that foot in his mouth. He did that five times, and each time he got his toes within sucking range, he gave me a gummy smile as if to say, 'foiled again'.

'Please let me dress you,' I begged him. 'We can't go outside if you haven't got your suit on.'

I resorted to holding his little ankles a little more firmly, with the result that Forester stiffened dramatically against my grasp. Now I didn't think I would be able to get his legs into the jumpsuit without breaking them.

I suddenly realised why mothers always seem to wipe their babies' faces so roughly. You only get one pass at it. As soon as a baby figures out what you're trying to do, the game is up and they will do everything they can to avoid you. Just as Forester was doing right now. Even as I got one leg into the jumpsuit, Forester flipped over onto his belly. I flipped him onto his back. In all the times I'd watched Kara and Ed dress him, Forester had never been quite so energetic. Now he was like a fish freshly hauled out of the water, hurling himself from side to side until I was ready to throw him and myself back into a river. But then I noticed the cunning popper system that would allow me to open the suit out, drop Forester into the middle of it, and pop the damn thing shut again around him.

'Thank God.'

It took me fifteen minutes to get him into that jumpsuit.

'You better not mess your nappy,' I told him when the last popper was done up. 'Because this isn't coming off till tea-time.'

I still had to dress myself.

I put Forester down on his back on the bed while I changed out of my pyjamas. I could see him behind me, reflected in the mirrored door of the wardrobe, using kung-fu moves against an invisible assailant. And then it struck me that if I could see him, then he could see me too. It didn't seem appropriate to be naked around my best friend's baby, so I closed the wardrobe door and changed with my back towards him.

I had that red polo-necked sweater with its particularly tight neck-hole stuck halfway over my head when I heard the thud.

I whirled round, jumper still half on my head like a nun's red wimple.

Forester was not on the bed.

He was in the gap between the bed and the cot.

On the floor.

Oh my God. I'd killed my best friend's baby!

I flew across the room to where Forester now lay. He beamed up at me and waved his arms and legs like a starfish. Not dead. Not paralysed. Not even all that surprised, by the look of him. I was the only one having a near-death experience.

I picked him up and sat down on the edge of the bed until I could breathe again. Forester stuck his fingers in my nose. It was okay. He was fine. But the reality of having to watch a baby the whole time had been made abundantly clear. In less than thirty, maybe even twenty seconds he had wriggled his way from the centre of a king-size double and executed a death-defying belly-flop onto the carpet.

I managed to finish dressing while keeping a hand or toe on Forester at all times. Yes, at one point, I held him still on the floor with my foot while I used both hands to zip up my trousers. But I definitely couldn't leave him on the floor while I went to take a leak. My beautiful home was a baby death-trap. There were sockets for tiny fingers to go into. Splinters from the floorboards. God knew what he might catch from the dirt underneath the bed.

There was nothing for it but to take him with me. I sat on the porcelain with Forester on my lap. So much for worrying that he would have to see me naked. Now he would have to see me pee. He didn't seem too bothered. He laughed and reached out towards the basin. I handed him the electric toothbrush to keep him occupied. And I covered his ears. The whole experience was making me feel incredibly shy. So shy that it took me an age to squeeze anything out, even though I had been absolutely busting.

And then I had to get up and pull my knickers up while still holding onto him. The bathroom floor was much too hard for Forester's little knees. Not to mention too unhygienic – neither

Ed nor I were particularly houseproud. I got up from the seat and tried a plié to get close enough to my knickers and jeans to haul them up again. They got stuck halfway up my thighs. Forester meanwhile happily waved the toothbrush like a conducting baton. And just as I managed to tug my trousers up again and was about to flush, Forester let the toothbrush fly. Straight into the pan.

'Shit.'

Not literally, thank God.

I fished the toothbrush out again and rinsed it off. It was Ed's.

For just a moment, I considered putting it back on the shelf.

'Another thing on our shopping list,' I told Forester instead, consigning the brush to the dustbin.

Time elapsed since we started to get ready for our jaunt? Forty-five minutes and counting.

Now I just had to open out that pushchair.

I'd seen Kara do it a hundred times. It was just a matter of pulling the handles away from each other and pushing down on that crossover bit at the back until it clicked into place. Easy. But I wasn't taking any chances. First I had to build Forester a fortress out of cushions from the sofa, where he could play safely should the pushchair erection take me longer than I anticipated.

It didn't. However, getting Forester into the pushchair did.

It was a reprise of our game with the jumpsuit – a game that Forester was intent on winning. Every time I managed to get one of his arms into the harness, the other one popped free. Did he really need the harness? I wondered. We could get to the shops and back without Forester falling out of his pram, surely? But even as I weighed up the risks he leaned a little too far forward – he still wasn't that practised at sitting up straight – and I had a vision of him doing the same while we waited to cross a road and pitching himself head-first into the traffic.

He had to have those straps on.

And he did, just as the pushchair folded up like a concertina with Forester still inside it.

'Oh my God.' I wrenched the thing back open. I clearly hadn't fully locked the pushchair in its open position.

'Are you all right?' I asked him, as if he could have answered me.

He merely looked a little surprised.

I hauled him out and started the process again.

One step forward and eight steps back. I had never appreciated how many steps there were to my front door.

When eventually I had Forester strapped into a safe and stable pushchair, I found myself standing at the top of those steps like a mountaineer pondering the assent of K2. Not only were there eight steps, those steps were tall and narrow. I remembered why Ed never let Kara carry the pushchair down on her own, but walked backwards down them in front of her, holding the front of the pushchair up so that Forester looked like a little Indian prince held aloft by his manservants. Now Ed wasn't there. And neither was Kara.

Not for the first time since I'd started this adventure, I wondered whether the sensible thing was to quit. Ed had been gone for almost two hours. He would be home again in another four. If I missed one Saturday afternoon at the shops it was hardly a tragedy. Dropping Forester down the steps on the other hand . . .

But I couldn't stay in all afternoon. That morning, Ed and I had used the last of the milk. Our cupboards were bare but for a couple of packets of pasta. If I stayed in, I would have to dine on plain penne pasta with nothing but olive oil to make it palatable. I'd already wasted half my morning getting Forester dressed to go outside. I was going to Marks and Spencer's Simply Food.

I couldn't carry Forester *and* his pushchair down those steps, but I could certainly carry them separately. So I unstrapped the baby one final time, laid him down on the rug in the hallway with my handbag by his side to amuse him and carried the pushchair down into the street. I allowed myself a moment of pride in my achievement and ingenuity, which was interrupted by the door slamming shut.

The fire brigade were there in less three minutes. I'll be eternally grateful to the woman in the next street who set fire to her kitchen with her chip pan at eleven that morning so that the firemen were close enough to save Forester's life. And mine.

They made quick work of the heavy-duty locks that Ed had promised me would make our lives so much safer. We opened the door just in time to see Forester cough up a bright pink hairball. He'd got into my handbag and eaten half a gonk keyring.

'No harm done,' said the smiley-faced chief as he checked Forester's breathing passages for fluff.

Not to Forester perhaps. I had lost years off my life, I was sure.

'Baby brain,' the fireman commented.

'What?'

'Baby brain.' He tapped me on the head. 'My girlfriend started forgetting things the moment she got pregnant.' He obviously thought I was Forester's mother. 'Though she never manages to forget the things she wants to give me grief for when I get back at night. I'll wait here with the baby, if you like,' he added. 'While you make sure you've got *everything* you need for the day.'

I would have commented that he really didn't need to talk to me like an imbecile but he had just got me back into my house and right then he was arranging the straps that held Forester into his pushchair. Properly.

'Thanks for your help,' I said meekly when I had retrieved my handbag and showed him my front-door keys to prove that I definitely had them this time.

'That's all right,' he said. 'You've got a lovely nipper. All right, gorgeous?'

Forester bestowed another big smile.

30

When the firemen were back in their engine and off on their next job, I found myself simultaneously proud to accept the compliments on behalf of Forester and faintly annoyed that the officer hadn't questioned whether I was Forester's mother. Surely I didn't look old enough? But of course I did. I was reminded of a girl in my class at school who had found herself pregnant at fifteen. Her son would be fifteen himself by now so I was definitely old enough to be pushing a pram full of six-month-old. It didn't necessarily mean the fireman thought I looked any older than twenty-five.

Nevertheless, I spent an inordinate amount of time checking myself out in shop windows as I walked that morning. If I had a baby of my own, would I be a yummy mummy or just plain mumsy?

People definitely reacted to me in a very different way while I was pushing Forester's pram. On a good day, I would usually get a whistle or two from the builders who were permanently encamped in our neighbourhood improving and extending the little houses that had been built for railway workers and now housed doctors, producers and lawyers who could barely afford their vast mortgages. That morning they didn't even look up from the *Sun*. That day, different people smiled at me. Specifically women. Women walking alone smiled openly. Women walking with boy-friends or husbands gave me secretive smirks and hugged their other halves tighter. Women walking with their prams nodded and beamed.

We exchanged smiles of understanding. One woman whose baby was mewling like a cat with its tail stuck in a mousetrap rolled her eyes at me in hope of sympathy. I gave her a sympathetic nod in return.

It was as though I had been given a day pass to another world, a world where people were friendly. The trauma of simply getting out of the house was forgotten as I pushed Forester past a row of adoring pensioners at a bus stop.

'Isn't he lovely?' an old lady cooed.

'Haven't you dressed him up nice?' said another.

'Thank you,' I said serenely. Yes, that's how I found I was feeling. Serene.

And then the sun came out, melting the last of the frost on the cars. For the first time that year it felt as though spring might really be just around the corner. I had stepped out in my all-weather puffa jacket but was actually starting to feel a bit hot. I checked Forester's jumpsuit. He was looking a little pink too so I tugged down the zip to give him some air. Then I checked my watch and realised that I had been walking for so long I had completely missed Forester's lunchtime, and my own.

I chose a café that had so many prams parked outside it, you might have mistaken the place for a baby-equipment supplier. But I took it as a signal that this place was baby-friendly in the extreme, the kind of place where you could ask them to warm up a pot of baby goo while you sipped a cappuccino and imagined you were really in Italy, where apparently everyone loves kids. Except the English tourists.

A very Italian-looking man noticed that I was struggling to open the door while hanging on to Forester's pram and leapt up to assist me. His smile was so disarmingly lovely that I felt the urge to tell him that Forester wasn't my baby. But then he sat back down next to the highchair containing his own baby and directed that lovely smile back towards his other half, who was spooning something snot-coloured but organic into the infant's mouth. There was yuck-spooning in progress at just about every table in the room.

So I was disappointed when the waitress hardly cracked a smile as she took Forester's bottle and jar of free-range chicken and pesticide-free carrots from me.

'Excuse me!' a woman called from the other side of the room. 'You've brought me the wrong bottle. Mine has the blue top. Tommee Tippee.'

The waitress rolled her eyes and said to her colleague, 'I'll Tommee Tippee the damn thing over her head.'

She was definitely not a mother herself. She didn't understand.

I unstrapped Forester from his pushchair and lifted him onto my knee. He was being very good and had clearly enjoyed the walk. In fact, he gave me the kind of goo-goo gaze he normally reserved for Ed.

I felt more proud than I had done when *Let's Talk London* won a national broadcasters' award.

'See?' I told him. 'We can have a lovely Saturday lunchtime in a chi-chi little café just like your mum is in Paris.'

The waitress returned with my cappuccino, a sandwich and the baby gunk.

Tommee Tippee mother watched in envy as Forester obediently opened his mouth for every spoonful and finished the entire jar with the very minimum of mess. He didn't even protest as I dabbed away a single spot on his chin.

'He's a very good eater,' Mrs Tippee commented as she passed me.

'It's just a matter of being patient,' I said.

I even got away without having to strap Forester back into his pushchair again. The waitress returned with my change just as I was sitting Forester down and the gorgeous Italian-looking guy said, 'Let me,' and did the honours while I put my change back in my purse.

'Beautiful baby,' said the Italian guy's wife. 'So well behaved.'

'I think they're relaxed when we're relaxed,' I told her.

What a fraud.

After that, to the park. I wheeled Forester to the playground where Kara and I had encountered Julia and her cracked nipples all those weeks ago. We stopped and watched the older children swinging, sliding, starting fights. One little boy who hadn't long learned to walk came barrelling towards the railings and, unable to stop himself, smacked headlong into the bars. I was the nearest adult and set him back on his feet. I rubbed at the sore spot on his forehead.

'Naughty bars,' I said.

The little boy looked at me and nodded.

'Thank you,' his mother said to me.

'I wish I'd managed to get between him and the fence,' I said.

'It's a nightmare when they start walking,' the mother sighed. 'They're so much more portable at that age.' She smiled at Forester. 'First one?'

'Yes,' I said.

'You got your figure back quickly.'

'Thanks.'

'Takes for ever to tighten up round the tum though, doesn't it?' She jerked her head towards my midriff. 'There's a good legs, bums and tums class at the gym I go to. I'll give you the times if you like.'

I had been enjoying the fantasy that I looked as though I could be Forester's mother up until that point, but now I made a note to renew my gym membership.

As I watched a genuine mum give her one-year-old's bottom the squelch test, I decided it was time to go home. Forester wasn't making a fuss but he almost certainly needed changing too.

And it wouldn't be long before Ed got back from Bristol. I hoped.

31

Despite the fact that I had just learned I had a mother's midriff, I left the park on such a big fluffy cloud of domestic peace that I decided that when Ed came back that evening, I would be the first to apologise. More than that, I would tell him I understood why he had been so annoyed that I had assumed my best friend's antics should disrupt his long-held plans. In fact, I was feeling so good I decided I would cook for him.

Well, I wasn't exactly going to be cooking. I've never been very good. But I bought a raft of ingredients from Marks and Sparks that I thought would go well together. A young girl let me jump ahead of her in the queue because I was pushing a pram.

Forester and I got home without incident and this time I knew exactly how to handle the steps. First I unstrapped Forester and carried him up to the house, then I put the front door on the latch *and* wedged it open with a carrier bag full of food while I dealt with the pushchair. Far easier to collapse than to open.

I settled Forester in his car seat on the kitchen floor and set to preparing the big meal. I read the instructions on those M and S packets over and over until I was convinced I had a timetable that would ensure all the various components would be ready at the same time. I lined up the plastic cartons in the order in which they were to go in the oven. I was determined that it should be a peace offering and not a burnt offering.

I was so pleased with myself that I grooved around the kitchen. Forester seemed faintly impressed when I juggled two apples for his benefit. I was a veritable domestic goddess: preparing a meal, amusing the baby. The only thing I hadn't managed to do was change into a cocktail dress. Or change Forester's nappy. But he still wasn't complaining and I couldn't smell anything awry.

At six o'clock, about the time I expected my loving husband-to-be to arrive on the doorstep with a bunch of conciliatory daffs, the telephone rang. I slipped off one oven glove to take the call. With the other oven glove, which was shaped like a crocodile, I intended to give Forester a little puppet show while I chatted. Perhaps the caller was his mum.

It was Ed.

'Hello H-Bum,' he said. It was my least favourite of his nicknames for me.

'Hello Fat-Arse,' I replied. 'I hope you're calling to ask me whether I want you to pick up a bottle of wine at the off-licence on your way past. In which case, yes, I do. Make it a red one.'

'Actually, darling, there's been a bit of a disaster.'

I made the oven-glove crocodile echo my cocked head gesture of anticipation while I waited for Ed to explain.

'I'm still in Bristol.'

'You're still in Bristol?'

'Scotty's car broke down. I don't know when we'll make it back.'

'What happened?' I asked.

'I don't know. Something to do with the transmission. It was spluttering most of the way down here.'

'Then why didn't you take your car?'

'I didn't know Scotty's Audi was going to stop altogether, did I?'

'Have you called the AA?'

'Of course we have.'

'And how long will they be?'

'Could be a couple of hours.'

'You're kidding!'

'Weather's bad here – lots of cars breaking down. That's a worst-case scenario though.'

'It had better be. Did you win the match?' I asked in resignation.

'Of course we did. I was a complete hero. How was your day with Forester?'

'Oh, we had a pretty good time.'

'What did you do?'

'We had lunch at a café. We went to the park.'

'And how was your first nappy change?'

I didn't say anything.

'Heidi. He probably needs his nappy changed by now.'

I managed a laugh. 'For God's sake, Ed, Forester and I are doing fine.'

'See? I knew you didn't need me getting under your feet.'

'Say hi to the boys. Remind Scotty to phone Clare too, won't you?'

'He already has.'

'Ed,' I said then, 'you're not sitting in the car, are you? Promise me you're sitting on the lay-by even though it must be cold.'

'Glad you care,' he told me.

When I put the phone down, I felt a little warm glow despite the fact that my plans for a romantic evening had been scuppered. Ed seemed a lot happier than he had been when he left the house that morning. I was disappointed that he wasn't there with me but Scotty's car had broken down. There was nothing Ed could have done about that. I was satisfied that it wasn't an excuse so he could keep on drinking with the Bristol team. He hadn't sounded drunk. He had sounded as though he was calling from a lay-by. If they had already called the AA, then they might be on the road again in an hour or so and Bristol was only a couple of hours from London if the traffic wasn't bad.

I fished my dinner out of the oven and ate it with one hand while I continued the puppet show for Forester. He liked it best when I grabbed at his nose with the crocodile's soft red mouth. After a few passes I found I could make him squeal and thump his legs up and down just by opening the croc's mouth by half a centimetre. Not quite a laugh but getting there.

'I thank you, Forester Knight.' I made the crocodile take a bow.

Seven o'clock passed without further news from Ed. I lay on the sofa with Forester between my legs, trying to push himself up into plank position with a small hand on each of my knees.

I'd given him another bottle and a meal of two types of goo. I'd taken the jumpsuit off and turned the heating up rather than try to get him to put on a cardigan. He was still wearing the baby-gro he'd been dressed in when Ed left that morning. And the nappy. In the corner of my vision the Pampers packet loomed like a rebuke. I'd carried Forester into the bathroom with me four times that day. He'd had several bottles of milk and juice. There was no way he didn't need changing. My resistance was tantamount to cruelty.

The moment had come.

I picked Forester up and carried him across to the changing mat. I called Ed's mobile one more time in case he was pulling into our street at that very moment, but the call went straight to voicemail. Perhaps his battery had run out.

'The thing that worries me most,' I told Forester as I undid the poppers on his baby-gro, 'is not what I am about to encounter but the fact that you may have been sitting in it all day long without complaining. You realise I'm going to use that fact against you as soon as you turn eighteen?'

Forester kicked his legs straight up in the air.

Tentatively, I started to peel open the straps on his nappy. I took a deep breath before the moment of revelation. Forester, too, seemed to be holding his breath. Applying the sticking-plaster removing principle, I lifted Forester by his ankles and whipped the dirty nappy from beneath him. I spread a wet-wipe beneath his raised bottom to stop any muck from getting onto the mat, then lowered him down onto that. Whereupon Forester peed. Straight up into the air. And my face.

Had I known that would happen, I would have let Forester stay in a damp nappy until Kara came back from Paris if I had to. But for some reason, that night it only made me laugh. I cleaned my face with a wet-wipe. And then Forester laughed back at me – a proper laugh out loud, not his silent movie-actor guffaw.

'You had your revenge, eh?' I joked with him. 'I promise I will never again let you sit in a dirty nappy for eight hours.'

With Forester in a new nappy, and not complaining or obviously turning blue around the legs where I'd fastened him up too tight, we retired to the sofa once more. I lay back against the cushions with Forester on my chest and he twisted a handful of my T-shirt in one of his fists for a while. I blew little raspberries on the top of his head.

'Are you sleepy?' I ventured. I was certainly feeling sleepy. 'Shall we have a little snooze?' I suggested.

In time Forester's fist relaxed. I felt his body grow slightly heavier against mine. When I glanced down at his face, I saw his eyelids were dropping, and soon he was in the land of Nod.

I felt a bubble of elation rise in my chest. At the same time, tears prickled my eyes. I'd fed a baby, changed a nappy and now I had got him to sleep.

I could cope.

32

Of course, not long after I persuaded Forester to close his eyes, the phone rang again.

With some difficulty and by practically dislocating my shoulder, I was able to reach the handset on the coffee table without disturbing the baby at all.

'Hello,' I whispered into the receiver.

'Hey, Sweetcheeks, it's Scotty.'

'Thank goodness. I hope you're calling to tell me you're on your way at last.'

'Eh?'

'You're not. Talk about hoping against hope. Oh well. Is his lordship feeling too guilty about leaving me alone with the baby all night to talk to me himself?'

'I don't know,' said Scotty. 'Is Ed there?'

'Of course he isn't.'

'Oh. Okay then. Where is he? I've been trying to call his mobile.'

'Isn't he with you?'

'No.'

'You didn't let him walk off down the motorway on his own in the dark?'

'Motorway? What are you talking about?'

'Where's Ed, Scotty?'

'I'm asking you.'

'No, I'm asking you. Where are you?'

'I'm in Newcastle.'

'You're supposed to be on the motorway near Bristol. Your car's broken down.'

'Has it? I bloody hope not.' The tone of Scotty's voice suggested that he thought I was losing my marbles. 'I'm in Newcastle all weekend at my little brother's stag party. Bit bloody boring so far. All his mates are teetotal family boys. That's why I wanted to ask Ed the name of that club he went to when he was up here.'

'A strip club?' I said quietly.

'Er . . .' Scotty coughed to hide his embarrassment. 'Well, you know . . . It is a stag night, H.'

'Scotty, what's going on? Ed told me he was going to Bristol with you.'

I heard a crackle of static down the line. 'Hardly any signal here, H. Will you tell him to call me on my mobile as soon as he gets in?'

Scotty was cut off, or hung up on me.

Where the fuck was my fiancé?

33

Once again I jabbed Ed's mobile number into the phone and once again I was passed straight to voicemail. Scotty's car was supposed to be on a lay-by on the M4 but Scotty was in Newcastle. It meant only one thing. Somebody was lying.

What to do? After I couldn't get through to Ed I called Kara, but Kara didn't pick up her phone either. Too busy being in love. Who to call after that? I had never been the kind of girl who bothered her mother with romantic dilemmas. Mum came from a generation of women who still believed that men had to be forgiven almost anything, infidelity included, because they just *aren't like us*. I could have called Eleanor, but I wanted to talk to someone who would at least consider the possibility that I was overreacting. Since her husband ran off with her sister, Eleanor was of the opinion that most men could do no right and the only cure when one went astray was to get yourself a new one.

What about Flo? I called Flo. No answer.

I sat on the sofa with my mobile phone and scrolled through the rest of numbers in my address book frantically. Should I call Clare and see if she knew why Ed was using Scotty as an alibi? But perhaps Scotty was using Ed as an alibi too? God knew what I would start if I called up Clare.

But I had to talk to someone. The AA couldn't help me. They were unable to tell me whether they had picked up anyone answering Ed's description that night and since I didn't have Scotty's registration number they couldn't look him up on the database. Not that it was certain Scotty's car was involved at all. I gave in and phoned Clare. Scotty and Clare's home phone rang and rang and rang. No answer.

And that's when I found myself calling Sophie.

I liked Sophie well enough but not well enough to ever call her for a chat. Ed and Sophie's husband, Zach, talked pretty much every day and arranged for the four of us to hang out every month or so. Sophie had often said, 'We should go out on our own, you and I. Have a girls' night.' But we never had – something always came up – and now that Sophie was three months pregnant, a night on the town fuelled by bright pink cocktails that tasted like ethanol was suddenly even less likely.

But there was something about Sophie that made her seem like the right person to call at that moment. The very first time I met her I had liked her. I couldn't say that about many of the girls who followed Ed's rugby team. At heart, I felt that Sophie was warm and wise. I knew she would be discreet. And sensible.

She picked up the phone on the first ring.

'Hello?'

'Am I interrupting anything?'

'Are you kidding?' she said. 'I'm married and pregnant. I never do anything any more. Is that Heidi?'

'It is.'

'How are you, sweetheart? How come you're not out on the town on a Saturday night, kicking up your heels while you still can? I tell you, I wish I'd done a whole lot more before I got myself up the duff. I'll never wear low-rise jeans again for a start. I'm sitting here like a bloody beached whale and it's only fourteen weeks. What are you up to?'

'I'm babysitting for Kara.'

'Again? Ed says you're babysitting every night these days. I hope I can rely on you for babysitting favours half so much,' Sophie laughed. 'Where's Kara gone this time?'

'Paris. For the weekend.'

'All right for some! How on earth did she persuade you to have the baby overnight?'

'It's a very long story. Listen, Sophie, I've got a problem,' I said. 'At least, right now, I think I've got a problem. I'm rather hoping that when I tell you what's going on over here you'll be able to give me a straightforward interpretation and tell me that I'm being a total idiot.'

'You're not going to ask me a baby question, are you? Remember I haven't actually had mine yet. I'm just as clueless as you are – probably more so. Have you tried giving him some milk? Changing his nappy?'

'It's about Ed,' I interrupted. And I poured the story out. The rugby match. The breakdown. The call from Scotty in the north.

Sophie didn't say anything much while I talked, and the very fact that she didn't interrupt me soon started to seem like a very bad sign. Eventually, when I had finished, I heard her take a deep breath. 'Oh, Heidi,' she said, 'I really hoped it wasn't true.'

It seemed that everyone knew except me. Well, everyone except me and Scotty. No wonder Clare had been so jealous of my engagement ring; she wasn't coveting my soon-to-be-married status so much as my fiancé. They had been seen whispering to each other at the rugby-club party, before Ed passed out. They were hiding out in the corridor by the cloakroom. Lucy saw them and said they seemed pretty close. Ed had kissed Clare on the forehead. She had given him a hug.

'I told Lucy she was being ridiculous. You and Ed are getting married in four months,' Sophie continued brightly. 'Perhaps nothing really happened. After all, they were only seen hugging, which isn't in itself a crime. Perhaps he really did just want to get away from the noise at your place this afternoon and he thought you wouldn't let him if you knew the rugby match had been cancelled two weeks ago. I don't think we should go jumping to conclusions just because he used Scotty as his alibi and Clare isn't at home right now, though. Clare is so hung up about Scotty; she'd cut her right arm off to get him up the aisle. I'm sure she wouldn't be so stupid as to do anything with Ed that might get back to Scotty somehow and jeopardise her chances of that.'

'But what about all the secretive phone calls?'

'I'm sure there's a genuine reason. Heidi? Heidi? Are you all right? Are you crying?'

Of course I was bloody crying.

'Look. Let's think about the best-case scenario,' said Sophie.

'What on earth is the best-case scenario?'

'I'll have to come back to you on that,' Sophie admitted. 'But please give Ed a chance to explain when he gets home tonight. He's a wonderful man and you guys are getting married. He hasn't stopped going on about the wedding since he decided to ask you. We've had nearly eighteen months of it at our house! He thinks you're the queen of the world, and he's so concerned that you get exactly the wedding you want . . . That isn't the behaviour of someone who's cheating on you.'

Except that we all know that a guilty heart makes more effort, I thought to myself. Just as Steven had made more effort prior to leaving me and my heart in pieces. Just as I had made an effort to make love to Ed the night after I almost let Steven kiss me.

'Heidi,' said Sophie. 'I'm going to get Zach to drive me over to your place right now.'

'No, don't,' I said.

'He won't mind. He's only had one beer so far this evening. I'm not leaving you there on your own with the baby.'

'Sophie, stay where you are.'

Just a week earlier she had been confined to bed by her GP so that she wouldn't lose the tiny life she was carrying inside her. The last thing I wanted was for her to get up from her comfortable sofa and drag herself halfway across London because I couldn't get a grip on myself. What if the late-night trip triggered some kind of problem with Sophie's pregnancy? I would never be able to forgive myself. Or Ed.

'I'm going to be fine,' I lied. 'My little brother is staying here for the weekend. He'll be back home in a minute.'

Understandably, Sophie took very little persuading to stay put. 'Well, if you're sure,' she said. 'But you can call me whenever you want to. Okay? I won't be going to bed for ages yet. And even when I do go to bed, I'll be awake for ages trying to find a comfortable position that doesn't upset the bump. I can't believe I've got another five and a half months of this . . . You call me any time, you hear?'

'Thank you.'

'I'm sure it will be okay,' she concluded. 'There's just been some misunderstanding.'

A misunderstanding. That's what it had to be.

Clare was probably out with her friends. She wouldn't be anywhere near my fiancé. And perhaps Ed was playing reserve for a rugby team he hadn't told me about. Perhaps there were two Scottys – all Ed's mates had such interchangeable nicknames: Scotty, Barfy, Burpy. After the first ten or so I gave up trying to fit the stupid name to the stupid face. It was quite possible that I had missed another Jock.

But I was being ridiculous. What is it that detectives say? The simplest explanation is almost certainly the right one. Ed had lied about the rugby match and insisted he had to leave the house because he had a secret rendezvous with somebody that day. If you had told me a month before that Ed would be capable of being unfaithful to me within weeks of our wedding, I would have protested hard. But back then I wouldn't have believed I was capable of infidelity either, and look how close I had come.

34

It was nine o'clock by now. Forester had slept on against my chest while I spoke to Scotty and then to Sophie but now he started to stir, as though he had sensed the change in atmosphere like a baby barometer. He gave a little whimper that seemed like a three-minute warning.

'Ssssh, Forester. Go back to sleep,' I tried. I stroked his head.

He balled up his fists and pushed back against my arm.

'Sssssh-ssssh-ssshhhh.'

His eyes were still closed but I could see that they were screwed more tightly and his open mouth began to widen into a grimace. His pale cheeks grew redder.

'Rock-a-bye baby on the tree top.' I sang the only lullaby I could remember but my voice was wobbling as I tried to keep myself from crying again and Forester wasn't convinced. 'Please, darling,' I pleaded with him. 'Give me a minute while I work out what the hell I'm supposed to do.'

'Waaaaah!'

Our entente cordiale was over.

Now Forester sent up a cry that was somewhere on the decibel scale between a smoke alarm and a cat being stretched between two Rottweilers. I tried everything I had seen Kara and Ed do to calm him, going through the three basic reasons a baby cries: uncomfortable, hungry and tired. He had seemed perfectly comfortable just moments before the screaming started. When I offered him a drink from his juice bottle it seemed to offend him and only make the crying worse. And if he was tired, he was damn well going the wrong way about dealing with that.

'Hush little baby.'

I got up. I sang. I carried him about the room. I stroked his head. I patted his back. But nothing seemed to appease him. The crying only became louder, more anguished. Now I was dealing with a cross between a Second World War air-raid siren and the roaring of Hercules attempting to escape his bonds. Forester banged his head against my chest now. I tried to keep him close to me but he strained against my arms with more force than I could possibly have imagined from a body so small. He threw back his head and gave me a technicolor view of his tonsils. He thumped his tiny fists against my shoulder. His legs and arms stiffened as he tried to break away.

'What's the matter? What's the matter?' I had never seen him quite like this before. 'What's the matter?' He just cried on.

How long did he cry for that night? Five minutes? Ten? An hour? Two hours? All I knew was that Forester cried until I was ready to cry myself.

And still no sign of Ed. No word from my fiancé, wherever he was. Whatever – *whoever* he was doing.

'Forester, please.' I tried to interest him in his bottle again, but he squealed so hard and loud in my ear that the only thing I could do was put him down on the cushions at the opposite end of the sofa from me and hold my head until it stopped ringing. Then I sat on my hands and just stared at him.

I remembered reading about an experiment in which teenage students were given realistic baby dolls to care for over a weekend. The dolls were fitted with computer chips that made them mimic a real baby, crying at roughly the same intervals throughout the day and night. Those computerised tears wouldn't stop until the student had fed, changed or simply held the baby for the proper amount of time. More than half the students failed to care for their baby doll for the whole weekend, either shutting the baby somewhere they couldn't hear the crying or simply removing its batteries.

'Where are your fucking batteries?' I asked Forester.

All the fears I had managed to suppress for a brief wonderful period that afternoon came rushing back to me and I just stared at Kara's baby. Once again he was an incomprehensible alien being I just didn't know what to do with. I couldn't communicate with him and he was raging against something he couldn't communicate to me. He thrashed his arms and legs against the cushions and screamed as though I was pinning him down, though I was no longer anywhere near him. I felt like an RSPCA officer facing a dog gone rabid. My duty was to look after this child, to pick him up and try again. My instincts told me to run.

But now he was howling as though he was in pain. Perhaps he was. I couldn't get close enough to tell. I picked up the phone and thought about dialling for an ambulance. But an ambulance could take for ever to come at closing time on a Saturday night. The only thing to do was put him in the car and take him to the casualty unit instead.

So I bundled him into the back of Ed's car, praying that I had strapped his baby-seat in the right way. I knew it wasn't meant to go in the front seat but I had no clue whether he was still supposed to face backwards. It wouldn't seem to fit that way so Forester ended up behind the passenger seat, facing forwards. It seemed okay. He cried anyway. Perhaps I hurt him when I tried to get him strapped in.

I crunched the gears and struck out in the direction of Chelsea and Westminster Hospital but I must have taken a wrong turning somewhere pretty early on, driven in the wrong direction at a roundabout or something, because soon there were no signs for the hospital any more. I turned into a side-street, intending to loop round and head back the way I'd come, but that only locked me into a one-way system I'd never noticed because I generally travelled on foot. I got out of the one-way system only to find myself on a flyover. From the flyover to a bypass. It wasn't long before I sailed past the BT Tower.

But while I'd been getting lost, a peculiar thing had happened to Forester. I'd turned the stereo in the car so high I almost didn't notice he'd stopped crying. Glancing behind me for just a second lest I run into the back of another car, I saw that he had one of his feet in his mouth again, chewing quite contentedly on his toes as he watched the world outside flash by.

Whatever had ailed him was quite forgotten. And I remembered now that Kara once told me the car always left Forester blissed out. There had been nights when he first started teething when Kara drove for an hour to induce sleepiness in her son. It seemed to working for me now.

'Are you okay?' I asked him.

He regarded me with wet eyes.

'It's all right.' I forced myself to reach behind and squeeze his foot to comfort him. Or me.

But God only knew where Forester's pleasure trip had taken us. Those few landmarks I had recognised on the way helped me guess we had been heading due east. Any moment now, I thought, the sun would rise and I would be sure.

We had been on the road for almost an hour by the time Forester calmed down. As I drove, too scared to slow too much in case Forester started crying again, I strained to get a look at the street signs. But London street signs are for the most part so badly placed – they're always so high on buildings you can't see them without sticking your head right out of the car window or they're obscured by years of dirt, graffiti and estate agents' boards. Otherwise they're simply absent. London is one of the worst cities in the world when it comes to signage.

I didn't know what to do. During the daytime, and without a passenger who might start screaming at any moment, I might have pulled up to the kerb and waited for someone friendly-looking to happen by. Someone who looked as though they could direct me back to civilisation. But there was no one remotely civilised-looking in the area where I found myself at closing time on that Saturday night.

As I slowed down to peer at a rare street sign that hadn't been placed especially for the pigeons, two women stepped out of the dark shadow of a shop door. Thin as a pair of abandoned greyhounds, wearing mini-skirts and no tights in what was definitely jeans and jumper weather, they looked disappointed when they realised that I was a woman and not a potential customer, immediately slackening their struts back into a slouch. But then one of them caught sight of the sleeping baby in the back of the car. She gave Forester a little wave and blew a tender kiss at him across her waggling fingers. I found myself returning her smile.

35

Sod it, I thought. I could have driven on for ever, ending up in Essex or beyond before I saw a comprehensible road sign. I stopped my car at the kerb, kept the engine running for Forester and, making sure the doors were locked, rolled down the kerbside window just half an inch.

'Excuse me,' I called. The girls were already sauntering back to sit on the shop door-step and couldn't hear me over the noise of the car engine. I rolled the window down another inch and shouted again. 'Excuse me.'

One of the girls turned round – the one who had smiled at the baby.

'Yeah?' she called back. Not exactly friendly, but not quite 'fuck off' either.

'I'm lost,' I said.

'Aren't we all,' her blonde friend laughed.

'No, really. I'm lost. I need directions.'

'Ask a policeman,' said the blonde girl.

The smiling girl was back at my car window now. Her face was softer than it had looked in the split second when we first made eye-contact. I rolled the window all the way down so that she could lean her elbows on the sill.

'Don't take no notice of her,' she said, jerking her head back towards her companion. 'Lovely baby you've got there. How old is he?'

'Six months.'

'Same as mine.'

'You got your figure back quickly,' I said nonsensically.

'I do a lot of exercise,' she grinned. 'So, you're lost. Where are you trying to get to, love?'

And when she said the word 'love', something broke inside me. Some thin membrane that had been keeping the tears from blinding me as I drove through London's empty streets with my best friend's baby in the back of my car. 'I'm sorry,' I sobbed. 'I'm really sorry.'

'Hey.' The girl reached her skinny arm in through the window. 'Hey. Don't worry. You cry all you like.' She stroked my shoulder and I must have flinched. 'I'm not going to hurt you,' she said perceptively. 'We're both mums. I know how bloody difficult it can be. I'm on your side.'

'I'm . . . I'm . . .' The sentence I was trying to get out was totally obscured by sobbing and snorting as the tears covered my face, the steering wheel and the smiling girl's hand as she passed me a Kleenex from her handbag. And then somehow she was sitting next to me in the passenger seat. Of course, she had just reached in through the open window and popped the lock.

'What's your name, love?' she asked, as I accepted another tissue.

'Heidi.'

'Hey! That's what my little girl's called!'

'The six-month-old?'

'The twenty-month-old. The six-month-old is Jordan, after her father's favourite trainers. I'm Stell. That's short for Stella.'

'This is Forester,' I said, introducing Stella to the chap in the back who was now wide awake again and gazing at our passenger with something between trepidation and wonder. She had a fabulous streak of silver in the back of her hair. She noticed him looking at it. 'You can play with it if you like,' she said, unclipping the streak from her ponytail and passing it across.

'Now, let's get you out of here.' She turned back to me. 'Where are you headed?'

'Where am I now?'

'This is the Hackney Road.'

'Hackney? I'm in Hackney?'

'Actually, you're in Bethnal Green.'

'I need to be in Chiswick.'

'Crikey, Dorothy,' Stella laughed. 'You're a long way from Kansas City. Got an A to Z?' She was already rummaging through the glove compartment.

It turned out that I did have a map. I hadn't driven in so long it didn't even occur to me to look. Stella flicked through the pages until she found our location, pointing out the junction we now sat on with an artfully extended red nail. Then she helpfully gave me an overview of our position using the front-page scheme where all the other pages are drawn side by side to give you an idea of the way Hammersmith relates to Kensington and so on. I really was on completely the wrong side of town.

'Perhaps your best bet would be to go up to the M25,' Stella said ominously. 'Lise,' she shouted to her friend on the shop step. 'She only wants to go to bloody Chiswick, don't she? What do you reckon? M25?'

Lise shrugged her shoulders. 'How should I know? I haven't got a bloody car.'

'Miserable cow,' said Stella. 'Look, I can show you where you are and where you should be but I don't know anything about which roads are one way and that.'

'Anything would help me.'

'You know what, I don't think I should really let you drive all the way back to West London in your state in any case. Do you know anyone who lives a bit nearer who might let you stay for the night? Then you can drive home in the morning. London's a whole lot easier in the daylight.'

'I don't think so,' I sniffed.

'Well, I'd invite you to stay at my place but I'm not exactly set up for guests. Are you sure you don't know anyone? Got no friends in Dalston? Hoxton? Hackney?'

'Hang on,' I said. 'There is one person.'

I got that card out of my wallet one more time.

'There we are then,' said Stella. 'Give him a call.'

'What? My ex-boyfriend? At this time of night? I can't.'

'He owes you, I'm sure he does. All my ex-boyfriends owe me.'

Over the next fifteen minutes, the whole story came out. I turned off the engine and wound up the window so that Forester wouldn't get cold. Well, apart from an inch-wide crack at the very top – Stella was desperate for a cigarette but didn't want to blow smoke onto the baby. She held the glowing tip of her fag out of the window and stretched up for a suck on the filter every now and then like a hamster getting water from a drinking bottle stuck through the bars of its cage.

She was a good listener. She pulled all the appropriate faces, convincing me for quarter of an hour that she really, really cared. Perhaps she'd just had a lot of practice, listening to the tales of hundreds of men whose wives really didn't understand them. Or perhaps she did care. She squeezed my hand when I felt the tears start to well up again, as though she might squeeze them back where they came from.

'Ring that Steven bloke,' Stella said when I had finished. 'He sounds like he won't judge you for needing help. Besides,' she continued, 'I think that people come back into our lives for a reason. I really do.'

'My best friend said exactly the same thing.'

'Great minds think alike. Except there's no way I'd leave my baby with an amateur like you.' She squeezed my hand again. 'I'm joking. You're doing fine with the baby. Look. He's happy as a sand-boy back there.'

I held Steven's card in one hand and my mobile phone in the other. 'What should I say?'

'Just say you need to come over. You can explain everything when you get there.'

I dialled.

'Hello?'

He sounded as though he had just woken up.

'Did I wake you up?'

'It's three in the morning, so I think you can safely assume that you did. Sarah?'

'No,' I paused. 'It's Heidi.'

I imagined him sitting to attention, propped up against his pillows. It certainly sounded as though he was suddenly paying more attention.

'Heidi? Heidi! What? Er, what can I do for you?'

'I need to come over to your house,' I said.

'Now? From Chiswick?'

'No. From Bethnal Green. I'm on the Hackney Road.'

'You are? Why?'

'Trying to get a baby to sleep. Look, I'll explain when I see you. Where's your house?'

He gave a street name, which I repeated out loud. Stella immediately started to look for it in the index.

'That's only a minute away,' she said happily.

'Have you got someone there with you?'

'Stell,' I said. 'A new friend.'

'Is she coming too?'

'I've got to work,' she said.

'It's just me and the baby. I'll see you in a couple of minutes,' I told Steven.

'I suppose I'd better ask the Brazilian hookers I'd got for the night to go home,' Steven said resignedly. 'I'll keep an eye out for you. The bell doesn't work.'

'So, he's okay for you to go round there?' Stella confirmed.

'Yes.'

'I knew he would be.'

'Thanks for helping me,' I said to Stella.

'My pleasure.'

'See you again sometime.'

'Yeah. Not if you can help it, eh?' Stella's face was beautiful when she smiled. 'See ya, Forester. Great name.'

She kissed her fingertips and pressed the kiss to his forehead.

'What about your hairpiece?' I asked, as she climbed from the car without it. Forester had pretty much decimated the weird silver rat's-tail already.

'I've got plenty more of those at home. Good luck, Heidi. Who knows, perhaps you'll get back together with your ex, then it won't matter a flying fuck what your fiancé's getting up to behind your back.'

'Yeah,' I said. 'Goodbye.'

Stella clipped away towards Lise.

I turned the car engine back on and pulled away from the kerb. Stopping at the traffic lights moments later, I looked into my rear-view mirror and watched as Stella leaned in at the passenger window of another car. Before the lights had changed from red to green, my friendly stranger was inside the car, which was making a U-turn and taking her away. To where? To what? I had the car heating turned up full but still shivered.

36

Outside Steven's house, I pulled the car up to the kerb but didn't dare turn the engine off in case Forester woke again. As promised, Steven was watching out for me. I saw his shadowy figure at the window of the tall town house with its front door painted almost the same shade as my own. Moments later, Steven opened that front door and walked out to meet me. I opened the car door but still didn't get out.

'It's been a very long time since you turned up at my door in the middle of the night, Heidi Savage.'

'I'm sorry,' I told him. 'I didn't know where else to go.'

He kissed me on both cheeks. 'Well, I'm glad you thought of me. Why don't you turn the engine off and come in? Or have you changed your mind?'

'If I turn the car engine off the baby will wake up again,' I said pathetically.

'So you're planning to sit out here all night? Turn the engine off. I'll deal with Buster in the back. You go on into the house and warm up.' He touched his fingers to my cheek. 'You're freezing.'

My legs really were shaking as I climbed the steps to Steven's house. I wasn't quite sure how I got there. I definitely wasn't sure what I was doing there. Steven walked up the steps behind me, holding Forester's car seat in one hand. He pressed gently against the small of my back and guided me through the front door.

'Let's go in here.'

Still with his hand on the small of my back, Steven steered me into the sitting room and placed Forester's car seat down carefully in front of the big bay window from which he had been watching for my arrival.

'I already made some coffee. Thought you might need it.'

'I only drink decaf,' I told him.

'Well, I need some with full caf,' he yawned. 'Tea? I think I've got camomile.'

'I'm sorry to have got you up in the middle of the night,' I began.

'I'm sure there's a very good explanation. Let's just get some drinks and then you can start filling me in. Hey, you know what? I think I might have some brandy round here somewhere. Do you fancy one?'

'I've never fancied a brandy in my life,' I said, 'until now.'

Steven disappeared in the direction of the kitchen, leaving me alone to take a look around the room. I'm not sure what I had expected his home to be like, but I certainly hadn't expected it to be like this. At college, we all had identical furniture in our identical rooms and any individuality had to be achieved on a shoestring, with posters and scraps of gaudy tie-dye brought back from trips to India or Africa taken during the long vacations. During the time that Steven and I spent in Leeds together, squeezing ourselves into his single bed night after night, his room was decorated with a huge map of the world, bristling with pins marking the places he had visited on his travels. I loved looking at that map, working out where my own pins would have gone. Until I was twenty-one, it would have been just England and France. That was it.

The map was still there, hanging in the hallway. It was the first thing I noticed as I came into the house. I wondered whether it was the same one. If so, it was properly framed now and peppered with so many pins it looked like one of those relief maps you have to make from cardboard in first year geography class.

The sitting room was pleasingly minimalist. The walls were painted off-white, the original floorboards stripped and beautifully varnished, the furniture quietly chic. Italian, I guessed. Maybe from Heal's. He was in advertising and could probably afford it. There were a couple of big black and white photographs on the wall, framed in stained ash. Landscapes. Seascapes, actually. The only garish touch was a colourful fabric-sided Wendy house, which stood in the bay window. Isabelle's. It said so on a hand-carved wooden sign that hung over the door.

'We could get inside that, if you like,' Steven said when he came back into the room with two steaming mugs (coffee for him, camomile tea for me) and a bottle of brandy. 'I call it the 'paddy hut'. Isabelle gets inside when she's in a bad mood. And I'm assuming that you must be in a bad mood, since I don't imagine you generally spend Saturday nights driving round East London with a baby in the back of your car for fun. What happened, Heidi? Did your boyfriend forget to put the loo seat down? Leave the cap off the toothpaste?'

I burst into tears as quickly as if he had just bonked me on the nose with a mallet.

37

'Ed's not just my boyfriend,' I began. 'He's my fiancé.'

'Your fiancé?'

'We're supposed to be getting married in June.'

'This June?' Steven raised his eyebrows.

'This June.'

'That's in just three months' time.'

'I don't know why I didn't tell you. It just didn't seem to come up.'

'No wonder you didn't call me when you got the roses.'

I nodded in confirmation. 'They were beautiful though,' I said.

'Well,' Steven sighed, 'Heidi Savage is getting married.'

'I might not be,' I snorted. 'Not after tonight.'

'And where is . . . your fiancé? I'm sorry, I've forgotten his name.'

'His name is Ed.' I coughed the name out. 'And I don't know where he is, except that he isn't where he should be and I think he's probably with someone else.'

I explained about the rugby match. The car breakdown. The phone calls.

'He's having an affair,' I concluded bluntly.

'Well.' Steven pulled a sympathetic face. 'I can see why that would be your first thought.'

'Isn't it your thought?'

'Well, not necessarily . . . Although . . .'

'Although what?'

'Things haven't been all rosy with you guys, have they? Otherwise, I would have known you were engaged. Why didn't you tell me?'

'Steven,' I sobbed, 'I don't know. I don't know what's been wrong. All I ever wanted was to get married and live happily ever after. Now the happily ever after bit seems like a life sentence.'

'Which part of it?'

'I don't know,' I said again. But I did know. 'Having children.'

'Don't you want to have children?' Steven asked me.

I glanced over at Forester, who was dozing in his car seat like infant Buddha again. If he had been awake, I might not have said what I said next. But Forester was sleeping and Steven made me feel as though all judgement was suspended that night.

'It sounds like blasphemy to say it,' I began, 'but I'm really not sure I do.'

'I don't think I'd be good at it,' was the first of my reasons. 'Everyone keeps telling me that it all comes naturally; that when the midwife puts the little bundle in my arms, I'll know instantly what to do and I'll be so overcome with love that nothing will seem too much trouble. But it doesn't always come naturally, does it? I mean, if this whole thing about maternal love being the strongest love of all were true, why isn't Isabelle's mother here in London with you right now? Why is Kara in bloody Paris with some man she met off the Internet?'

'Kara's Kara,' said Steven, 'and you are definitely not like Sarah. What else are you afraid of?'

'I'm afraid of getting fat. I'm afraid of the pain of giving birth. I'm afraid of breastfeeding. I'm afraid of not breastfeeding in case my child grows up all sickly. I'm afraid of not being able to look after the baby on my own.'

There is nothing worse than being left holding the baby – that's what I wanted to shout at Kara when she told me she was pregnant. The hard work, the sleepless nights, the money, the *lack* of money, the *stigma*. Coping with that all *on your own*. It made me feel cold with fear just to think about it. I couldn't even operate a pushchair without a co-pilot. Sterilising bottles, knowing when to move on from milk to solids, making a decision about jabs? So much responsibility for another human life!

And that was assuming there were no other complications. Only days before Kara discovered she was pregnant, we had a guest come onto the radio show to talk about raising a child born with Down Syndrome. Her husband walked out on her when the amniocentesis results came through positive and she refused to have a termination. Her daughter was an absolute delight – she came into the studio and sat all quiet and cuddly on Eleanor's lap while her mother talked to Flo on the other side of the glass – but the little girl would never be fully independent. She'd never quite grow up. What would happen when the mother got too old to take care of her adult child? How could anyone handle the worry of that? Even at thirty it seemed Kara was old enough to have an increased risk of her baby being born with some congenital complications. We'd covered that nightmare on a show the previous March.

Let's Talk London was a great resource when it came to finding out about the very worst. You could raise your perfectly healthy child like a professional and still have that child turn to drugs (Is Your Child Taking Drugs? Wednesday 7 August). Or be kidnapped by a stranger on their way home from Sunday School (Is My Baby Really Dead? Friday 1 October). Or they might just grow up to hate you (What Did We Do Wrong? Monday 16 January). You could devote eighteen years of your life to this creature that had grown inside you only to have it forget to send you a sixtieth birthday card. As Kara and I sat on her sofa that afternoon, I went through a thousand hideous scenarios in my head: disability, desertion, destitution . . . How could she cope? How could anyone cope with all that?

For the first time ever, the rant that had been building inside my head for seven years made itself audible.

'Why do you think you'd have to look after the baby on your own?' Steven asked when I had finished.

'Why don't you tell me?' I replied.

38

'Why did we split up?'

Steven's eyebrows dipped momentarily. 'What?'

'Tell me, Steven. Why did we break up? We hadn't been arguing. The sex hadn't gone off the boil. At least, not for me it hadn't. And there was no one else. Unless you were lying,' I added.

'I wasn't lying,' he half-laughed. 'There was definitely no one else.'

'So why did you tell me it was over?'

This time it was his turn to say, 'I don't know.'

'That's not good enough,' I goaded. 'That's what you said to me back then. But there always is a reason and you've had seven years to think of a good one.'

'It's not important now, surely.'

'Then it won't matter if you tell me the truth. Did I have halitosis? Did you hate the way I dressed? Was it something about the way I pronounced "tagliatelle"?'

'I really don't know,' he said. He ran his finger around the rim of his glass. 'And believe me, for months, if not years after I did it I would wake up in the middle of the night in a cold sweat, wondering if I had made the most stupid mistake in the world. You were perfect, Heidi. I want you to know that more than anything. You were the perfect girlfriend. Beautiful, funny, kind, the perfect friend above all else. The times we spent together were some of the happiest times in my life.' He poured another slug of brandy into my glass.

'I don't think I need any more,' I said.

'I do,' he replied. 'Didn't expect the Spanish Inquisition tonight.'

I gave him a mock scowl. 'I must insist you carry on. It's important.'

'I suppose I thought I was doing the right thing. I got this idea in my head that it was time for a change. We were young. We were really young, when you think about it. I just didn't believe that we could possibly last for ever, having met so early on. There were so many things I wanted to do. So many places to see.'

'More pins to stick in your map.'

'You could say that. And I just thought that I wouldn't be able to do them with you. With anyone, really. You had another year of training to go through at the BBC and I didn't want to hang around London any longer at that point. And I didn't want to go travelling on my own, thinking of you waiting patiently for me in our flat. Either you would be resentful because I was never around or I would be resentful because I couldn't go everywhere I wanted because I had to come back to you. I convinced myself that there was going to be too much temptation out there in the real world and it wouldn't have been fair to ask you to wait. I felt sure that eventually you would understand what I had done and perhaps even be relieved. I was sure it was only a matter of time before you got bored of me. It's hard to live out your dreams when you're tied to someone else. At least, that's what I believed then.'

'But you don't believe that now?'

'No. I don't.'

'Even after what happened with Sarah? She decided the same thing, surely, when she buggered off to France?'

'I know. What can I say? I still believe in love. More booze, I think. Or some booze. You haven't even touched yours. I feel at a disadvantage.'

I took a sip of brandy, but not properly, and the fumes made my eyes sting. I coughed.

'I'll get you a glass of water,' said Steven. He got up and went into the kitchen. When he came back, he sat down on the sofa next to me rather than in his armchair. 'Here,' he said. I was still coughing a little and he patted me on the back.

'Thank you,' I tried to say, but I didn't dare speak so I patted him on the knee.

He put his hand on top of my hand.

And as soon as it was clear I wasn't going to splutter all over the pair of us again, he moved his hand up to my cheek. He stroked me wonderingly and then he pulled my face closer to his. All of a sudden we were nose to nose. He tilted his head ever so slightly. Lip to lip. I could feel his warm breath tickling my mouth before we actually made contact. And this time we did make contact. His kiss, so strange and yet so familiar, even after all those years apart . . .

After a moment he pulled away. 'I'm sorry. I shouldn't have done that. Especially now I know you're getting married. It's just that . . . God, Heidi. This is all so . . .'

'Strange? I know.' I put my fingers to his mouth. 'But I don't know if I mind at all.' This time I put my hand on his face and pulled him towards me.

It was as though we were a pair of dancers, getting together again for a tribute show after years spent performing with other partners. The memory of me and Steven still resided in my body; in my arms, my legs, my blood. I let my fingers flutter down Steven's back in the way that always drove him wild with lust but made Ed say he felt like he was being bitten by a thousand mosquitoes. Steven weaved his fingers through mine, bending my wrist back oh so slightly so that I couldn't do anything but turn into his chest.

And before I could really ask myself what I thought we were

doing, we were standing up from the sofa, moving towards the door in a slow waltz. Then we were stepping backwards down the hallway, mouths still locked together, the pressure of Steven's thighs against mine telling my legs where to move. And then we reached the stairs and were slowly climbing up them, holding hands, still kissing. Kissing all the way to the bedroom door.

39

I was woken by sun filtering through the thin blinds in Steven's bedroom the following morning. He was still asleep beside me, his body curved protectively around mine like a shell. Like in the old days. This was the way we always slept together.

I lay very still while the reality of the situation took shape in my mind. Fragments of the previous night's events flickered like frames from a chopped-up movie reel. I remembered that kiss on the sofa, dancing our way up the stairs, taking my shirt off. I remembered the weight of Steven's body on top of mine, the heat of his breath against my neck as he pressed hard against me. Then I remembered Forester, and remembered that I was supposed to be taking care of him. Immediately I panicked that he wasn't crying. Why wasn't he crying? Was he alive? Where exactly was he?

I sat up as though I'd just been shocked with a cattle prod but I needn't have worried. A second later, as though answering my psychic call, a high-pitched voice pierced the silence.

'Daaaaaa-dddddy! Daddy! Daddy, come quickly! The fairies have left a baby in the sitting room.'

Followed shortly after by Forester screaming with extreme indignation as Steven's daughter, Isabelle, attempted to lift him out of her old travel cot, which Steven had set up for their tiny visitor.

'Shit,' I said, quickly struggling from Steven's sleeping embrace and desperately searching the floor for something – anything – to put on. I couldn't see any of my clothes.

'Wha—?' Steven started to wake up.

'Daddy!' Isabelle continued to shout from the other room. 'It's making a noise, Daddy. Make it shut up!'

Forester wailed.

I pulled on the nearest thing I could find, which was Steven's shirt – inside out – leaving him to follow me into the sitting room bare-chested.

'Put the baby down, sweetheart,' I tried to tell Isabelle calmly. She had him half out of his blankets.

'Who are you?' she asked wide-eyed before screaming 'Daddy!' loud enough to bring my father running from Southampton as well as her own. 'Daddy! Daddy! Daddy! There's a strange lady in our house.'

Steven came running so fast that he actually skidded in his socks straight past the door to the sitting room before he got to us.

'Issy,' he said, 'it's okay. Stop shouting. These are our visitors. This is Heidi and that is Forester.'

'Can I have Forester, please?' I begged.

'Give the baby to Heidi,' Steven pleaded.

Isabelle finally relinquished her hold on the baby, who was absolutely inconsolable, and was soon clinging to one of her father's hairy legs instead.

'What are they doing here?'

'Oh God.' I held Forester tight to my chest and skipped around the sitting room in an attempt to calm him down.

'I expect he's hungry,' said Steven. 'I'll put a bottle in the microwave.'

Isabelle followed her father out to the kitchen. Well, she didn't so much follow him as let him drag her there. She refused to let go of his leg.

'Daddy, who is that lady?' she persisted. And what is she doing in our house?'

★   ★   ★

295

Good question, Isabelle. What was I doing in Steven's house that Sunday morning?

In the sitting room, I hooked the tip of my little finger into Forester's mouth and he seemed a little happier as he sucked on that. He drank his first bottle of the day with one eye still on me, breaking my gaze only to sneak suspicious glances at the girl who had yanked him from his dreams.

Isabelle sat next to her father on the sofa with a glass of milk while I nursed Forester in a comfy chair. Steven smiled at me over the top of his coffee cup. It was a tired smile. Isabelle buried herself in the jumper he had thrown on and forced him to allow her to tuck in under his arm.

'So much for our lie-in,' said Steven.

'Yeah,' I agreed.

Beneath the small-talk that we managed in front of his daughter, I knew both Steven and I were having the same thought. Perhaps, in a parallel universe, a Steven and Heidi who hadn't split up seven years ago were having exactly the same kind of morning: dazed from lack of sleep, sitting at opposite ends of the living room in a state of extreme dishevelment, while two children competed for their attention with ever louder means. Except, of course, in the parallel universe, the two kids would have been *theirs*. The kids they had together three or four years after the big white wedding that wasn't cancelled.

'Tell Heidi what you've been doing at playschool this week,' Steven suggested to Isabelle.

'No.' Isabelle climbed down from the sofa and shut herself inside her Wendy house.

The conversation was over.

I was glad when the telephone rang and broke the silence.

'I have to get this, Heidi. Do you mind?'

'Of course not.'

Steven lifted the cordless handset out of its cradle and took it out into the hallway. I could still see him from where I was sitting. And hear him.

'Hi,' he said. 'How are you?' His voice was at once familiar and cool, like Ed's voice when I made the first overture towards making up after a fight.

'We're fine,' Steven continued. 'She's just having her breakfast. Yes, she got the clothes you sent. They're very pretty. And the birthday card. We had a party – your mother came over on the Eurostar.'

Could it be he was talking to Sarah?'

'Yeah. Your mother looked well to me but I guess she's been pretty lonely since your dad died. She'd probably appreciate a visit. We'd all appreciate a visit . . .' His voice tailed off.

On the other end of the line, the mysterious caller held forth. Steven nodded and leaned against the wall, shoulders slumped.

'Well, he sounds like a nice guy,' said Steven eventually. 'Let's hope this one sticks around. I'll get Isabelle. Isabelle,' he called, 'it's Maman. Come and talk.'

Inside the Wendy house, Isabelle gave a sigh. 'I'm playing.'

'Come and talk to Maman,' Steven insisted. 'Say thank you for your birthday presents.'

'They were boring,' Isabelle retorted.

Steven reached one long arm into the Wendy house and tapped his daughter on top of the head.

'Be a good girl,' he said, pressing the phone into Isabelle's hand.

Like her father, Isabelle took the phone out into the hall. Steven sat down opposite me again. He smiled, but it didn't go anywhere near his eyes.

'More coffee?' he said.

I told him I'd love one just to give him the excuse to get up.

★　　★　　★

297

In all the time Steven and I were together, I had never once seen him cry. I thought perhaps that might be about to change that morning. As he walked through the doorway with his back towards me, I saw his shoulders creep upwards. He shrugged them down again as though hoping to shrug a feeling away at the same time.

Eventually Isabelle danced back into the sitting room with the telephone dangling between thumb and forefinger like it was something she wanted to throw into the bin.

'I said thank you and I said next time could she send me something I actually want, like a Barbie house.'

'Issy, that's so rude!' Steven snatched back the telephone. 'Sarah,' he said hurriedly, 'I'm so sorry.'

But Sarah was gone.

'You cut her off,' Steven said to his daughter.

Isabelle gave me an appraising sideways glance as she told her dad, 'I know.'

'What are you going to do?' Steven asked as I finished my third cup of coffee. Proper coffee. I wouldn't sleep for a week.

'I don't know. I suppose I should go home and talk to Ed. I can hardly throw the book at him for sleeping with someone else now, can I?'

Steven gave a small nod of agreement. 'You don't have to go right away.'

'Sooner I go, sooner it will be over and done with. I'll call and see if he's back,' I said.

I reached into my handbag for my mobile. It was gone.

'That bloody prostitute,' I groaned.

Stella must have stolen my phone.

40

Minutes later, Forester was safely strapped into the back of the car.

'Call me as soon as you can,' Steven said as I climbed into the driving seat. He took my hand, which was on the window-sill, and kissed it. 'I'm glad you came to me,' he continued. 'And I'm glad we . . .'

'Don't say it,' I said. 'I know.'

'Call me.'

I nodded.

Steven waved until I turned the corner of his street. Waved rather frantically, I thought.

It took me a lot longer to get back to West London in the daylight. The Sunday drivers were out, as were the tour buses, stopping at random in front of all those places of interest Ed and I were always promising to visit ourselves one day. Ordinarily I would have been frustrated by the traffic, but that morning I was grateful for the slower pace. It gave me time to think through the previous night's events and prepare myself for what might lie ahead.

What exactly was I going to hear when Ed and I were face to face once more? I felt a stab to my heart as I thought of Clare, for in my mind the most likely explanation was still that Ed had been cheating and Clare was most likely to be the woman he had been cheating with.

I thought about all those hypothetical conversations Kara

299

and I used to have about infidelity, about how much we would be able to forgive and forget. A one-night stand? I'm pretty sure I would have considered that forgivable once upon a time. But now I knew that even a one-night stand was a signal of a much bigger problem. A one-night stand could mean so much more than the cliché implied.

How had we let this happen? How had Ed and I let things slide so badly since we announced our engagement? I saw now how uninterested Ed had become in our wedding plans. How many of those rugby weekends had been a cover for his affair? Why hadn't he just called the whole thing off?

Perhaps he thought it was easier to go through with the marriage ceremony and deal with the fallout later. So many people would be disappointed if the wedding was called off: his cousins with their expensive air tickets from Australia, his parents, my parents. Was he going through the motions to avoid embarrassing them? Had I been going through the motions too?

No. No, I hadn't. I loved Ed. I remembered that moment of glittering promise when he and I first met. I hadn't really had high hopes for an evening at the theatre with a very forward dentist but Ed was instantly so warm and so funny. So attentive. Afterwards, as we had drinks in a wine bar near the theatre, he had looked into my eyes when I told him about my job as though he had never heard anything quite so fascinating in his life. He kept looking at me like that right up until Paris, the proposal, and beyond.

I would never have believed that a relationship could feel so right. I'd been out with men who made me laugh over dinner but curled my toes in a bad way under the sheets. I'd dated red-hot lovers who didn't have a thing to say outside the bedroom. In Ed I had everything: a passionate and considerate lover, a generous and ever-thoughtful friend. He was enough for anybody. At what point had he decided that I wasn't enough for him?

I didn't want to let him go.

Please, God, I prayed. Show me what I can do to make things right again. Let there be an innocent explanation for Ed's disappearance. Let him turn out to be worth fighting for. Let him want to work on this as much as I do.

I can forgive a one-night stand if he can.

As usual, there was no parking in the street outside the house. I circled the nearby roads and eventually found a spot on the next street. Then I turned off the engine and sat in the car for a while, savouring the silence. 'Right. Time for the showdown,' I said at last as I unstrapped Forester's car seat. 'Assuming he even came home.'

Oh, Ed had come home all right, and as soon as I put my key in the door, I discovered the real reason why there was no parking outside our house. It seemed that every person I knew, and a couple of policemen too, were sitting on every available surface in the living room.

'Jesus, Mary and Joseph,' cried my mother. 'You're home.'

Kara tore herself from Duncan's arms and fell on her baby like a mother greeting her son just back from the war.

'Is he okay?' she asked as she checked him over. 'Is my baby all right? What on earth happened? Where on earth have you been!?'

Forester screamed as Kara rolled up his trouser legs to check that everything was still in one piece and perfect.

'He's okay,' I reassured her. 'And so am I, if anyone's interested.'

'Where the fuck have you been?' Ed asked me.

41

'Why didn't you call one of us?' said my mother. 'Why didn't you call me? It wasn't just you we were worried about. You ran away with the baby.'

'Why don't you all ask *him* why I "ran away" last night?' I snarled, jabbing my finger at Ed. 'Why don't you ask him why he "ran away" from me first? Scotty, *you* could ask him. Since it was you he said he was in Bristol with while you were up in Newcastle. It was your girlfriend he went to shag.'

So much for my plan to approach things calmly. Ed's aggressive reaction to my return had made me forget I was going to be conciliatory.

'Yes, that's right. Ask my fiancé who he was with last night,' I raged instead.

I had never seen Scotty lost for words.

'Heidi,' Clare began. 'It wasn't . . .'

'You were with him, weren't you?'

'Yes, I was but . . .'

'Let Ed speak for himself now,' I snapped at her. 'I want to hear him tell me why he left me alone with a six-month-old baby to spend the afternoon with you. Excuse me, the whole night with you. Everyone knows you've always wanted him.'

Ed had his hand to his forehead as he sank down onto the sofa.

The entire room was silent as they waited to hear his explanation. Scotty and Clare shared an anguished glance over the top of Ed's stubbly head.

'Heidi, you are a bloody pain in the arse,' said Scotty eventually.

'I think we've got to tell her,' Clare told Ed.

'I was with Clare yesterday afternoon,' said Ed. 'Exactly as I told Scotty last week. I can't believe *he* forgot.' Ed glared at his friend.

'I'm sorry, Heidi. I was supposed to play along. It's my fault things got complicated.'

'I was in Bristol,' Ed continued. 'And I was in Scotty's car. But Clare was driving. Clare and I went to an auction together. I asked her to help me find a present for you – something for our wedding. She found out that a Victorian watercolour of a wedding scene was going to be auctioned in Bristol this weekend, so I picked her up and drove over there. I needed her to make sure it was the real thing. I didn't want to end up with a fake.'

'It's true,' said Scotty. 'At least I bloody hope it is.'

'It is true,' said Clare, and she gave Scotty that soppy look of hers, which confirmed that she only had eyes for one big lunk of hopeless manhood and it definitely wasn't mine. She took a sidestep closer to her boyfriend and he wrapped his arm protectively around her shoulder.

'Oh God.' Now it was my turn to be lost for words. 'Ed, why didn't you tell me?'

'I called you and called you last night but you weren't at home and your mobile went straight to voicemail.'

'My mobile was stolen,' I said.

'Actually,' said Ed, 'your phone was found in a gutter outside a house in Hackney. What on earth were you doing in Hackney?'

'I think we need some time alone,' I told him.

The policemen were already making for the door, happy that this case was closed as far as they were concerned. The rest of the search party would be slightly more difficult to get rid of.

★   ★   ★

303

Instead of sitting down with Ed and talking through the events of the previous evening, I found myself in the kitchen with Kara making tea and sandwiches for eight.

'So,' I said, 'Duncan knows about Forester at last.'

'Yes. And I nearly ruined your relationship in the process,' Kara said quietly.

'I don't think I can blame everything on you.'

She laid her hand on mine.

'What happened?' I asked.

'Ed phoned me, of course, as soon as he realised you weren't tucked up in bed. He caught me just as we were about to go up the Eiffel Tower. I still hadn't mentioned Forester to Duncan by then and I was tight as a violin string with the stress of it, wondering when on earth I would find the right moment. But Ed found it for me. As soon as he told me that he didn't know where you'd gone but you'd taken my baby with you, my priorities were suddenly very clear indeed. I told Duncan that I had to be on the next train to London. And then I told him why.'

'And he was okay about it?'

'No. No, he wasn't okay. He just stood there and started to go red. He didn't say anything for what seemed like a minute or two but could only have been seconds, then, very quietly, he told me that I should get out of his sight. Just go. He didn't say anything else. He didn't have a go at me for lying to him or leading him on. He just told me to go. And I went. I didn't even try to persuade him to come with me. I flagged down a taxi, grabbed my stuff from our hotel and headed straight for the Gare du Nord.

'I'd just missed one train and the next one wouldn't leave for two hours. I was frantic, Heidi. I called Ed every two minutes. You don't want to know what I was calling you, fucking off like that without leaving a note.'

'Irresponsible.'

'Maybe that was one of the words. But I guess that makes me Mrs Pot, eh, Mrs Kettle? Who am I to call you irresponsible?'

'I'm sorry.'

'No, I'm sorry. Let's be clear about that. I left you to cope with my baby for a whole weekend because I wasn't grown-up enough to say no to a free trip to Paris. I should have told Duncan the second he brought out the tickets. Instead, I was forced into humiliating him in the queue for the Eiffel Tower.'

'But Duncan was with you here when I got back!'

'Yes, I can hardly believe it. I honestly didn't think I would ever see him again. But twenty minutes before the train left for London, he came barrelling through the concourse towards me. He hadn't even bothered to go back to the hotel to get his bag. He'd been wandering along the banks of the Seine, cursing his luck, when he decided that he wasn't going to let me go home alone after all. He commandeered a *police* car to drive him to the Gare du Nord – thank God his French is better than mine. They made sure he got onto the same train as me and he held my hand all the way back to London. I needed him so much and he knew it.'

'I guess that makes him a keeper,' I said.

'Like Ed is. Where did you go last night, Heidi?'

'I think Ed should be the first to know.'

'Fair enough. So, am I still your best friend in the whole wide world? Can you ever forgive me?'

I chewed my lip as though I was thinking about it.

'It's just one more thing that will seem terribly funny when we're fifty,' I replied.

'Like the time you passed out on the loo at that restaurant . . .'

'That is never going to seem funny,' I said. 'Yee-uck. What is that smell?'

Kara wrinkled her nose in the direction of her son. Forester looked up at her with what I thought was a cheeky smile.

'Auntie Heidi,' Kara began. 'I don't suppose . . .'

'No way,' I said. 'No bloody way. I'm not going to be changing another nappy for a very, very, very long time.'

42

It was almost dark by the time my parents left for Southampton. Ed and I had circled each other uneasily all day,
knowing that as soon as we were alone, some difficult things
would have to be said.

As I closed the door behind my parents, Ed disappeared
into the kitchen to make two more cups of tea. We took them
into the sitting room and sat down at opposite ends of the
sofa.

'Well, you know where I was all weekend,' Ed began.
'And I think I have a good idea where you were. Steven said
he found the phone where you must have dropped it as
soon as you drove off. You spent the night with him didn't
you?'

'Yes,' I admitted, 'I did.'

It was so easy to be with Steven Gabriel again. The way our
mouths fitted together, just like the first time we ever kissed:
the right size, the right pressure, the right taste.

At the top of the stairs, he had lifted me from my feet and
carried me into the bedroom in his arms. He lay me down on
the bed as though I was the most precious thing he had ever
held in his life. He had smoothed my hair away from my face
and covered my cheeks in kisses as light as the touch of a
baby's fingers.

I knew it would be wonderful. It would be like the way we
made love back when we knew that we were *in love* with each

other. One of those times when the idea that two people can be as one actually seems to make sense.

He unbuttoned my shirt but never took his eyes from my eyes. He slid my jeans down over my hips but never took his lips from my face. His hands moved slowly over my naked skin, as though he thought we had for ever. Every cell in my body was vibrating at his touch.

But then, before I even knew I had started to cry, I felt the wetness of a tear snaking across my face and into my ear. I wiped away the wetness and let out a sob that surprised us both.

'What's the matter?' he asked me.

I struggled upright against the pillows. Steven climbed from between my legs and sat up next to me, still holding my hand.

'We don't have to do anything,' he said. 'Not until you've sorted things out with Ed.'

But I knew by now that Steven and I would never be together again.

'This isn't about Ed,' I said. 'It's about you and me. It's about more than you and me. Steven, there's one thing I never told you . . .'

Was it even fair to tell him after all this time? Was it just twisting the knife? Punishing him for something he couldn't have prevented? When Steven walked out of my life, I hadn't told him that I thought I might be pregnant. When the worst was confirmed, two weeks after Steven loaded the last of his worldly goods into the back of his best friend's car, I still didn't tell him. And I didn't tell him when I booked myself into the clinic to have a termination.

Afterwards I called for a taxi. A cabbie drove me through Chelsea on an unusually sunny April morning with a blood-stained pad between my legs. I can remember the way he chattered on about his morning at work, trying to cheer me up, oblivious to the real reason for my tears. I told him I'd just broken up with someone, not that I'd just had a termination. I can remember the song that was playing: 'Too Shy' by Kajagoogoo. The radio was tuned to a 1980s nostalgia show. I remember the way a mother pushing a pram over a pedestrian crossing scowled at us when the cab's brakes squealed in an emergency stop. I held it together until that moment but the anger on the mother's face had made me sob. It felt like she was angry with me.

And then, when it was all over, it started to seem as though it had never happened at all. Sometimes I thought about calling Steven up and telling him, 'You made me have an abortion, you shit.' And he would think I had gone bonkers, started making things up to make him feel guilty. It was the kind of thing some girls did – pretend they had been pregnant. Girls I knew.

So I kept my secret until I met Ed. I shocked myself when I told Ed about it on the weekend we spent in Norfolk. The night before we took a walk on that long, wide beach and he gave me a pebble to remind me every time I looked at it that it would take a lot to wear him down, to wear away his love for me.

'I don't care about your past,' he'd said, as he pressed the curiously warm stone into my palm. 'Not one second of it. Because I'm going to have the whole of your future.'

And suddenly, the future had become so much clearer. I knew so very early on that I loved Ed and that I wanted him to be the man I grew grey alongside, but until that weekend when Kara went to Paris and I went back to Steven Gabriel, the movie of our life together had sort of ended in soft focus at the exact moment when we walked out of the church as man and wife. Or woman and husband, as I preferred to put it.

As a much younger woman, I had daydreamed about the children I might one day call my own. All that had ended with the abortion. I had held my future child inside my body and let her go. I don't know why I thought the baby I gave up was a girl. I didn't ever ask. But I suppose I thought of her as a girl because she was so much a part of me. When I walked out of that clinic, I didn't just leave a pregnancy behind, I left behind a whole Heidi Savage that I thought I would never know again. Heidi Savage, future mother.

It was at that point I decided that I didn't deserve the chance to have another child. I clearly wasn't fit to be a mother. That's what I believed. Prior to the termination, I had considered the possibility that I could bring up a child on my own and concluded that I just couldn't do it. I was pathetic.

But after Kara's AWOL weekend I saw it differently. I looked back on my memories of my mother and knew that it wasn't easy for her either. These days everyone knows about post-natal depression. In those days, people were less sympathetic. She had a husband, a home, two beautiful children; how could she not be overjoyed? But it isn't possible to be strong all the time. And having a period of weakness isn't the same as being evil or an unfit mother.

When you break a bone, the fibres that form around the break are stronger than the broken matter they're replacing. My mother had come through her breakdown to become the wonderful woman who had just spent a sleepless night calling hospitals and hostels because her twenty-nine-year-old daughter had gone missing. She had always done the best she could and her best was good enough to raise me and James to adulthood.

I could do it, too. I had done it. It may have been for less than twenty-four hours, but I had cared for a child on my own. And Forester was none the worse for the experience.

He didn't get sick or even particularly worried. I had made him laugh his first proper laugh when he peed straight in my face.

Ed laughed too when he heard about that. It was the first indication he had made that he wasn't about to walk away from me.

'Come here,' he said, patting the sofa cushion next to his. 'Come and sit next to me.'

That night, I curled up beside him and started to dream about a different future. A future where children with names like Johnny and Winstona were part of the fun we could have together, not potential pitfalls to be avoided. I realised that in trying to map out my life so that I never came within an inch of possible heartbreak again I might as well have been trying to map a road route from Land's End to John O'Groats that didn't pass through any roundabouts. There had been a time when I thought I would never be able to drive across a roundabout, and all it took to get over that misconception was a bit of practice.

When I had finished talking, Ed and I remained in silence for a while. I breathed in the warm smell of him and smoothed my hand over the prickly stubble that had grown back on his head since the rugby-club dinner. I sat up and looked into his eyes. Even without proper brows to frame them, they were the kindest eyes I had ever known. The sexiest eyes. They started to crease at the corners.

'So,' he said eventually, 'is the wedding off?'

I kissed the very tip of his nose.

'Can I take that as a no?'

I nodded.

'In which case,' he said, 'I'd like you to have this.'

Ed got up and retrieved a small red box from the pocket of his jacket. Next thing I knew he was on one knee in front of me, snapping the box open to reveal my engagement ring, back in one piece from the menders.

'For the future,' he said.

He gently took my left hand and slipped the platinum band around my ring finger. And I cried all over again.

EPILOGUE

There were a couple of guests who hadn't been on the original invitation list when I got married to Ed, exactly as planned, three and a half months later. Despite the somewhat difficult circumstances under which their relationship began, Kara and Duncan were still very much together when I walked down the aisle and I was delighted to see them sitting side by side at the back of the church. Kara was wearing a hat decorated with a little Eiffel Tower in homage to my engagement and her own moment of revelation. And Duncan was the one who got up and carried Forester out into the sunshine when he threatened to add a howling descant to Ed's cousin's rendition of 'Ave Maria'.

'What a naughty baby,' tutted a familiar little voice as Forester was taken outside. Isabelle Gabriel was on her very best behaviour. She sat with perfect deportment on the third pew on the bride's side of the church, looking exactly like the angel child I had once imagined her to be, in a soft pink dress, matching gloves and a big straw hat with a wide silk ribbon. Along with my bouquet I carried the silver horseshoe she had made for me from tin-foil, for luck.

Two seats away from her, sandwiched between the eagerly attentive Eleanor and Flo, was Isabelle's father. As Ed and I processed from the church, Steven Gabriel smiled at me. And it was a smile that beamed back all the love I ever had for him, transformed into something better. I'd lost a fear and found a friend.

Outside the church, while our guests threw confetti and the photographer snapped his pictures, I wrapped my arms around my new husband and he held me close against him. I would never let him go again. I knew now that between us, within our four arms, we would create a safe, secure world. But the most important thing I'd learned was how much I could carry on my own.

THE END